CHINATOWN BLUES

A MAX LeBLUE MYSTERY

CHINATOWN BLUES

by Frank Lauria

Rothco Press • Los Angeles, California

Published by

Rothco Press

8033 West Sunset Blvd., Ste. 1022 • West Hollywood, CA 90046

Cover design by Rob Cohen
Cover image by Dewey Thomas

Rothco Press is a division of Over Easy Media Inc.

FIRST EDITION TRADE PAPERBACK ISBN: 978-1-945436-14-7
Electronic ISBN: 978-1-945436-15-4

For Jerry Boxley, a true artist...

ALSO BY FRANK LAURIA

Doctor Orient Novels

Doctor Orient

Raga Six

Lady Sativa

Baron Orgaz

The Priestess

The Seth Papers

Blue Limbo

Demon Pope

Max LeBlue Novels

Fog City Blues

Chinatown Blues

Melody Dawn Series

Melody Dawn

Horror Novels

The Foundling

Communion

End Of Days

Chapter 1

"Father Time is undefeated."
– John Wooden, Legendary basketball coach

Time flies when you're dead.

Think about it—all of us are the end result of the titanic struggle of a single sperm among millions to reach the sacred egg.

Ergo, every single one of us who gets to be born is a *winner*. That's on a good day.

On a bad day I weep for every last ragged soul on the planet.

Face it, we are all doomed from the jump, the blessed along with the rest of us.

Ergo, it all comes down to time.

Which is exactly why I take it day by day, grateful for every hour I'm breathing free air.

Because the fact is, I'm dead.

I went down with the Twin Towers on 9/11 and I've been underground ever since. My sad story goes like this: I was a DEA agent in New York until uber self-medication and a bitter divorce resulted in me being brought up on charges by Director and ex-pal Alvin Delaney.

Then on 9/11 Delaney offered me a deal. Agent Sam Devine —which *was* me—would be declared legally dead in the tragic collapse of the Twin Towers and go into permanent deep cover.

My mission: find where the drug and arms intersected. I would avoid charges and be back on the job. The position came with perks not usually afforded field agents. A plush apartment, fifty grand in cash, and a kilo each of cocaine and heroin.

A perfect starter kit.

Too perfect.

So I followed Delaney's town car after a meet. Followed it all the way to the apartment building where my ex-wife resided.

Coincidence?

Sure enough when Delaney exited the lobby the smiling woman on his arm was my widow Grace.

Was she grieving? Is Madonna a virgin?

Then it made sense. With me dead Grace collected my insurance and pension and Delaney had a clear field with my now wealthy widow.

So I jumped ship, made it across the border to Canada, and used my superior computer skills to create a new me.

Two years later I reentered the States as Max LeBlue and have been trying to live quietly in San Francisco and the Bay Area ever since. Along the way I dialed down my bad habits to a dull roar but I still enjoy a few drinks now and then.

Tonight was then.

I was staying at my Marin estate, an in-law cottage behind the home of Organic Phil, a local nutrition guru. From there I bicycled to Sausalito and caught the ferry to my town house, a sublet room in North Beach hosted by bohemian physicist Dr. Eli Safelli.

I avoid driving, especially in Marin where the cops are white and uptight. A stray traffic ticket, fender bender, whatever; if you're on the road you're vulnerable to a stop and search. These days law enforcement maintains data networks that can ID your ass in seconds.

I know. I helped set one up for the NYPD.

Of course my creation, which I named Donna after the song, was primitive compared to the cutting edge neuromancy practiced by our local cyber shamans. But I make it a point to stay updated and still have a select clientele for my services.

Which is how I manage to survive off the grid.

So far.

***

Approaching San Francisco by water is a major experience. The city is a jewel by any standard. However of late it's been losing its luster to greed.

I sipped my take-out coffee and watched the city emerge in three gleaming facets as the ferry rounded Alcatraz. The first was North Beach, a hilltop community of human-sized dwellings and small shops, a legendary cradle of the arts huddled next to the glass and steel towers of the financial district. While packed tight, these skyscrapers were artfully designed to complement and interact with each other.

But there was nothing artful about the third facet, a tangle of huge cranes and faceless monoliths advancing south, like concrete dinosaurs gobbling up every square inch of open sky.

A sad flaw in the gem.

Like a beautiful woman with bad teeth.

When the ferry docked at the Ferry Building I bicycled over to North Beach and hauled my wheels three floors to my flat on Chestnut Street.

Eli was there, distracted as usual.

"I lost an important file, I've been frantic," he said as soon as I entered the front door. "It's my paper on Dark Matter. I'm scheduled to present it in London this week." Eli peered at me accusingly. "It's gone I can't find it. Where have you been? I don't even have your cell number."

"Easy, I didn't erase your damn file," I growled as I sat behind his Apple and began a search. Cyber sweeps are part of my deal with Eli. He lets me rent a room in his apartment off the books and I keep his computer equipment humming.

Eli is constantly misplacing or erasing files so my presence is always welcome. This one wasn't hard to locate despite Eli chattering excitedly about his latest theory which included my personal favorite: entangled electrons.

"Sounds interesting. What happens in London?"

Eli grinned. "I'm staying at Claridge's. A suite. After the lecture there's a good chance they'll put me up at the Saville Club."

"Is your file titled 'Dark Matter and the Speed of Light'?"

"That's it. You found it. Thank God. Now I can sleep on the way over. I'm going business class you know."

That's Eli: a brilliant brain obsessed with upgrades.

I stashed my bike in the hall nook and went into the kitchen. Sanjin, the third roommate in the rent-controlled apartment, was seated at the kitchen table. He was writing something by hand, open laptop beside him.

He didn't look up.

"I'm brewing tea. Want some?"

"Thanks."

Engrossed, he continued scribbling. Sanjin was a math prodigy and had just become a full professor at Berkeley. He also made excellent tea.

"Trying to unravel the kinks in this formula," he muttered.

I said nothing, tiptoeing through the halls of genius.

Abruptly he slapped his pen down and went to the stove. Originally from Delhi, Sanjin was educated in London and earned his fellowship at an early age. Now he was a young professor, just thirty-three, slim and fit with penetrating dark eyes and an easy smile.

"What are you working on?" I ventured.

"Vibrational frequency theory." He set two steaming cups on the table. "I'm supposed to discuss it at a five-day conference in LA."

He picked up his pen and began writing again.

"Wouldn't it be faster on the laptop?"

Sanjin shrugged. "When you are trying to pluck the strings of the universe it is better to use your hand."

Still pondering that sip of wisdom I showered, changed clothes, and stepped out for a stroll.

***

A spring afternoon in North Beach is an old-fashioned Technicolor musical.

Pastel awnings, outdoor cafes, eccentric people, tourists, young lovers, street musicians, sunbathers, and dogs chasing Frisbees in Washington Square Park…all about to break out in a dance number.

I picked up a meatball hero and ate it on a park bench.

Always a good idea to eat before drinking. Distracts the body from the harm you're about to inflict on it.

I proceeded south pausing for an espresso before I crossed Broadway and stopped for a quick browse at the City Lights Bookstore.

I bought a copy of *Spook Country* by William Gibson. The title seemed to fit my mood. On leaving I made a quick right through Jack Kerouac Alley and found myself in Chinatown.

My destination was an herbal medicine shop on Jackson Street owned by my friend Doctor Jimmy Shu. Chiropractor, acupuncturist, herbalist, healer. Jimmy has on more than one occasion reconstructed my spine. He lets me use his herb shop as a mailing address for the few bills I receive each month, and I maintain his website and help expedite his mail order business.

We also like to go out and have a few drinks once in a while.

But when I entered his shop Jimmy didn't seem to recognize me.

"May I help you?" he said, voice flat.

It was then I noticed a tall Asian man in a silver gray Italian suit, Texas boots, Swiss watch, and French sunglasses pretending to inspect the herbs and roots displayed behind the counter. He didn't strike me as the organic type so I decided to play it straight.

"Yes," I moved closer to the counter. "I need some ginseng." A fuzzy cloud of tension filled the room like static electricity. I ignored it. "And uh, some fresh ginger too."

The two men stood stock-still, poised like cats with arched backs.

A second later Jimmy reached under the counter. "Yes we have ginseng."

At the same time the Asian turned and I saw something metallic in his hand. A snub-nosed automatic.

"Hands where I can see them," he said calmly.

The gun was pointed at Jimmy.

I took a step back. "Is this a bad time?"

The man smiled. "For you maybe."

Wrong answer.

Among its many virtues a hardcover novel makes a dandy weapon.

My short, swift, spinning backfist extended so the sharp corner of the book caught him just below the sunglasses breaking his nose. Blood spotting his shirt he staggered back and dropped to one knee but held on to the gun.

Not a good sign. Obviously a pro.

One hand covered his nose while his pistol waved back and forth between Jimmy and me trying to decide who to shoot first. From the corner of my eye I saw Jimmy lift a .38 from beneath the counter.

I also glimpsed the muzzle flash of the man's gun and was halfway to the floor when I heard the shot. As my belly hit the wood I heard another shot.

Ears ringing I rolled over and saw Jimmy standing behind the counter with a stunned expression, staring in disbelief at the still-fuming barrel of his .38.

I squinted through the smoke.

The man's sunglasses had been dislodged and for a moment I thought the bloody splotch in the center of his face was the bullet wound that killed him. Because he was lying motionless with the automatic still clutched in his lifeless fingers.

Then I saw the blood seeping from the hole in his chest. I watched the dark stain spread over his silver jacket and slowly pushed myself erect.

"Oh fuck," Jimmy said, almost to himself, "oh fuck."

A numbing exhaustion smothered the adrenaline surge and a brief chill shivered through my bones.

Oh fuck indeed.

Here I amble into Chinatown to pick up my mail and within five minutes I'm an accomplice to a homicide of some man I never met. My carefully constructed house of identity cards was about to come crashing down.

"Shit. I'm sorry," I said. "Maybe I overreacted."

I only half-believed this but I needed Jimmy to focus.

He didn't.

"Jimmy."

My sharp tone drew his attention from the body.

He seemed surprised to see me.

"You better shut down, right now."

Jimmy nodded and went to the door, the .38 still in his hand. He put up a sign that I assumed said *Closed* in Chinese and came back.

"Do you want to call the police? I'll testify it was self-defense."

I regretted the words as I said them, well aware of the unpleasant consequences. But in my world you don't leave a friend hanging. Yes it's a dumb code to cling to for a man in my position but it's all I have.

So it came as some relief when Jimmy said, "No police."

"Do you have any large plastic bags?"

"What?"

"You don't want blood on your floor."

"Oh," he said absently. He went into the back and returned with a floral-patterned shower curtain. Fitting.

My skin oozed cold sweat and I was still shivering lightly as I helped lift the man's body onto the plastic curtain. We wrapped him up as is, one hand still clutching his gun, and then dragged the body into the back room where Jimmy worked with his patients.

We both took a break. I lit a cigarette and wondered if Jimmy had any booze tucked away.

"Can I bum one of those?" Jimmy said, voice strained.

"You smoke?"

"I do now."

I gave him a light. "You want to tell me what just happened?"

"The new Triad."

"Triad?"

"Developers, Tongs, politicians."

I gestured at the corpse. "Which part is he?"

"Developer's hit man."

He dragged on his cigarette and coughed.

"Some alcohol might clear your throat."

"Yeah, good idea."

He rummaged around in a file drawer and fished out a bottle with a Chinese label. He took a swallow and passed it to me.

It tasted like 200 proof gasoline and burned its way through my throat into my belly where it boiled like an undersea volcano.

"Whoa what is this?" I said when my vocal cords recovered.

Jimmy almost smiled. "Chinese moonshine."

Whatever, it definitely helped gather my scattered nerves.

"You think this guy was here to kill you?"

"Maybe not this time. He threatened my family instead." The vehemence cut through his quiet tone like a razor.

"What did he want?"

"They want this building."

"They?"

"New World Developers."

I made a mental note to look them up and nodded at the body. "We can't leave him here."

Jimmy's usually impassive expression sagged. "I need to figure this out."

Grateful for the numbing effect of the alcohol I sat in a padded leather chair and waited. Jimmy's therapy room included a massage table, various heat lamps, a movable tray with small bottles of oils and potions, a refrigerator, and a huge, old-fashioned pharmaceutical cabinet with at least a hundred small drawers. My chair was behind a black mahogany desk. Jimmy was perched on the massage table, head down.

I smoked my cigarette and waited. Jimmy was slender with large capable hands and an air of dignified confidence. He was on the good side of forty with sharp features and intelligent eyes. When he lifted his head his eyes were clouded.

"Late tonight I can move him."

I looked at my watch. It was nearly six.

"What do we do until then?"

"I must go back home, make sure my wife and daughter are okay. You don't have to come back."

"Think you can handle dead weight by yourself?"

Jimmy stepped off the table. "You've helped a lot already, Max."

"Any idea where to take him?"

"Not yet."

"I'll meet you here at eleven."

Jimmy looked at the body and shook his head sadly. "No. Meet me at Mr. Bing's."

***

The streets were crowded with neighborhood residents returning from work. Many were carrying bags of take-out food. The restaurants were already in full gear and tourists milled about looking for a General Tso's Chicken.

Still stunned, I hopped the 12 Pacific bus and settled down for the long ride to the Mission. I like buses. Gives me time to think. In this case I kept asking myself why I was getting

involved in this mess past the initial skirmish. I hadn't shot anybody. In fact the one blow I struck was in self-defense against
an armed man.

Okay I might beat a manslaughter rap but old Delaney
would be right there waiting to chew me up and spit out the
bones the moment I left the courtroom.

On the other hand if I helped Jimmy dispose of the body
efficiently both of us were clear. That is until our unknown
developer began to wonder what happened to his attack dog. At
that point Jimmy would receive another visit, or worse.

Not your problem I told myself. Yeah right.

It was still a bit early for serious drinking and the unpleasant
business facing me later that night put a damper on the festivi-
ties. I was due to meet my lady friend Nina at the bar where she
holds court later that night.

I got off at Fifteenth and Mission and started walking over
to Valencia Street. A few years back the hood was territory of
artists, junkies, Latino gangbangers, radical bookstores, store
front organizers, rock bars, great cheap burritos, and low rents.
San Francisco's East Village West so to speak.

And both neighborhoods have suffered the same fate over
the years.

Gentrification.

Better known as castration.

To be honest some of the changes are user-friendly. Such
as the creation of a Parklet complete with bike racks in front
of Four Barrel, an industrial-sized coffee emporium. For those
who have yet to be gentrified, a Parklet is a simple wooden deck
placed over two parking spaces so as to create a space where
people can sit.

This one came furnished with counters and stools, so the
mass of twenty somethings might have a place to park their
laptops and sip their expensive coffee outdoors. Not like those
early Mission cafes with sagging couches, chessboards on the

tables, shelves of books, people reading newspapers, and dollar espresso.

For there's the rub. The emporium starts at three bucks for the house coffee and works its way to six or seven for those wishing to indulge in exotic brews poured by hand.

The Parklet was jammed with smug young techies so I decided to go old school. I walked a few blocks to a place called Muddy Waters, got the coffee of the day for a buck seventy-five, and took a table at the window. Back to the wall, eyes on the street. Old habits of an undercover narc. I sipped my coffee and opened my new book. As I started to read I noticed the corners of the pages were marked with red ink. It dawned on me that it wasn't ink but blood from the recently deceased's broken nose.

I read for about an hour or so before I moved on. With apologies to Bill Gibson I left the novel behind unfinished.

DNA can be a bitch.

The bus ride, coffee, long walk: none of it dispelled the sense of foreboding floating over me like a vulture with keen eyesight. In a few hours I was going to help Jimmy Shu get rid of a body.

Pro bono.

Not exactly the sharpest razor in the shave kit.

It was barely eight but Nina would have started her shift. Along the way I stopped at a Taqueria for a burrito and the obligatory beer. I also ordered a burrito to go.

The Lone Palm has all the requisites of a good bar. It's off the beaten path, it's dimly lit, frequented by interesting characters, and the bartenders play good music.

It also featured a bartender with a world-class ass. My significant lady Nina.

At the moment Nina was royally pissed at me.

A couple of years back I helped rescue her cousin from the motorcycle gang that had kidnapped her. I also helped rescue Nina from the same gang. In the process we became very close.

After things settled down we took a long, lazy vacation in Mexico and became even closer. Nina even had my name tattooed on her fabulous bun.

Problem was I had too many demons I couldn't share.

Nina knew I had an ex-wife but very few details. She had been patient but I made no secret of the fact that I intended to stay a bachelor.

However Nina is Latina and her patience blew like Mount St. Helens.

Currently she was in her glacier stage. She was talking to a young couple at the end of the bar and pretended she didn't see me come in.

Hoping to melt her resistance I slid the aluminum wrapped burrito across the bar. Nina's eyes went from the burrito to my lame smile then back to her customers.

I sat quietly waiting my turn.

However I was working up a fair helping of outrage. It had already been a tense fucking day. And okay, I couldn't commit fully to a relationship but how did that suddenly make me a bad guy?

Nina's voice punctured my indignation.

"Hello, Max."

"Hi."

"Are you drinking tonight?"

"Patron."

She poured a healthy measure of tequila and when I put a twenty on the bar she pushed it back.

"Thanks for the burrito, Max. That was nice."

I gave her a manly shrug and lifted my glass. "Here's to you, kid."

My Bogie toast went unnoticed. A customer at the end of the bar caught Nina's eye and she drifted off.

The Patron burned away some of the tension. The belt around my belly relaxed a notch and I took my first deep breath since I stepped into Jimmy's shop. It felt so good I took another.

Nina moved into view. "The air in here isn't that fresh.".""

She was eating the burrito.

"You're right. How about a refill?"

"If you promise to drink it slow."

I lifted my hand. "I hereby swear."

She gave me a long look, honey eyes searching my face, then moved away.

Wondering what that was about I dutifully sipped my Patron.

Except for the gruesome task looming ahead I was starting to feel better. The bar was starting to fill up with unwired hipsters who liked to have a drink and talk things over. The girls were attractive and the boys wore long pants. I watched Nina expertly mix and serve drinks and listened to the Eagles welcome me to the Hotel California. Halfway down my tequila I decided to step out for a cigarette.

The street was quiet. I moved away from the entrance and lit up.

After a few contemplative puffs I was pleased to see Nina come outside to join me.

"Thought you gave it up."

She folded her arms as if chilled.

"Ceremonial occasions. Spare one?"

We stood for a few moments in the semi-darkness without speaking. Then Nina turned and gave me that searching look again.

"Max…Max, I think we should stop seeing each other. Just for a while."

What the fuck?

My elevator suddenly plunged fifty floors sucking the air from my stomach.

"Is…there somebody else?" was all I could muster.

She looked away. "Nothing like that. I've been thinking about us and maybe this is the best thing. I seem to need a lot more than you can give right now."

No matter how tough, cold, cool, dangerous, famous, rich, powerful, sophisticated, strong, handsome, or smart you are, once a woman gets under your skin you become just another prom date sweating inside your rented tux.

And I was no exception.

My throat was tight, my heart was stammering, and my emotions were howling like a lost dog.

"Just like that?"

"Not just like that, Max," she said softly. "You just haven't been listening."

"To what?"

"Sorry, Max, I've got to go back to work."

I heard that.

She dropped the cigarette and stepped on it. Now there was a metaphor.

As I watched her go inside, I felt as lonely as the day I became a homeless, nameless fugitive. Numb, I began walking until I saw a taxi and took it back to North Beach.

The capper to a perfect day.

Back in the hood I checked into Specs and found a spot at the corner of the bar where I could stew in self-pity and tequila. Until I remembered the dangerous task ahead. Emotions are one thing. But that corpse was stone real.

I compromised on a margarita and checked my watch. An hour to go before my meet with Jimmy. Time to put on my game face.

For the next sixty minutes I nursed my drink and carefully compiled a to-do list which I jotted on a paper napkin. I ordered a coffee and went over the list again. Then I went outside for a cigarette and burned the napkin.

Old habits.

Mr. Bing's is a dive bar down the street from Jack Kerouac Alley at the edge of Chinatown. The music is loud, the drinks are cheap, and the clientele is dicey. Tourists, hustlers, Chinese wise guys, strippers from the clubs nearby, transients, and people with problems…like me.

I was early but it seemed to be a peak hour. The Boss was on the jukebox and everyone there was born to run. A white-haired dude was chatting up a pair of heavily made up ladies, two Chinese men in suits were engaged in a heated conversation, and the bartender was serving beers to three female tourists in tank tops who seemed amused by everything.

The bartender was a short Asian man with a wide smile and quick moves who immediately came over when I sat down.

Another drink would have dulled whatever facilities were still on duty after the hits of the day. So I compromised.

"Patron straight with a Coca-Cola back."

The bartender grinned. "No Patron. How about Hornitos?"

"Sure."

I didn't intend to drink the tequila anyway. It was the Coke I needed.

As the drinks were placed in front of me Jimmy arrived. He looked tired.

"I'll have the same," he said, taking the stool beside me.

He waited until the bartender served him and moved away before speaking.

"Everything's ready…I think. My first time."

"I made a list of things we could use tonight," I said leaning closer. I went through the items as the music went from *Sympathy For the Devil* to *Thriller*.

Jimmy nodded. "I've got all of those." He tossed down his tequila and looked at me. "I needed that. I just tucked in my little girl for the night."

I gestured at my drink. "You can have this one as well."

He hesitated then drained the glass.

"Ready for this?"

I tried to sound reassuring but I had co-defendant's remorse.

"I've I made some preparations."

"Then let's do it."

Jimmy's preparations were impressive. The body was where we left it but there was a large cargo dolly beside it. Jimmy gave me the plastic surgical gloves I asked for and I partially unwrapped the corpse. Gingerly, lest the dried blood might somehow liquefy, I prized the man's wallet from his jacket pocket.

Jimmy also produced the small portable vacuum cleaner I'd requested. I used it to carefully go over the body and remove traces of the herbs in Jimmy's store. Forensics are sophisticated these days. Just watch TV.

As I rewrapped the body Jimmy dragged over an empty trunk and put it on the dolly. Then we lifted the corpse and placed it inside the trunk.

That's when Jimmy really surprised me.

"This way," he said rolling the dolly to an inside door.

The door led to a long unlit tunnel that smelled of stagnant water.

Jimmy led the way, his flashlight stabbing through the dank darkness.

"There's lots of these tunnels in Chinatown," he said, "came in handy during prohibition. This one goes directly to my storeroom across the street."

As we walked half bent over, the low rumbling of the dolly's castors sounded like a funeral dirge in the tight space. The tunnel was long and my back was starting to stiffen when Jimmy unlocked a door and pulled the dolly into a room stacked with barrels and crates neatly labeled in Chinese script.

"My van is parked in front. I'll go out and open the door."

So far Jimmy had earned high marks for efficiency.

I waited until the van's side door was open then rolled the dolly outside. We grabbed opposite ends of the trunk and lifted it into the van. It was heavy and my back started to protest in earnest.

Jimmy put the dolly inside, slid the door shut, then went back to lock up his storeroom. As I got into the van I checked the street. Jimmy's tiny storeroom was on Grant Street, which was virtually deserted at that hour. We had dragged the body almost a city block underground.

Jimmy started the motor and slowly pulled away. I checked the side mirror. There was nobody around. The transfer had taken less than three minutes. We were fine unless a traffic cop found us interesting.

"Where are we taking this guy?"

Jimmy shook his head. "Haven't figured that part out yet. Any suggestions?"

I had thought about it. "Yes. Head over to 280 south."

"What's there?"

"Devil's Slide."

Jimmy cocked his head as if uncertain. "Not much room. We'll have to work fast."

"We will. Take the Pacifica exit."

Twenty minutes south of San Francisco, Pacifica is a bucolic seaside community where people fish off the pier and surfers rule the beach. On a clear day you might spot a hang glider or two circling the steel blue water.

Pacifica is also the home of Sea Bowl, a deluxe bowling alley with a large parking lot. Jimmy pulled into the lot and stopped in a far corner. We both got into the back of the van, took the body out of the trunk, and put it near the side door.

That done we exited Sea Bowl's lot and slowly turned south for HalfMoon Bay. The twelve mile stretch begins as a winding mountain road through a wooded area then becomes a narrow two lane snaking around the edge of a sheer cliff.

Two hundred yards below heavy surf crashes against some very sharp rocks and the only thing that keeps you from going over is a ridiculously low guard rail.

Add to that the regular mud slides that accompany the rains and you get the name Devil's Slide.

It was a clear night and what little traffic on the road could easily be seen coming. At the moment there was none.

"Now."

At my word Jimmy stopped the van and turned off the light. Like some crack pit crew we exited the vehicle, pulled open the side door, and opened the plastic curtain around the body. The blood had dried but was sticky which made it a bit like peeling off tape. The gun was still clutched in his stiff fingers. I gave the weapon a tentative tug but the dead man's grip wouldn't yield. So be it.

I took him by the shoulders, Jimmy by the feet, and we hauled the body out of the van.

"On three," I grunted, wary of my back.

We swung the corpse once, twice, and over the guard rail. He bounced off the rocks far below and disappeared under the booming surf. Ninety seconds later we were heading toward Half Moon Bay.

As soon as we reached the bottom of the curved stretch we turned and drove back to the city. Along the way we disposed of our surgical gloves, the bloody shower curtail, and the trunk. We also emptied the contents of the portable vacuum.

The last item was the wallet.

The name on the driver's license was Peter Ng and he used to live in Oakland.

I wrote down the numbers on his license as well as those on his credit cards. Then I dropped the cards and the wallet down a sewer. The only thing I kept was a business card tucked behind the license.

The company name was New World Investments, the name on the bottom was Taylor Kingston. His title was CEO. One the back of the card was a handwritten phone number with a 301 area code—Beverly Hills.

"I think I need a drink," Jimmy said.

He found a parking space in Chinatown and before leaving the van I swept the back with a flashlight.

"Looks clean," I said. "Are you okay?"

"Like I said, I think I need a drink."

We walked to Specs and found a table in the back. Part museum and all Bohemian, it is one of the last of the real San Francisco joints. Best of all it's reasonably anonymous

Jimmy ordered cognac. I stayed with tequila. He drained his glass. So did I.

"I owe you, Max," Jimmy said as we waited for another round.

"That's the liquor talking."

"No seriously,. If you hadn't walked in…anyway I owe you big time. Or better yet—*lifetime*."

The waitress arrived which spared me a reply.

Jimmy drank most of his cognac and leaned forward. "You really knew what you were doing tonight."

"You were fairly well-prepared yourself."

"Yeah well I haul stock back and forth through the tunnel, but you," he leaned closer, "you knew about the details."

I shrugged. "Military training."

"They don't teach forensics in the military." He leaned even closer. "Is that why you get your mail at my place?"

"I'm ducking an ex-wife." It was partially true.

Jimmy knocked back the rest of his cognac. "My address is your address, Max. Now and forever."

His eyes were bright and I could see the booze had re-booted his fading adrenalin. As for me it had faded, or rather plummeted, into an abyss in the middle of my chest where my heart used to be.

I had managed to ward it off but now there was no excuse. My task finished, it was time to face my life.

There was nothing there.

Nina's abrupt severance had sent me adrift from the only link I had with humanity leaving me in deep space without a helmet. And the worst thing was that when I thought it over—I had to agree with her.

Any sane female would have cut me loose years ago. Sure I saved her life but since then I've kept my emotional distance. She'd never even visited the flat in North Beach, which reminded me. I had been hoping we'd go there tonight.

"You okay, Max?"

I looked up from my glass. Jimmy's glazed eyes peered at me with concern.

I smiled. "Thinking about the one that got away."

He nodded. "I know all about that."

Sorry Jimmy, I thought, *you've got a wife, a daughter, and a business. You don't know what it's like in deep space. Not yet.*

"Sooner or later New World Developers is going to send out a search party," I said, to change the subject.

That sobered him.

"It's my family I'm worried about. I can take care of myself."

"Is there somewhere they can stay until this blows over?"

He gave me a sad smile and shook his head. "Both my wife and I were born here. We're paying off our condo and Christine is in school. We're also helping out her parents and they live in Chinatown too. Got nowhere to run, Max."

"One thing you need to do."

"What's that?"

"Get a new gun. Lose the old one."

"Yeah sure, of course. You see what I mean, *details*."

I snorted and shook my head. "That's basic criminal procedure. Don't you watch TV?"

"Only kid shows lately. Which reminds me. They get up early."

"Go home. It's been a tough day."

He nodded wearily. "Sure has. But, Max…?"

"Yeah?"

"Where do I get a new gun?"

I heaved a deep sigh. "Let's talk when I pick up my mail."

He got up to leave. "Tomorrow then?"

"I won't be moving around much tomorrow," I said with a modicum of certainty. "Day after okay?"

"See you then, Max." He shook my hand. "And thanks."

I watched him go, his shoulders slumped, his head down, body heavy with worry. Home and family was a double-edged sword. As for myself I had already fallen on my blade.

With Jimmy gone, my obligations dispatched, I felt free to indulge in a bout of anger turned inward. Commonly known as a ferocious depression.

I had a few more tequilas, furious at my inability to negotiate some kind of detente with Nina. Furious at being locked in a situation which prevented me from pursuing Nina rather than letting her go. Furious at volunteering to bury other people's bodies.

It must have shown because the patrons were avoiding my gaze. I remember thinking I wasn't drunk and arguing with the waitress when she refused to serve me another double. I recall heading for Golden Boy Pizza when I left the bar.

I don't remember how or when I got home.

Chapter 2

"Got burned so bad I'm still smokin'."
— Angela Strehli, Blues singer

It was late morning when I woke up.

But I wasn't in bed.

I was on the floor beside my bed. Somehow I had wrapped myself in a blanket and stuffed a pillow beneath my aching head. As I started to get up my ribs were raked by a sharp pain. I had to roll on all fours in order to crawl onto my mattress.

I took a deep, careful breath and was relieved to find my ribs weren't cracked. I took off my shirt and saw a large bruise on my chest. My brain too, felt bruised. I lay back and tried to remember.

An hour later I opened my eyes. My headache was on the front burner and I was hungry. However fixing breakfast was out of the question. I hobbled to the bathroom and took a long hot shower. Then I took a short cold shower and a few aspirin.

Mobile if not nimble I dressed and went out.

It was past noon and lunch in North Beach was in full swing. Mario's has good strong coffee so I got a large take-out and sat outside contemplating the ruins of my life.

Besides everything else my black out was worrisome. That's the fallacy of trying to drink away your problems. You wake up feeling like shit, your old problems are still there but now you have a new one.

So much for the fucking sermon.

Truth was my life had been pulled out from under me. Again.

Nina was the woman I had yearned for all my life, even if I didn't know it. Apparently my prior acts of nobility on her behalf had a shelf life. To be fair until now I had given Nina only half a person. But the whole person was toxic.

For both of us.

I couldn't expose her to the kind of evil lurking in my world.

Ergo I was fucked.

"Max."

The female voice triggered a shower of reactions: joy, relief, gratitude, and abject disappointment when I saw it wasn't Nina.

It took a second to recognize the blonde lady smiling at me. Leslie was the cocktail waitress at Spec's. She had served us drinks the night before. The smile was reassuring but I was wary. I still couldn't remember what happened between closing time and home that caused me to wake up with sore ribs.

"Leslie what's up?" I ventured cautiously.

"Thanks for last night. That was awesome."

For a stricken moment I wondered if we had hooked up. To be sure Leslie was lovely with long blond curls and wise blue eyes but at that point I couldn't handle anything more complicated than a handshake.

"Awesome? Usually I'm average."

"Oh come on, Max. Most guys wouldn't have stepped in like that. You're a real Galahad."

A series of blurred images slowly came into focus. Stepping out of Spec's into the courtyard and lighting a cigarette. Leslie there outside talking to a tall dude with a ponytail. Clearly she's not enjoying the conversation. She pulls away and starts back inside. He grabs her arm.

She slips free. He grabs her again and yanks her back. Hard.

That's when The Preacher descended and the fury fell over me like a dark curtain.

It wasn't the booze that caused my black out. It was the uncontrollable rage that over the years I had come to name The Preacher.

"Uh, was he your boyfriend?"

"Wannabe. Bad news. But I think you convinced him to fuck off permanently."

"Um how so?" I said treading lightly lest I had gone too far.

"Oh he thinks he's bad because he used to box. But you took his best punch and bent him in a pretzel before you kicked his ass into the street."

"Hope I didn't draw a crowd. I would uh, hate to embarrass you."

"Don't be silly, Max. It all happened so fast I was the only one who noticed." She beamed up at me and I could see infatuation lighting her cornflower blue eyes.

Nina used to look at me that way.

"You want to have a coffee or something?"

I didn't but her plaintive tone hit home.

I had already disappointed my share of women so I said, "Sure."

"Do you like Trieste?"

"Yeah, good call."

Trieste is another hold out from the golden era. Steeped in tradition the café is located on the triangle where Grant meets Columbus. It stands directly across from the Church of Saint Francis made famous by Lawrence Ferlinghetti's fine poem. Every Saturday afternoon various opera singers perform to a packed house. The place is cramped and filled with old guard bohemians which makes finding a table an adventure. However it serves good strong coffee and fresh pastry both of which I badly needed to clear my foggy senses.

We found a table in the rear which was fairly anonymous since at the Trieste everybody is looking at everybody else and no one sees anybody.

Leslie chatted while I ate my Danish and dipped into the conversation here and there. I learned she graduated from Bennington and had a day gig in public relations which put her in touch with the city's local celebrities from Sean Penn to Metallica. She said all this with becoming modesty and I found myself charmed by her fearless intelligence, not to mention her ripe sensuality.

But all I could think about was Nina.

And then as the sugar and caffeine ignited the ashes of my brain I remembered the dead man I had heaved over Devil's Slide. I made a mental note to get on the computer and dig up his vital statistics.

"So what are you doing these days, Max?"

"Uh, you know I'm a tech geek. Private clients, work at home, that kind of thing."

She was about to ask where I lived until I diverted the conversation.

"I'd be glad to help you update your web page."

As I said it I realized it sounded like a techie seduction line.

Leslie leaned closer and put her hand on mine. It felt like cool water on desert sand. "You've already helped a lot," she said quietly, her pink mouth curled in a mischievous smile. "But maybe we can trade services."

The husky tone in her voice suggested it could turn out to be a memorable afternoon. She didn't know her Galahad was a knave in dented armor, creaky with defeat.

"Yeah that sounds good," I said, pretending I had missed the point.

A few minutes later Leslie finished her coffee and said she had to run. We both promised to email. I waited until she had gone and went directly home to find out exactly who the late Peter Ng really was.

I used Eli's big Apple computer to run down Ng's credit card numbers, DMV records, and bank records. Hacking into police and FBI databases I searched for criminal history. Then I opened Interpol.

Finally also checked his immigration status.

In a few hours I had compiled a detailed profile of Peter Ng.

Thirty one years old, son of a Chinese father and Vietnamese mother.

Educated in England, left Cambridge after a year and lived in London. Became an English citizen and soon after moved to New York where he made a fortune in real estate. While there he married Sara Sun, a Chinese -American graduate of Harvard Law School. He then formed XTech, a corporate security firm.

Ng had no criminal record anywhere and believe me, I tried. Which left one glaring question.

Why would a wealthy entrepreneur risk everything by acting as a low rent strong arm man for some developer?

My guess was Jimmy had been right. Ng intended to kill him and didn't want any potential witnesses. Like a hired hit man—or me. So Ng was there to execute Jimmy personally.

Which implied he had done it before.

My sugar and caffeine breakfast burned out and I went to my room for a nap. On the bed this time.

I woke up famished. A shower loosened up my aching body parts and I went out to get some food and pick up my mail. It was a short walk from North Beach to Chinatown and when I got to Jimmy's shop it was still open.

Jimmy was busy with a customer when I entered and after concluding the ancient Chinese woman wasn't a threat I wandered around the shop.

The sharp musky scent of the herbs and roots stored in the glass jars and wood bins was oddly reassuring as if I'd been transported to a simpler time. Except killer wolves were circling just outside the portal I reminded, sniffing the dark vibes of the previous day's violence.

As the elderly lady shuffled out wheeling her shopping cart behind her Jimmy reached beneath the counter and produced a thin stack of envelopes.

"Usual bills," he said, handing them over. He paused and peered at me.

"You okay?"

"Except for a wicked hangover and some bruised ribs I'm dandy."

He half pushed me into the back room. "Step into my clinic."

Jimmy had me strip down to my shorts and sit on the massage table while he brewed some special tea. After I drank the bitter brew he told me to lie face up and close my eyes. Then he switched on the overhead heat lamp. Five minutes later I began to sweat. Within ten minutes it came in torrents. My body was drenched.

Jimmy produced a large towel and dried me off. Then he gently rubbed ointment over my bruised ribs and chest. Finally he covered my legs with a cotton blanket and told me to lie still. I felt an icy warmth seep into my muscles and bones, like ginger and jalapenos mixed with hot gin. And then Jimmy started expertly dotting my skin with acupuncture needles.

When the process was finished I rolled off the massage table feeling as fresh as a twenty-year old. Well maybe thirty-nine.

Jimmy smiled. "You must be hungry."

"I arrived hungry."

"There's a good place up the street. Szechuan okay?"

"Right now I could eat the Great Wall."

Jimmy locked up and we walked a block to a small restaurant called Lucky Moon.

The food was excellent but I could sense something was troubling Jimmy. I waited for him to tell me but I had an idea what it might be. Odd how I could read everybody except myself.

He spooned some black rice onto my plate. "I don't remember you having bruised ribs last night."

I told him what happened after he left Spec's.

Jimmy shook his head. "I was pretty well wasted myself. Linda has been giving me icicle eyes all day."

"Yeah but you managed to make it home without assaulting anyone. Considering our situation it was stupid."

"It's not stupid to help a girl in trouble." He leaned closer. "How was she, or don't you remember?"

"Strictly platonic. The bleeding hasn't stopped from my previous disaster."

"Must be tough."

I was too busy digging into the scallion pancakes and pepper shrimp to answer.

Finally he sat back and sighed heavily. "I'm sorry I got you mixed up in this."

"Something happen today?"

"As a matter of fact…" he looked at me sharply, "how did you know?"

I shrugged. "Intuition. You seemed worried."

"I'm worried alright. New World Developers left a message on my home answering machine. Some male secretary said they would like to schedule an appointment."

"He leave a name, this secretary?"

"Taylor Kingston."

"He's the CEO of New World. Ng had his card and number."

Jimmy flinched at the mention of Ng's name but his expression remained stoic. "What do you think I should do?"

"Calling you at home was definitely a message. Schedule the meeting and have me along. I'll make sure everything is recorded."

"Once you show up with me you're in deep shit."

"I'm already in deep shit—I just ate a chili pepper. Schedule the meeting."

"And oh, Max?"

"I know. You need a piece."

"Thanks. Maybe I should take Linda to the pistol range."

"Maybe you should send Linda and your daughter out of town somewhere."

"She's still in school, Linda would panic. If things get heavy I'll send them to Disneyland in Florida."

"Let's hope it doesn't come to that. At this moment Mr. Kingston is worried. That's why the sit down. To size you up."

Jimmy polished his glasses. "Okay I'll call tomorrow. But don't forget the gun."

"Alright but no guns at the meeting. As far as they're concerned you're a small time problem. Their enforcer could be anywhere. They're not even sure he visited you at all."

He nodded thoughtfully. "Of course. You're absolutely right. They just want to make sure."

When he looked up the stress clouding his features had cleared. He took a deep breath and smiled. "Thanks,, I feel a lot better."

I smiled back but I knew it wouldn't be that simple.

***

After dinner as I walked home I started planning how I would bug the meeting, perhaps plant one right in Kingston's office. I went over available devices.

Anything to keep my mind off Nina.

I was so engrossed I didn't see the large black Mercedes until it pulled up alongside of me. The door opened and a young Chinese man stepped out. He had a blond pompadour, a pale blue suit, and a Glock nine. The Glock motioned me inside the open door.

One eye on the gun I crawled inside.

Blond boy closed the door behind me and got into the front seat. The car was roomy with soft leather seats and head cushions.

It had to be roomy.

Seated beside me, an innocent smile masking his hard, alert eyes, was a very large man with a shaved skull. When I say large I mean big enough to qualify for statehood.

"Please forgive me," he said, "we need to talk."

"Who are you and what the fuck is this about?" I snapped. Too quick.

The smile faded and his eyes drilled into mine.

"I'm going to make you an offer you can't refuse."

Then he laughed.

Chapter 3

*"Everybody has a strategy until they get
punched in the face." –* Mike Tyson

"I've always wanted to say that." The big man said, still chuckling.

The driver and the blond gunman were also amused.

The only one not smiling was me. My brain was frantically sifting through a thousand possibilities. All bad.

He seemed to read my scattered thoughts.

"My name is Albert Chan. Again, please forgive my crude manner of introduction."

He pressed his huge hands together as if in prayer and regarded me carefully over steepled fingers.

"However it is urgent. For both of us."

As I took a deep breath and settled down I noticed Albert's diction had a slight British twang. Maybe Hong Kong. I also noticed his chest and shoulders threatened to burst through his custom tailored suit. Probably steroids. His bald dome looked like a glass turret on a pin striped tank.

Aware of my position I dialed down the attitude.

"Whew you scared the hell out of me," I said mildly. "So tell me, Albert, what's so urgent?"

He clapped his hands in delight. "Max, you are all I'd hoped."

Max?

That stopped me. My precious anonymity had been shattered like a Ming Vase.

"I wasn't aware I was so famous," I said with all the cool I could muster.

"Infamous. Were you aware there's a bounty on you?"

I shrugged. "I've heard rumors."

It was true.

Since I helped break up their drug and human trafficking operation, the Vandals motorcycle gang had put a price on my head. Still it was disheartening to know the news had seeped all the way to Chinatown.

"Takes talent for one man to piss of so many dangerous people."

"It's a gift."

"Word is you rescued a couple of girls they had kidnapped."

"Why the interest in my legend Albert—do you intend to collect that bounty?"

"I need a man with your skillset."

"Pissing people off?"

"We know that you're a friend of Doctor Chu."

"A client."

"Who receives his mail at Doctor Chu's shop."

"In return for my computer services."

"Which are considerable, Max. I've seen Doctor Chu's website. You've made him global."

When I didn't respond he said., "Now why would you receive your mail at an herb shop in Chinatown?"

"I'm dodging a vindictive ex-wife."

It was my standard but it carried credibility. Especially in California.

Hands still pressed together Albert nodded sagely. I wasn't sure if he bought it but neither was he.

"How did you know I get my mail there?"

Albert opened his hands and grinned.

"The mailman is *Chinese*," he said as if delivering the funniest joke since the chicken crossed the road.

Again the boys in the front seat laughed. Again I didn't.

Then his grin compressed into a serious expression. "We know everything that happens here. We *are* Chinatown."

His eyes bored into mine. "That's why New World asked us to look into the matter of one of their missing representatives."

"New World?"

"Developers. Mister Peter Ng went to see Doctor Chu about selling his property yesterday. He disappeared."

"Why don't they go to the police?"

"They will. But first they come to us. They want us to convince people to sell to them."

"I see."

"No you don't, Max. I was raised here. My grandparents still live here, and their friends. We will accept a consulting fee for looking into the Peter Ng matter but we will block any effort to turn Chinatown into a fucking theme park. This is a community and we will protect it."

Some might say it's a ghetto, I noted, but my sympathies lay with Albert. I was sick of greedy developers who swallow traditional neighborhoods like canapés and spit out malls. New World's tactics were clear evidence of their lack of community spirit.

"They especially want us to force Doctor Chu to sell," Albert said, making sure I understood. He put a huge hand over his heart. "My mother and my sister go to Doctor Chu. So we will protect him."

"You keep saying we. Who exactly is *we*?"

"Sun See Huang Benevolent Association, what's known as a Tong. You're the computer geek—Google us."

"Okay. But I still don't understand why I'm here."

"We know you were with Doctor Chu yesterday. You were seen at Mr. Bing's bar together and again at Spec's. Which gives us a hole card, Max."

Ace of spades, I thought. I said, "Hole card?"

"We can throw you to New World for Ng's disappearance, keep them off Doctor Chu's back, and still collect our generous fee." He smiled thinly. "Maybe I can even collect that bounty."

"This is bullshit, you can't prove any of this."

"This ain't no court of law, Max. However as said, I am going to make you an offer you can't refuse."

Nobody laughed this time.

"We have a problem only an outsider can solve. Someone with your special abilities. You help us solve our problem and we will protect Doctor Chu and his family. We will also make sure you stay under the radar."

I didn't have any choice and Albert knew it.

"So what's your problem?"

He took a deep breath and grunted and for the first time I saw the ferocity behind his cheerful front.

"There is a serial killer working Chinatown."

"Why me?" I said lamely. "You were raised here, know the territory…"

"We believe the killer is a Caucasian who is targeting Asian women."

"What about the police?"

"The police see these murders as low priority. First because all of them were sex workers. And second because all of them were Asian. I know because many detectives are on my tab. They are stupid and corrupt. In fact they still have not tumbled to the fact that they are dealing with a fucking serial killer."

I almost said those three little letters but his eyes stopped me.

As a former Marine, New York cop, and dead DEA agent, I'm familiar with intimidation. So I can attest with confidence that the expression on Albert's face was certifiably scary.

"And if you're thinking FBI forget it. Nobody wants the feds nosing around town; not the SFPD, not me, and not you. That's why you, Max, are the only man for the job. You have experience. And strong motivation."

Motivated? I was now.

I understood how Albert's benevolent offer of protection for Jimmy could easily turn ugly. Which left me two options.

Fight or flight.

Within hours I could be in San Diego or Seattle, have a new ID within a week, bulletproof passport within four months. Only problem was I was far from bulletproof. The Chinese connection extended from Mexico to Vancouver. And it meant abandoning Jimmy Chu to the wolves. If not to Albert then to New World, most likely both.

And then there was Nina. Just the idea of leaving her behind tore me apart. As if roots were being forcibly yanked from my soul leaving a barren wasteland.

"I'll need expenses," I said wearily, "and the names of the dead females. Who they worked for…"

Albert's granite features melted into a smile as if made of silly putty.

He reached behind him and extracted a thick manila envelope.

"Good to have you aboard, Max. You'll find everything you need in there. Finish the job and there's twenty-five more."

When his hand dipped into his jacket I half expected to see a weapon. Instead he produced a business card. On the back, written in ball point, was a phone number.

"This is where you get off. We'll be in touch."

I hadn't been paying attention to the scenery outside the tinted windows, fascinated by Albert' lethal presence, like sitting eye to eye with a giant cobra.

The car stopped and unceremoniously let me out on the corner of Broadway and Columbus, a few steps from Spec's.

I needed a drink but I had to make sure I wasn't being followed by one of Albert's conveniently stationed soldiers.

I took a circuitous route stopping off at the Grant and Green bar which gave me a view of the street. One Hennessey, a long scan for a possible tail, and out the door. I cut through Jasper Alley and back up to Grant. The street was deserted. Just to make sure I circled the block before finally going home.

Paranoid? Fucking A.

Chapter 4

"Money has no home."
—Amarillo Slim, Poker Champion

The envelope Albert gave me contained twenty grand in cash as well as seven photographs of provocatively attired Asian women.

Information was written on the backs of the pictures. There was also a list of names and numbers of escort services around town. Crude, but enough to start.

And start I did.

I began by Googling the Sun See Huang Benevolent Association. There wasn't much there: established 1911, Albert Chan President. Ben Hung Vice President, Lyn Sun Treasurer. Address, phone number, short mission statement community service etc. and a message box. The one photograph was of Albert, smiling like a sly Buddha.

Undaunted I hacked into the SFPD database for the official reports on the murders and any evidence they had discovered. The files also had crime scene photographs of the murdered women. Reluctantly I printed those out for future study.

Nosing around I discovered three other Asian women had been murdered under similar circumstances outside of the Chinatown area. Two victims had been found in the inner Richmond district which was multi-Asian—a rich blend of Thai, Vietnamese, Burmese, Filipino, and Chinese.

Another female was killed in the Tenderloin, a hood populated by addicts, drunks, transients, and gang members. The rent was low and the risk up there in the red zone. Then again so was having sex with strangers.

Clients tended to regard prostitutes as disposable.

That added up to ten women in eighteen months which called for a major task force.

From the dates I was able to track my quarry's timeline. The killer had gone out of Chinatown after the first three.

The next was in the inner Richmond leaving a gap of five months. Then two more in Chinatown and another in the outer Richmond.

After a gap of five months a prostitute was murdered in North Beach. Then another in the Richmond and finally one in the Tenderloin. The last occurred only forty days before.

The scumbag was quite clever, spacing his victims between different police precincts to obscure the pattern. Still, any competent homicide detective should have caught the similarities.

Every victim was a sex worker, every victim was Asian, and every victim had been strangled.

Not rocket science. Just simple logic—if you bothered to look.

The detectives working the inner Richmond and the Tenderloin had an excuse. The boys in North Beach had a lot to answer for. Especially if they were on Albert's pad.

I understood why my new friend was angry. So long as it wasn't at me.

It was after three a.m. when I turned off the computer and went into the kitchen for a nightcap. But the scotch didn't help. I was the lonely guy in a Sinatra torch song.

Except the music had stopped.

There I was, just another boy grown old sitting in an empty kitchen staring at the bottom of my glass as if it contained what little future I had left.

I struggled to keep from calling Nina.

Two scotches later I went to bed, switched on the TV, and fell asleep watching Bruce Willis in *Die Hard* take shit from the bad guys, the good guys, and his ex-wife. Story of my life.

***

The next day, after much inner discourse and not a little apprehension, I called Nina.

"Max?"

Her voice was instantly soothing

"Yeah."

"I'm glad you called."

"I wasn't sure you wanted me to."

"Can we meet somewhere this afternoon?"

"Mario's or Borderlands?" I said, naming cafes on both sides of town, "your call."

"Mario's."

It was within walking distance of my place. A spark of optimism.

"I'll be there at two."

My mood rocketed from dismal to manic in sixty seconds. Until I reminded myself a motorcycle gang had a price on my head. The DEA had me on their want list and a Chinese gangster had me on a string.

Not what I'd call an eligible suitor.

Sill I fidgeted like a kid on his first date. I tidied up the apartment and kept checking either the mirror or my watch.

What I saw in the mirror wasn't encouraging. I carried various souvenirs of my rumbles with life and my skin was drawn drum-tight over sharply angled cheekbones. My deep set green eyes looked like they were staring out of a foxhole.

But as I walked across Washington Square Park there was a lift in my step.

I arrived ten minutes early and took a window table in the corner.

Mario's Bohemian Café is another North Beach original, blessed by a phenomenal location, a wine and beer license, and a phenomenal location. To its credit, the place lived up to its name. Compared to the high-tech caffeine mills around town Mario's was a nostalgic oasis, low key, friendly and real.

The big clock on St. Peter and Paul's church had just struck two when I spotted Nina crossing Columbus Avenue. She wore a black leather jacket over a pale blue blouse, skinny black jeans, and red heels that highlighted her graceful stride.

I watched her glide closer with a mixture of anticipation and apprehension. Her shy smile and demure kiss didn't raise my hopes.

"Hello, Max."

"Good to see you."

"The other night…" she blurted as soon as she sat. "… I got it all wrong."

"Now you tell me."

"What?"

"I might have avoided the hangover."

Not to mention the bruised ribs, I thought. Still I liked where this was going.

Nina had an expressive face. Her emotions were right there as large as a movie screen. And what I saw in her dark Modigliani eyes melted my resentments.

She took a deep breath. "Here's the thing. You risked your life to save me and my family. We've been close, very close for two years. Do you really think that I would betray you in any way? Because at this point I find your secretive bullshit insulting."

Her fiery gaze had my complete attention.

"I love you, Max, but I won't be insulted."

"Okay, you're right. I have secrets."

To my relief the waitress came to take our order.

We both decided on cappuccinos and pastry. As the waitress left I realized I had no choice. Either I came clean or Nina would walk. But after years in storage the truth didn't come out easily.

I decided to give her the Cliff notes to start with.

"I'm a former drug agent from New York. I was officially declared deceased on 9/11 so that I could go undercover and trace illegal arms traded for drugs."

Nina's expression relaxed. It wasn't as bad as she thought. I wondered what she had in mind.

"So you're undercover?"

"Not exactly. I'm a dead fugitive."

The waitress came with our order and we took a brief coffee break. I was also starting to loosen up. A bite of a fresh apple turnover, a sip or two of strong cappuccino, and I was ready to cop to the hard part.

"I found out that the man who put me in that position, Alvin Delaney my superior in the DEA, was romancing my soon to be ex-wife. With me officially dead my ex would collect the insurance and pensions. Delaney was the only man who knew I was still alive. I figured his next move would be to take me out."

I drank more coffee. Nina was quiet.

"So I jumped ship. Crossed over to Canada and acquired my new identity. I got myself a green card, immigrated to California, and started a small computer business. Then I met you."

Nina put her hand on mine. "So that's why you're so secretive. You believe the DEA is still hunting you."

"That—and the fact that the Vandals have a bounty on my head."

Her hand tightened.

"I didn't know that."

"Neither did I. Yesterday it became official."

"Max that's awful." Her eyes were wide and for a moment she seemed disoriented.

She had been kidnapped by the biker gang. It couldn't be easy to erase the experience. Outwardly Nina had recovered well but I knew all about nightmares and sleepless hours rerunning the horror.

"It's me they want, not you," I said quietly. "Me."

It didn't reassure her. For a few minutes we silently ate our turnovers.

Nina looked up.

"The other night…" At that moment she resembled a Madonna mourning a lost savior. "…the way I sprang it on you. It all came out wrong. I was so full of these feelings I guess I exploded."

I let that settle. I had left out significant details in my confession including my new employer the Chinese mafia.

I leaned across the table and lowered my voice.

"A little while ago you said you loved me. Did you mean that?"

She gave me a wicked smile.

"Take me home, Max."

***

"…and when they have eyes for you it's heaven."

The line from Allen Ginsberg's poem drifted lazily though my brain as Nina nestled against me. She felt as warm as a house cat against my naked skin, and as familiar. Locked together minutes earlier we had touched souls.

Sounds corny but sex is definitely a cosmic enterprise.

However at the core of everything is entropy. When Nina woke up I'd still be lying to her. And because we were so close she'd sense it.

And Nina wasn't a three-strike girl. Two and I'd be out.

"There's something else," I said later, while we shared a joint. "I've been hired to investigate a serial killer."

She pushed herself up and her weight fell on my bruised ribs.

"Hired, by who?"

"Same people who told me about the Vandal's bounty."

"Why you,?"

"They heard I was good at finding lost girls."

She settled back down into a fetal position.

"If it wasn't for me you wouldn't…"

I kissed her neck. "…if it wasn't for you I'd still be lost."

"I missed you like crazy, Max."

Six little words that lit up my world.

We stayed in bed for hours, listening to music, talking nonsense, enjoying the solitude. It was getting dark when we got up to forage for food.

"I'm not insulting you by keeping these things from you," I ventured as we raided the refrigerator. "I'm trying to protect you."

Hot button.

Nina straightened up, eyes blazing.

"Fuck that bullshit, Max," she seethed, "I'm here for you no matter what. That's my idea of a relationship."

"Fine, baby," I said quietly. "You know I'm on that page too. So are we still good?"

Nina groaned. "Yes we're still good, Max, except nothing has changed."

"A lot has changed." I gently pulled her close. "Give me a few months. We'll go back to Mexico and talk it over."

"Why can't I stay here with you?"

"I have two roommates and one bathroom. Do the math."

She shook her head and laughed.

"You never told me you had roommates."

"I never told you where I lived."

Nina sighed and kissed me. "Talk about baby steps."

We made love there in the kitchen, by the light of the refrigerator.

***

The glow lingered long after Nina left.

I returned to my serial killer project with renewed energy if not enthusiasm.

Poking around the internet I found that six of the victims were registered with two local escort services. One was located at the edge of Chinatown on Stockton. It was named The Green Star.

There are lots of escorts in San Francisco. The back pages of the local papers feature a sugary array of seductive ladies wearing little more than heavy makeup and a phone number.

There are also live nude shows at bordellos posing as theatres, a goodly number of strip clubs, massage parlors, and God knows how many amateurs working the rich streets. Conventions, sporting events, cruise ships, fleet week, and human need, all combine to feed Moloch's insatiable maw.

Armed with a makeshift private investigator license I'd printed up before leaving, I walked to the Green Star. Along the way I passed the Condor, the Hungry I, the Roaring Twenties, Hustler, Centerfolds, and the Garden of Eden. All busy strip joints and all within shouting distance of the venerable City Lights Bookstore, which amplified the echo of the Beat Generation.

Free love, jazz, and poetry.

First thing they forgot about was *free*.

Indeed the city was among the first to unionize working girls and strippers. Sex is to San Francisco what guns are to Dallas.

During the afternoon Chinatown's Stockton Street is a seething fishbowl of busy Chinese ladies browsing the endless food markets, old guys smoking cigarettes, workers expertly wheeling hand carts loaded with iced fish, packed buses, shoppers trailing wheeled carts, cars circling endlessly for a parking space, designer moms flaunting skin tight knock-offs, flocks of gawking tourists, and dicey characters like me.

I caught a reflection of myself in a store window. With my leather jacket, black T and shades I looked like a PI following somebody. Hardly innocuous. No wonder Albert Chan had picked me out so easily. I made a mental note to adopt a meeker look.

The street action becomes more sedate as one walks past the block-long excavation pit that will someday house the new billion-dollar subway line connecting the Embarcadero to Chinatown.

Normally a seventeen minute walk.

But then I'm naturally leery of subways in earthquake zones.

The Green Star Escort Service was located at the edge of the Stockton Tunnel, on the second floor of a three story building that badly needed a paint job. I climbed the stair and saw the number above an unmarked door. I tried the knob. It was open.

Two Asian women sat at desks facing each other. The younger one wore a telephone head set. The other lady was over fifty with a bee -hive hair style that precluded phone wear. Instead she was pecking at the computer with red lacquered nails. Both of them looked startled when I stepped inside the small room.

I smiled and half bowed. "Sorry, I was looking for the Green Star. This is the number but there's no star."

My lame humor did nothing to lighten the situation. The younger one looked at the older one who snapped to attention like a switchblade

Her smile was a red slit and her tone was sharp.

"May I help you, sir?"

Sir implying I might be delivering pizza. I decided to keep the phony PI license in my pocket and tried to look confused.

"Is this the…escort service?"

My discreet tone did the trick. The woman's smile widened and she nodded. "Yes. Did you wish to make a booking?"

"Uh yes, thank you."

She stood up and I saw she was tall. The beehive hair made her taller and in heels she towered like a Vegas showgirl.

With military flourish she presented me with a business card. "Please call us anytime and we will make appropriate arrangements."

I decided to string it out.

"I was hoping for…discretion," I said, lowering my voice on the last word.

The woman's expression relaxed a notch and her manner became almost friendly. She took a pen from the younger woman's desk and extracted the card from my hand. She wrote a name and a number on the back.

The name was Ky Sin.

"Miss Sin is a woman of utmost discretion," she confided, "you can tell her whatever you desire."

"Are you Miss Sin?"

She put a lacquered fingernail to her lips.

"Discretion."

That didn't leave me much to say but thank you and goodbye.

On the surface my visit had been a meaningless exercise. I could have (and would very soon) hacked into their computer but I wanted to get a personal feel. How did their ladies register I wondered as I walked back. Did you need a resume or was it all who you know?

At the same time the encounter stirred something in the back of my memory. Something unfocused but strong enough to make an impression, no matter how dim.

On my way home I veered onto Jackson Street and stopped at Doctor Jimmy's shop. An elderly gentleman wearing round spectacles, a striped scarf over a striped suit and yellow slippers was engaged in a spirited monologue in loud Chinese while Jimmy weighed, packaged, and labeled various roots and herbs.

It was a big order so I helped myself to some Goji Berries and waited.

The elderly man continued his one-man harangue without a word of response from Jimmy. It took a while but finally Jimmy filled two shopping bags with gnarled roots, pungent herbs, dried flowers, and slabs of mummified mushrooms.

Jimmy broke his silence to say something in Chinese. The elderly man raised his voice and shook his head vigorously.

With a sigh Jimmy opened a ledger book and wrote down an entry.

On his way out the elderly man paused to squint at me with disapproval as if I was eating his personal Goji berries and breezed past.

"That's Mr. Ling," Jimmy said, after he left, "he hasn't paid me for three months."

"You don't cut him off?"

"Can't do that. Mr. Ling is ninety-seven years old. My herbal teas and soups are keeping him on his feet."

"What was he talking about?"

"Same thing everybody around here is talking about. People getting evicted, rents too high, prices…and our hypocrite Mayor Yen."

I gave him a what-can-you-do shrug. Yen, the first Asian elected mayor had previously been appointed on a promise that he would not run when his term ended.

A promise he promptly broke. Since then San Francisco has become a go-to town for rich tech companies and predatory developers bankrolled by hedge fund money.

Jimmy returned the shrug and smiled.

"No bills today, Max."

"Yeah but plenty of news."

I went on to tell him about my encounter with Albert Chan. "He even knows I get my mail here," I said, "but he doesn't really know what happened to New World's hit man."

"Around here they call him Shark Boy," Jimmy said with a rueful snort.

"Because he's a killer?"

"That too. But mainly because he likes shark fin soup."

"Seems to keep him big and strong."

"He was born in Hong Kong. Nobody knows how he made it to America but they say the triad arranged it. They recognized his assets at an early age. Now Albert Chan's Tong is extremely powerful."

"How did he do it?"

"The old-fashioned way. The former leader of the community was gunned down. They never caught the killers. Shark Boy showed up at the funeral in a white suit."

"He must have looked like a circus tent."

"Careful, Max, he's no clown. Albert Chan is as smart as he is dangerous."

"The good part is he promised to protect you from New World."

Jimmy's expression was incredulous. "You believe that? Anytime it suits his purposes he'll toss me under the bus."

"At the moment I suit his purpose."

"You sure, Max? You sure it's not a set-up?"

I didn't mention that Shark Boy hadn't turned me over to the Vandals for the bounty. Still that was a temporary stay.

But isn't everything?

Metaphysically I was fucked on every level.

The sole constant in my turbulent universe was Nina.

"Listen, Max."

I looked up from the gloom. "Yeah?"

"We want you to come for dinner."

"We?"

"Linda and me. You've never been to our place for dinner. It's time, Max. I want to introduce you to my family."

I was reluctant but acutely aware that refusing was not an option.

"Sure, great," I said, "I just hope I won't disturb Linda."

"She's looking forward to it. Tomorrow at seven. Here's the address."

I took the card uncertain if I'd see tomorrow.

Chapter 5

"The universe is eating itself…"
— Depak Chopra

Back home I went through the grinding process of compiling a bio on each of the victims. By midnight I had profiles on four.

Vera Wu: immigrated from Shanghai with her parents. Father owns a small grocery, busted for gambling in 2007. No other arrests. Vera graduated from Central Chinese High School and went to college in Arizona. Shortly before the end of her sophomore year she dropped out and returned to San Francisco. Six months later she registered with the Green Star escort service.

Kim Yee: born in San Francisco, Galileo High School, entered Marin Community College, dropped out during her sophomore year, registered with the Green Star, one arrest for misdemeanor possession cocaine, one arrest methamphetamine, one arrest felony assault knocked down to misdemeanor, suspended sentence, one arrest solicitation, thirty days county. Local girl makes bad.

Kate Sweet (ne Katherine Chow) graduated from the prestigious Lowell High School, scholarship to Berkeley, completed two years. Cross checking showed she had registered with the Green Star in mid semester of her sophomore year. Odd choice of study for a Berkeley coed.

Lili Belle (ne Lily Chung) arrived in San Francisco as an exchange student from Hong Kong. Background and visas hazy to my cynical eye. I got the impression her papers were doctored. Married to one Philip Chin, registered with the Green Star one month after her marriage.

Short honeymoon.

Eighteen months later she divorced Chin after getting her green card.

In less than a year Lili's path to citizenship led to an early death in a cheap pad in the Tenderloin.

My mood shifted from diligence to outrage and I felt The Preacher begin to stir. I suppressed my primal instincts and took a scotch break.

It's been my experience that emotion distorts deduction. So rather than gnash my teeth I went into the kitchen for my bottle of Glenmorangie.

I find scotch more contemplative than tequila, especially the traditional eighty-six proof batches now dwindling as the corporations absorb the old school distillers and cut the product to eighty proof.

I cleared the kitchen table and laid out the crime scene photos of the four girls connected to the Green Star. I placed the profiles I'd just compiled below their photographs.

Then I poured a double and sat at the table sipping my drink while I mulled over the facts. There were a number of coincidences.

Three in fact.

Most obviously, the victims were all working for the Green Star.

The second coincidence required a minimum of study.

All the victims were clad in full-tilt lingerie: opera length stockings, frilly garter belts, black lace thongs, and remarkably high heels.

And to me equally remarkable was the fact that three out of the four had dropped out of college to pursue a career in the world's oldest profession.

Two is a coincidence, three's a trend.

I could only assume they needed the money. Could well have been drugs, I mused, making a note to interview the friends and family members listed on the homicide reports.

I also noted the detectives that filed said reports: Alvin Lee, Samuel Vance, and Martin Riggs.

Another scotch and my thoughts wandered off to Nina.

Could we make it work now that I had peeled away the outer layer of my secrets? Or did I merely extend my stay of execution.

I made a list of everything I needed to do the following day. And Nina was at the top.

***

Early the next morning I hacked into the Lowell High School database and found an address and phone number for Katherine Chow's parents.

They were in the neighborhood, a single family home on Vallejo off Hyde.

It was officially known as Russian Hill but I had dubbed it upper Chinatown for the preponderance of affluent Asian families who resided there.

My phony ID was in order so I sat in an outdoor cafe on Polk Street and called the Chow residence over a designer coffee.

Mrs. Grace Chow answered and when she heard my name her response surprised me.

"Oh are you from the real estate office?"

"No, ma'am, I'm a detective." I didn't mention what kind.

There was a long pause. "Yes, well we already spoke to the police. Do you have some new information?"

"No, ma'am, I just need to ask a few questions, if you can spare five minutes. I'm in the neighborhood."

I heard a deep sigh. "I see, well if you can be here in a half hour. I have an appointment."

Fortified by caffeine I trudged up two steep hills to Hyde Street where Tony Bennett's cable car climbs halfway to the stars.

Standing above Hyde on Vallejo, the Chow residence rested on a tall, flagstone base reminiscent of a Mayan Pyramid. The house itself was colonial with picture windows on both sides of a white door at the head of the stairs.

The woman who answered looked like she stepped out of a Rolls Royce. Slim and regal with porcelain skin. Mrs. Chow's black hair was perfectly cut as was her light gray flannel suit. She wore understated black pumps, a pearl necklace, matching earrings, and an antique emerald ring on her third finger left. It was clear where Kate Sweet got her looks.

I was silently grateful that I had thought to wear a blazer for the interview.

The woman's expression was polite but reserved as she blocked the front door, both hands clasped in front of her. Standing at the top of the stairs she loomed over me like a schoolmarm.

'I'm sorry to intrude like this," I said.

"Thank you. I don't have much time. We are in the middle of preparing this house for sale. What is it you wish to ask?"

"Your daughter was enrolled at Berkeley is that correct?"

The question seemed to make a crack in the porcelain exterior. For a second her expression softened.

"Yes, they gave her a scholarship." Her tone carried a trace of pride.

Abruptly the door behind her opened and a man appeared. He had long slicked back hair, a gold necklace, rose tinted glasses, and a heavy gold ring encrusted with diamonds. From Rolls Royce to Low Rider.

"What's the delay?" he said brusquely. "Is this the real estate agent?"

"He's a detective who came to ask about Katherine."

Her voice wavered when she spoke her daughter's name.

"We already spoke to the police," the man growled. He resembled a bulldog with greasy hair.

"Yes I know, Mr. Chow, this is a follow up in case you might recall something…"

"We already told the police. My daughter left home and got her own place. We didn't know what she was doing for a living."

He shook his head and for the first time I glimpsed a spark of humanity in his clenched features.

"If she had stayed with us…who knows…"

I could see I wasn't going to get much more so I pitched the one curve I had prepared.

"I understand your daughter had a scholarship. Did she tell you why she left Berkeley?"

The question landed like a live grenade.

A steel curtain dropped over their faces and suddenly they looked alike.

"She did not say why, Detective," Mrs. Chow said, her tone a razor. "Excuse us now. We have an appointment."

Like clockwork figures they withdrew in unison behind the door. The only sound was the lock clicking shut.

I left with more questions than I came with. I could understand the quick house sale. Even fixer-uppers were fetching over a million these days. However the Chows weren't exactly grieving parents. Most would be grateful for a police follow up. Was it family shame? That didn't explain the sudden shut down.

Could be my hunch had legs. But I needed more than one sample.

***

Vera Wu's father had a fruit and vegetable store in a neighborhood teeming with similar shops, some larger some smaller, displaying the same wares. The fish stores had their fresh catch on ice, the fruit stores had bin after bin of oranges, mangoes, papaya or cherries or whatever. Supplies changed every few days depending on the season.

A narrow door decorated with large white Chinese characters was the only thing that separated Wu's shop from another just like it. The interior was dim with a cash register in the rear and the two cramped aisles. Two women wheeling shopping carts jammed one aisle so I stepped back outside and browsed the bins. I selected a papaya then tore off a bag for some cherries. As soon as I did the short white haired woman attending the outside left her chair, waddled over, and started scooping cherries into my bag.

"*Tze, tze,*" I said, which in Chinese means thank you.

Her weathered face broke into a spidery network of lines when she grinned.

"*Bo ca chi,*" she said, which roughly means you're welcome.

"Do you speak English?"

"Yes I understand."

"You work for Mr. Wu?"

"I am…" she groped for the word, "…mother in law."

I nodded solemnly. "I'm a detective. I'm investigating the death of Vera Wu."

Her sunny smile clouded.

"Vera my granddaughter."

The grave sorrow that shaded her face made me almost sorry I asked.

"Was she good in school?"

The old woman's expression brightened. "Very, very good. Very smart. Get high marks. Go to college in Ari..zona."

"Why did she leave college?"

Grandma's creased face folded into a dark scowl. She lifted her withered hand but before she could speak a thin man with a pencil moustache appeared at the entrance and shouted something I didn't understand but he was obviously scolding her.

To her credit Grandma Wu scolded right back in rapid-fire Chinese.

A few people stopped to watch the argument. When the man noticed he stopped yelling and looked at me. "You want to buy papaya?"

"Yes but…"

"Five dollars everything, cherries too."

Grateful for the bargain I gave him the five. "I'd like to talk to you…"

"No talk now, business hours. Goodbye."

As he huffed back inside I looked at Grandma but she had retaken her chair by the side of the outside bins and sat with her eyes averted. A couple of shoppers stared at me curiously in hopes of further drama but I decided to walk away before I drew a bigger crowd.

So far I was zero for two.

The third college dropout on my list was Kim Yee.

I had already antagonized enough people that morning so I went home for a working lunch. I had done background on the victims but now I wanted to dig a little deeper and check out their families.

Sure enough I found interesting similarities.

Mr. Paul Chow declared bankruptcy some years back and the house he was preparing to sell had been in danger of foreclosure. The bankruptcy coincided with Katherine Chow's decision to leave school.

Vera Wu's father Fred Wu wasn't bankrupt but he was deeply in debt. Credit cards, car payments, lease, bank loans; you name it and he was behind.

However he had been in financial trouble since his daughter was thirteen so there was no connection there. Most of America was in deep financial shit when Bush Jr. left office. So I kept digging.

In anticipation of an afternoon visit to the jewelry store owned by Kim Yee's parents, I checked their finances. Until five years ago Mr. Yee had ideal credit. Then everything turned sour and there was a flurry of missed payments. At present he was barely keeping up.

And yes, five years ago Kim Yee dropped out of Marin Community College.

So what I reasoned, lots of kids drop out when their parents can't afford the exorbitant tab for a college education.

But lots of kids don't register with the same escort service and wind up murdered.

While I was at it I looked up Lily Chung's ex-husband Philip Chin.

I didn't have to dig very deeply.

Turns out Philly, as he was known to his friends on Facebook, had been married three times in the past five years. And each of his blushing brides was from China.

Not only that, they all had registered with the Green Star.

His profile picture showed a man of thirty-five or so, with a white wall haircut and diamond earring, sporting a pale blue tuxedo jacket and red striped bow tie. Most likely his standard wedding outfit.

Rather than trouble another set of bereaved parents I decided to squeeze Philly and see what came out.

Philip Yuen Chin was in good shape financially. He had a solid 401K, a tidy stock portfolio, and owned a two bedroom condo in a high rise in the Tenderloin.

Turk Street is a rough hood. To get to Chin's apartment one has to walk a gauntlet of dealers, hookers, junkies, muggers, and winos. Once inside the lobby however you were in a better world.

Chin lived on the eleventh floor and answered the buzzer promptly. I had called earlier under the pretense on doing a follow-up investigation. He never questioned my credentials and agreed to a visit without hesitation.

There was a dramatic view of the city from his terrace but if you looked straight down you could see the people sleeping on the sidewalk.

I know this because Philly invited me in and proudly showed me around his place. It looked like downtown Vegas.

So did Philly.

I was somewhat taken aback by the man who opened the door. He looked older than his Facebook photo and definitely heavier. Only his earring was the same.

He was short with a barrel chest and hefty shoulders, like a wrestler. His black silk shirt was open to the navel displaying the flashy gold chain around his neck. Equally flashy was his toothy grin.

In turn I flashed my phony ID.

"Detective LeBlue."

"Please, please come in, Detective," he said, throwing open the door as if to show he had nothing to hide.

"Nice place," I said.

Actually Philly's place had the charm of an airport. A white plastic table and chairs in the kitchen area. A three stool bar made of faux wood with a neon Corona Beer sign above it. A white leather couch, chrome framed white chairs, and a chrome coffee table. I could see an unmade bed in the room beyond.

"Take a look on the terrace. The view is awesome."

When I came back inside he was pouring white wine.

"Drink?"

"Thanks that would be great." I wanted to put him at ease about my visit.

He brought me a glass and we settled down on the chrome chairs.

"Were you still in touch with Lily after your divorce?"

His grin didn't waver but his dark eyes were wary.

"Sure we stayed friends. She was a nice girl. We still went out once in a while. You know, to clubs and stuff."

"When was the last time you saw her?"

"Maybe two months before she was killed."

"How did you find out?"

"Her girlfriend Ginger. She was the one who called the cops when Lily didn't answer her calls. I had to go down and identify the body. Closest relative."

"You have a lot of close relatives.

"What do you mean?"

"You've been married three times in five years."

"You know how it is." He gave me a man-to-man shrug. "I like women too much. But when they come to America they forget how to be a wife."

I gave him an intimidating stare. "Is that why they register with the Green Star escort service?"

Philly's grin finally deflated.

"What's that got to do with Lily's murder?"

"Maybe everything. You tell me."

Philly's grin came back, strained this time. "You know how it works, Detective. Chinese people here have relatives there—nieces, cousins—want to come here, don't have papers. Easy way, they marry an American citizen. The relatives pay me to marry them and bring them here."

"You still haven't mentioned the escort service."

"When these girls arrive here they're in debt to family. Must repay loan. That's between girl and family. I already collect my fee."

"Bullshit."

I got to my feet and stood over him using a well-worn interrogation technique.

"I do know how it works, Phil. You collect your fee on both ends. The family in China and the girl herself. She has to pay you both off. Isn't that right?"

His affable demeanor vanished, leaving behind the wary eyes and teeth bared in pre-strike mode. As his head receded into his shoulders he resembled a snapping turtle.

"Okay, Detective LeBlue, what do you want?"

I backed off a step to give him breathing room.

"Who's your contact at the escort service?"

He seemed confused by the question. "What contact? Look if this is about money we can come to arrangement."

"Money? Okay let's talk money. What happens if the IRS looks into your stock portfolio? Or if the FBI looks into importing women for prostitution? Human trafficking…"

"Okay, okay I got it. The lady I deal with is called Ky Sin."

Now I knew he was telling the truth. So I pressed it.

"You kept in touch with Lily after the divorce."

"Sure. She was happy to be in USA. Had apartment, green card…"

"And you were still collecting your fee."

"Why you asking me this?"

"Because somebody murdered Lily."

"You think I did it? When she dead I can't collect my commission."

"Do you still have a key to her apartment?"

"Yes. Why?"

"We're both going over there now."

Lily Chung's apartment was still in disarray. I recognized the overturned coffee table in the living room and rumbled bed from the crime scene photos.

It was a renovated two-bedroom in a run-down building two blocks from Phil's place on the edge of the Tenderloin war zone. Unlike Phil's luxury condo there was little protection from the human misery just outside the plaster walls.

Lily's clothes hung neatly in the closet and the bureau drawers were undisturbed suggesting the motive wasn't robbery. It also suggested she had been strangled in the living room and her body dragged to the bedroom to be staged. The upended lamps and chairs were practically a trail to her bed.

"Did she ever mention having a problem with a client? Anything strange?"

"Not to me. She might have told Ky Sin."

I kept looking but there was nothing to find.

"I haven't been here since she died."

Phil's voice seemed to echo in the empty apartment.

For a second I almost felt sorry for him. Then he said something that woke The Preacher up.

"I'm going to have to get this place fixed up."

"Fixed up?"

"For the new girl."

I held myself back.

Only one fast shot to his belly.

As he slowly folded to the floor, sucking air like a fish, I walked to the door.

"What the fuck…was that for?" he wheezed after me.

I kept walking.

"For the new girl."

Chapter 6

"Anyone who can pick up a frying pan owns death."
– William Burroughs

Two years after leaving the perfume department at Macy's Jem Ming was making real money.

She was first generation Chinese and her father worked as a house painter to support his family of four so there had never been much to go around.

Her mother Lin didn't speak much English but she did the shopping, cooking, and took good care of her two girls Jem and Tang. She made sure they could read, write, and count. Taking them each to a store front school every day. By the time Jem got to first grade she had no trouble with her schoolwork.

What did trouble her was the drab sameness of her life. Disappointed that he failed to have a son, her father Gu Ming remained distant. At home there was nothing but homework after dinner and then bed. Nothing like the families she saw on TV.

A gawky teen Jem grew to be a pretty girl, taller than most with a good body. She had lots of admirers but was too smart to get involved with the local boys. Jem had bigger plans.

She knew her way out of Chinatown was through college. So she kept her head in the books, got a part time job as a salesgirl at a local jewelry store to help with family expenses, and didn't go on her first date until junior year in high school.

She lost her virginity in her senior year. Jem and her boyfriend planned to attend the same college that September.

In July however, things changed.

Her mother announced the family needed money, Jem would have to take a full time job. Her sister Tang as well. Her little sister had been at the top of her class in high school and she would have to drop out. It broke Jem's heart but she obeyed her parents' wishes. It was the way she had been raised. The traditions of two thousand years were bred into her DNA.

Jem found work at a Macy's and her sister took over the job she had at the jewelry shop.

However even with the extra money it didn't seem to be enough. As usual Jem didn't question her parents but one evening something happened that opened her eyes.

Her father did not return home after work. Hours later they received a phone call. Gu Ming was in the emergency room. He was the victim of a severe beating that left him with two broken fingers, a broken rib, and facial bruises.

At first Jem believed her father had been mugged. It was her boyfriend, Greg Han, who told her the truth.

"Everybody around here knows what happened to your dad," he said gently. He looked away as if embarrassed. "It was the Tong. Your father owes them money."

"But now he can't work."

Greg shrugged. "They made him an example to the others. Half of Chinatown owes money to the Tongs one way or another."

What Greg left out was that her father was a gambler.

Jem found that out later. She had stopped believing her mom's excuses and made her tell the truth. She also found out how much her father owed.

"Fifteen thousand, ten percent a week," her mother said as if reciting a prayer. She began to cry.

For her mother's sake Jem made a decision.

There was a salesgirl at Macy's who had been a stripper in Florida. She had confided to Jem that she made more in a night stripping than she made in a week at Macy's. Her name was Susan Wagner but she worked under the name Brenda Fury.

Susan stayed at Macy's for a few months then left. She had registered with an escort service. Jem was shocked when Susan broke the news during their lunch break.

But now Jem saw it as the only way to protect her mother and sister.

She contacted Susan and asked her how she could register.

At first Susan was skeptical. However when Jem told her about her father, Susan agreed to help.

Jem was still working at Macy's so Susan helped her shop for a new wardrobe while Jem still had an employee's discount. Then she gave Jem instructions on make-up and hair to enhance her natural beauty.

The other lessons were more advanced and Jem had trouble relating to them. She nearly backed out until she remembered her mother and sister. They were depending on her.

Susan arranged her first date.

She let Jem use her apartment. It was only for an hour, at four hundred dollars an hour.

It was the worst hour of Jem's life. She cried afterwards. The man had been crude and insensitive and had bad breath. Jem was left with two hundred dollars after paying Susan and the escort service their commission.

A few days later Susan contacted her. She had a private client. Susan's end would be one fifty an hour plus tip. Reluctantly Jem agreed.

This time it went a little better but Jem felt depressed afterwards. Still she had made four hundred and fifty dollars in a couple of hours.

"Think of it as going to the dentist," Susan said, counting out the money. "Except you've got to make them think you enjoy it. That's how you make your tips, and pick up steadies. With your looks you won't have much trouble. But you've got to learn fast. It's a jungle. C'mon I'll buy you a drink."

Welcome to the jungle Jem thought, gathering her things.

When she returned home Jem found her mother waiting. With no explanation she gave her mother three hundred dollars.

"I'll take care of Daddy's debt," she said flatly, "but Tang must go back to school."

Her mother accepted both the cash and the ultimatum without questioning the source.

For the next few months Jem continued to work as a salesgirl nine to five and as an escort three nights a week. She no longer paid Susan a commission and the money she earned paid down her father's debt and supported her family while her father was still recovering from his injuries.

*****

Finally Jem quit her day job and became a full time escort, six nights a week. At the same time she moved into her first apartment.

At the end of the first year her father's debt had been paid, her sister was scouting colleges, and Jem had thirty seven thousand dollars in a savings account.

One day while shopping at a boutique Jem ran into Susan who seemed happy to see her.

"Hey, girl, you're looking fine, how's business?"

Jem had to admit Susan was looking exceptionally good. She was driving a Mercedes convertible and wearing a designer suit that made her look like a successful tech executive. Her hair was perfectly cut and she was flashing a set of emerald earrings and matching necklace.

"Well I'm not looking as fine as you," Jem said. "Did you hook up with a sugar daddy or something?"

"Better than that. Come on I'll buy you lunch and tell you all about it."

Susan took her to The Slanted Door and explained the source of her newly acquired wealth. She had moved to the executive side of the escort business.

"Here's how it works, we put your photograph on our website. When the john clicks on your picture, he's taken to your *personal* website. Now here's the best part. You have a video on your site and a Skype set up. Depending on what the john wants to spend, he can either download your video or have

Skype sex with you in person. And if you want to take a live date that's fine. We charge a monthly fee for maintaining the site plus a percentage of your online action. As for live dates ten percent sounds fair."

More than fair, Jem thought. The escort services took thirty percent.

"But I don't have a video and my computer…"

Susan airily waved away her objections. "We can take care of all that. In a couple of months you'll be making more money and working less."

Actually it was expensive to get started on Susan's website *High Class Sluts*. However the photographs and the five minute video were very professional, even flattering, and in three months Jem was making plenty of money.

The video income alone more than paid for her monthly expenses and she had learned how to keep the johns online longer during her Skype sessions. It added up.

In fact Jem had become something of a Skype star. She had a closet full of various costumes, wigs, and erotic devices to entice her viewer into lingering past the time limit. After that the john was on pricey overtime.

As an added benefit the fee for her live dates had also gone up. Jem soon acquired a serious bank account and modest stock portfolio. She leased a BMW convertible and moved into an apartment with a view of the bay. Jem also made sure her mother was comfortable and put some money away for her sister's education.

She even acquired a sugar daddy.

Gregory was older, or the far side of fifty, and he visited her once a week on Skype. He liked her to pose for him in lingerie and indulge in erotic conversation before they both masturbated. Afterwards he liked to talk at twenty dollars a minute.

Even at a distance Gregory was hard to take. He looked okay, no better or worse than her older, gray-haired clients.

But there was something oily about him, unclean. So when he requested her address, Jem was quite reluctant.

"Oh but I'd like to send you a present," he said, surprised that she turned him down, "a very nice present."

Intrigued, Jem gave him Susan's office address. The next day Susan called to say a messenger delivered a package.

Gregory hadn't exaggerated. The gold bracelet set with three small diamonds was elegant and expensive. There was a card inside with just a phone number.

"Work this john," Susan said, admiring the bracelet, "he's a gold mine. If you need advice just call me."

At the end of the next week's Skype session Gregory asked if he could see her live. To discourage him Jem quoted an exorbitant fee, three thousand an hour. Without so much as an eye blink, he agreed.

That's another thing about Gregory, Jem thought as she smiled for the camera, *his eyes*. His gray eyes were unblinking and empty. While three thousand dollars an hour was tempting, she remained undecided.

"Let me check my schedule," Jem said, "call Susan tomorrow."

"No call me directly, do you still have the number I left in the box?"

"Yes."

"Use it to get in touch with me. I live in Berkeley."

"Sure, fine, Gregory. Thanks for being so understanding."

Jem felt relieved when the connection was severed and Gregory's image left the computer screen.

Susan airily waved off her objections. "Of course he's creepy. He's a *john* for chrissakes. That's why he's willing to pay three grand for your company. You should be flattered."

She had a point. Many of Jem's clients were hardly attractive and they paid a lot less. The next day she called Gregory.

Still careful Jem arranged to meet him in a public place where she could size him up safely. As a concession she wore the bracelet he'd given her.

On first meeting Gregory seemed harmless enough: paunchy, round-shouldered, thinning gray hair—with a large bald spot she'd never seen on camera—very pale white skin, and gray eyes that seemed to disappear inside his pasty features. The only things expressive about him were his hands which moved constantly.

Gregory seemed shy in person as if having the Skype screen between them gave him confidence. Certainly Jem preferred it but three thousand an hour was too good to pass up. Especially now that her sister would be entering college. Not to mention the potential for more in the future.

They met at a café in the Cow Hollow neighborhood which bustled with boutique shoppers and young matrons wheeling strollers. Soon after they arrived however Jem noticed Gregory was starting to perspire.

"I'm sorry, is it hot in here?" he said, mopping his brow with a large blue handkerchief.

"A little," Jem said, pretending not to notice. But she chalked it up as another in a long list of turnoffs.

However she relented and told him to meet her in an hour at the Sunset Motel.

He seemed relieved. "I'm crazy about your body. If I could paint I'd have you pose for a nude portrait."

"That's very sweet, Gregory. But remember no cameras."

"Don't worry. And here's a little something extra for you."

He discretely pushed five hundred dollar bills across the table.

"You are very nice. See you at the Sunset in an hour."

Jem scooped up the bills and left the cafe to prepare for her client's pricey session.

The first place she went was Susan's apartment where she bought two grams of coke. She usually avoided drugs and alcohol but she needed something extra to go through with this session.

Everything went as usual. Jem posed provocatively in lingerie and high heels while Gregory watched with his flat gray eyes and rubbed himself.

He was still sweating and kept mopping his neck and face with the blue handkerchief.

Then he beckoned.

As she knelt down beside his chair Jem tried to pretend he was on the other side of a computer screen.

Until she felt the wet handkerchief drop over her neck and begin to tighten.

Chapter 7

*"I don't like being alone after I'm finished being
by myself."* — Marianne Faithfull

I woke up early and took a run around Washington Square
and up a few steep hills to ease my anxieties. I worked up
an appetite but the anxieties buzzed around my breakfast
like flies.

The two appointments I had that day were worrisome.

While honored by Jimmy's invitation to meet his family my
social skills were lacking after years of living alone. I didn't want
to frighten his wife and little girl.

To that end I went shopping for a gift for his daughter. A
few years back a picture book would do the job but these days
kids are way ahead of Walter the Farting Dog.

I went to a computer game shop. Like most ironclad bach-
elors I'm wary of kids and they of me so I wanted to make a
good impression. I bought an electronic pad that contained five
games. The salesgirl said it was endorsed by the teachers association. Sold.

From there I went to City Lights Bookstore and browsed
until I found a volume called *The Cartel* by Don Winslow. I say
volume because it's a big novel and weighs a bit.

I hauled it across the street to a restaurant called E Tutto
Qua, Italian for 'it's all here'. Over white wine and a civilized
pizza I started the novel and didn't want to stop until I realized
it was time to go home and do some work. Along the way I
bought a bottle of good wine and a bunch of flowers for my
hostess.

My bases covered I went home and hit the computer until it
was time to shower, shave, and look presentable.

Jimmy lived on the outskirts of Chinatown on Russian Hill. He owned the second floor of a two story house on Pacific.

He greeted me at the door with his wife Linda. His daughter peeked at me shyly from behind her mother.

"Thank you for the flowers, Mr. LeBlue, they're beautiful," Linda Chu said.

She was a lovely woman, tall and graceful with long black hair, flawless skin, intelligent hazel eyes, and an easy smile.

"Please, Mrs. Chu, call me Max."

She glanced at Jimmy and nodded. "Of course, Max. Please call me Linda. And this is Christine."

Reluctantly the young girl came out from behind her mother. "Hello, Mr. LeBlue."

Christine favored her mom, tall and skinny with hazel eyes and her dad's soulful expression. Despite her shyness she radiated an exuberant innocence that won me over instantly.

"You call me Max too okay?" I said extending the wrapped game pad. "Here, Christine, this is for you."

Wide-eyed she looked from the wrapped gift to her parents. When her mother nodded approval she took it.

"Say thank you," Jimmy said.

Christine stared up at me. "Thank you, Max." A moment later she was tearing off the wrapper.

"Let me fix us a drink," Jimmy said, leading me to the living room, "bourbon, scotch, tequila, or maybe a margarita, it's my specialty."

Linda disappeared into the kitchen along with Christine.

"Specialty it is," I settled into an easy chair while Jimmy got busy at an antique glass liquor cabinet with a fold out shelf that served as a bar. A large sofa sat nearby flanked by another easy chair. A large blue and red silk rug covered the hardwood floor and I could see the lights of the Bay Bridge from the windows.

There was a redwood bookshelf with the lower shelf dominated by children's books (so much for my insights) and the upper by leather bound volumes and hardcovers. A couple of abstract oil paintings reminiscent of Chinese calligraphy hung on the walls. All in all cozy and classy.

Jimmy returned with the drinks.

"Here's to good friends," he said, lifting his glass.

I tapped his glass with mine. "A rare breed."

The margarita was slightly chilled, light on the mixers and salt. A mild drink to start the day since I would be meeting Nina at the Lone Palm later and switching to straight Patron.

"Something smells good," I said noting the aroma wafting from the kitchen.

"Linda's a fantastic cook," Jimmy confided, "and she's learned to incorporate my healing herbs into her recipes." He beamed proudly. "Her idea not mine."

He clicked his remote and the high, sweet sound of Miles Davis's trumpet came over the speakers.

"I try to play Jazz and classical music to offset the electronic crap the kids listen to," he said, "even some good old rock and roll."

I lifted my glass. "Here's to musicians who play their own instruments."

Christine appeared bearing a serving tray heaped with tiny dumplings. She set the tray down on a glass coffee table.

"Thank you for the game, Max," she whispered. "I figured out the math game but the word game is hard."

I leaned closer. "I'll tell you a secret. Use your phone as a dictionary while you play the word game."

Her face lit up. "Ohhh I get it." Then she hurried back to the kitchen.

"She's really a math whiz," Jimmy said as he refilled my glass from a crystal pitcher. "Please try the dumplings."

They were warm and delicious. My social stiffness oiled by the second drink I settled back in my chair. "You have a nice family."

Jimmy smiled. "I'm thankful for my family, my work, my clinic. But..." His smile clouded. He looked anxiously at the kitchen and lowered his voice, "I'm not seeping well lately. This whole thing…"

"I know. Let's see what happens at our face to face with Taylor Kingston."

"Max, you don't…"

I waved him off. "Wouldn't miss it."

Linda had put my flowers in a vase on the sideboard. "They're beautiful. Thank you, Max, it was very thoughtful."

"I got through the word game," Christine said, "now I'm on the next level."

Linda set down plates of sesame chicken and spiced vegetables. "I'm so glad you gave her an educational game, most of them are so violent. All that shooting."

I had to agree but kept my opinions on the back burner during dinner.

Jimmy was right, Linda was a fantastic cook. She was also a health worker in a local hospital and had a lot to say about facilities for the homeless.

"Mayor Yen's appetite for tech companies has displaced thousands of former residents," she explained, "not only have they lost their homes but they have no access to basic hygiene facilities."

"Linda's passionate about this," Jimmy said, "we're very proud of her work."

I smiled and nodded, basking in the after dinner glow. It had been years since I'd attended a real family meal. Maybe it was the wine but I found I liked it. It filled a small part of the void inside.

Our conversation lingered long after dessert. Jimmy was explaining the basic science of acupuncture when we were interrupted.

"Max, can you help me with this last puzzle game?" Christine said, putting her new pad in front of me.

"Let Max talk to daddy," Linda said gently, "He was kind enough to bring a gift, we can't expect him to play it for you."

"No problem," I said winking at Christine. "I'll give it a quick look."

I studied the game, which entailed trying to trap an elusive elf and winning a pot of gold.

"My best advice is this." I gave the pad back to Christine. "Instead of chasing the elf, block his exits."

"Always good advice," Jimmy said. "More coffee?"

Two words which I interpreted as 'closing time'. Maybe I was over sensitive but it beat overstaying. I made small talk for a few minutes, praised my hostess for a truly fine dinner, and made ready to leave.

Before I could Christine came back, big hazel eyes glowing with pride. "I did it!" she announced holding up the game pad. "It says I'm number twenty out of four thousand and two. Thank you, Max, I love this game."

I grinned like a schoolboy all the way to the street. As I sat on the half empty bus I realized the family dinner had opened a door I'd kept locked for more than a decade. The realization made me uncomfortable, as if something had been released beyond my control.

It also amped my desire to find the psycho who had destroyed ten families to feed his obsessive lusts. Ten young women who had once been little girls like Christine.

***

While I waited for Nina to finish her shift at the Lone Palm I kept going over what I'd learned so far.

It wasn't much.

One way or another the victims and their families were in debt. Katherine Chow had a scholarship but these days that barely covers basic expenses. Strong traditional customs are still maintained in the Chinese community. Customs that stretch back two thousand years. But how far do they stretch here, today? Forcing a daughter into prostitution? Maybe.

But would a modern coed submit to the ancient ways?

None of my questions put me any closer to the man I was hunting. A man who had strangled ten women. And I was the only one who seemed to care.

Except for Albert Chan, I thought. He cared enough to pay me twenty grand to run down the killer. I tended to agree with Jimmy Chu. Shark Boy was using me. Anytime he was finished he'd throw me to the Vandals for the bounty and recoup his investment with interest. I made a note to google the dollar amount my head was worth.

"I'm proud of you, Max."

I turned and saw Nina smiling at me. She had come outside for a smoke break.

"For what?"

"You're still nursing your first drink."

She lit her cigarette with a small antique Zippo I'd given her.

"You've been lost in thought since you got here," she said.

It wasn't a reproach, just a question.

"Case I told you about."

"*About* is a slight exaggeration."

"I'd rather talk *about* us," I said.

"Very good, Max. I'll buy it for now."

"Want to go somewhere after your shift?"

"No. I want to go right home."

"Your place or mine?"

She leaned close and kissed me. Her mouth lingered then moved to my ear.

"Mine," she said softly, "it's closer."

That kiss swept away all distractions and for the rest of the night I was in the moment with Nina. A long, delicious moment suspended in a parallel universe where God was in his heaven and the devil was in bed with me.

Later, while listening to B.B. King's guitar and basking in each other's naked arms Nina sighed and asked me a hard question.

"You know, Max, I'm willing to stick it out. But is that what you want for us? You in North Beach with two roommates and me here never sure of when I'll see you again?"

"You know that's not what I want. In a perfect world…"

"In *this* world."

"In this world you and I would have to go to a neutral country, maybe Brazil, and start over. My computer skills translate anywhere in the world so I shouldn't have much trouble finding work. Or generating new identities if necessary."

Nina lifted her head. I could see she was impressed.

"So you have thought about it."

"Of course. A lot in fact."

She was quiet for a while then started lazily tracing her finger along my chest.

"That's a nasty bruise. Does it hurt?"

"Only if I breathe."

Nina gently kissed my ribs, lips and tongue warm on my grateful bruise.

"Is that better?" she whispered.

"Oh yeah."

Then she moved on and soon everything felt better.

***

When I woke up Nina was in her tiny kitchen making eggs, toast, and coffee.

I looked at my watch. It was barely eight thirty but I felt wide awake.

Amazing what love can do for your health.

"Where are you off to so early?" I said, as Nina started gathering her things.

"I'm seeing Jordan and I want to come back before rush hour."

She came back to the bed and kissed me.

"Get up. I made your favorite omelet. I want you to know what domestic bliss is like."

After breakfast Nina went to Berkeley to see her cousin Jordan Fuente who was doing post graduate work at the university. Jordan's mother and his sister Carla had moved to Chicago. Not for the weather but to avoid retaliation by the Vandals after two honest cops and myself rescued Carla Fuente and put the Vandals out of business for a few years.

And I was still getting the fallout, I brooded, as I rode the 12 bus from the Mission to Chinatown.

It was still early when I arrived at Jimmy's shop. Doctor Chu was consulting with a trio of elderly patients. A few minutes after I entered a delivery man arrived bearing a manifest. Jimmy made a circle with his fingers and pointed to the clock on the wall behind the counter.

I left and wandered over to North Beach. I stopped to buy a newspaper and walked to Café Trieste. At that hour the place is full of unemployed artists and freelance geniuses. In fact it was there I first encountered my flat mate, the celebrated bohemian physicist Eli Sarfetti. Currently holding court at some posh London club.

I found a small table against the window, drank my coffee, and read up on the local news. It was generally bad. A candidate for state senate Paul Wing had been caught in an FBI sting. As usual the Feds tried the perp in the media but a careful reading of their case showed it was obvious entrapment. Any good lawyer would get it tossed.

Then I focused on a smaller headline: *Richmond Woman Found Dead.*

Jem Ming, twenty, had been found in a motel room on Lombard.

A long way from Richmond. The story didn't mention a cause of death. I tried to figure some way I could get to the crime scene while it was fresh.

On impulse I called the sole contact I had in law enforcement. Newly promoted Captain Bob Lowell of the Petaluma PD, one of the honest cops I mentioned earlier.

"It's me, Bob."

"Max?"

"Yeah, congratulations on making captain."

"Bullshit. What's up?"

"I'm wondering if you know a straight cop in the SFPD."

"By straight you don't mean…"

"I mean honest."

"Are you on a case?"

"Yes. But I need police access. Know someone I can trust?"

"Detective Alvin Lee in North Beach. He's a friend. If it'll help I can call ahead and let him know you're coming."

"Great. I owe you."

"Forget it, Max. So what's this case about?"

"Long story."

"Let's get together for a drink. I'll be meeting Steve tomorrow."

"Tony Nik's at nine."

"See you there."

Captain Bob Lowell happened to be gay. Steve was his partner and worked the bar at the Top of The Mark.

Bob was under the impression that I was still with the DEA. An impression I never bothered to clear up. He was also the best lawman I'd ever worked with.

I recognized the name Alvin Lee from the police reports I hacked.

For the first time I felt a buzz of optimism. Maybe I could even convince the police they had a serial killer problem.

Then again it could have been the strong coffee. It's been my experience that a homicide detective's two biggest fears are a) the Feds and b) paperwork.

Serial killers attracted both.

I walked back to Jackson Street feeling a sense of cautious hopelessness. Once I contacted Alvin Lee I risked exposure.

Jimmy was behind the counter with a clipboard when I entered his shop.

"Good morning, Max. You look busy."

"It's the coffee. Thanks for last night, dinner was superb."

Jimmy grinned. "You were a big hit with Christine. She usually doesn't take to our guests."

"She's a great kid. You must be proud."

"Tell me about it when she hits thirteen. That's when the trouble starts. But most kids in the community respect their parents."

"Speaking of which. Do you have time to give me some background on this community?"

We went into Jimmy's therapy area where he brewed some soothing tea and schooled me on the ways of Chinatown. He began by explaining the centuries old family codes that still prevail today, then gave me a brief overview of who's who in crime.

"Back in nineteen seventy-seven, before you were born, Max…" he grinned at his own joke. He didn't know how right he was. "…there was a war going on between two street gangs; the Wah Ching and the Joe Boys. One night the Joe Boys heard some key members of the Wah Ching were at a restaurant called the Golden Dragon. So the Joe Boys went in and shot everybody in the place—except their targets. Killed five people including tourists, wounded eleven. One of the Wah Ching members who survived the shooting was only twelve years old. Today they call him Shark Boy."

"Another American success story. So you think it's possible that a girl would turn to prostitution if their family was in debt?"

"Depends on the debt. If the family owes money to a Tong they must pay or suffer serious repercussions."

I sipped my tea which was quite relaxing. "How many Tongs are working the neighborhood?"

"There are many Tongs, benevolent associations with roots in China. Mainly they act as banks, lawyers, and civil advocates for immigrants. But a few are fronts for criminal organizations with ties to the Hong Kong Triads."

"How many is a few?"

"Three. There's the Sun See Huang Tong, that's Shark Boy. Just as strong is the Wu Sing Ki. That one's headed by Victor Kang. The smallest is the Hip Wing which is run by a young thug named Billy Gin."

"Do the cops know all this?"

"*Everybody* knows it. Business as usual."

That about summed it up.

"By the way I took your advice."

"About time. What was it?"

"I scheduled a meeting with Taylor Kingston. Day after tomorrow at three p.m. Can you make it?"

"I'll be there with my recorder."

"And, Max…"

"Yeah, yeah, I'll have your piece too."

∗∗∗

I called Detective Lowell back and he gave me Alvin Lee's private number.

"Thanks for the hook up, Bob."

"You can tell me about it tomorrow night."

I phoned Alvin Lee from the street. I wasn't worried about him tracing my number since I was using one of my many pre-paid phones.

He answered promptly.

"Yes?"

"My name is Max. Detective Lowell gave me your number."

There was a pause. "Yes, okay."

"Can we meet somewhere?"

"Today?"

"As soon as possible."

"Can you tell me what this is about?"

"The dead girl on Lombard."

Another pause. "Okay how about Golden Boy Pizza on Green. Ten minutes."

Good choice, Alvin.

Golden Boy is an outdoor pizza dispensary which serves customers on the sidewalk from a window and has tables inside. Late at night it was jammed with party animals pouring from the bars.

Since it wasn't yet lunchtime there were tables and counter space available. It was totally anonymous and provided a view of the street.

I picked out a slice of vegetarian pizza from the window display and took a seat at the counter. Before the slice came out of the heating oven, a slim Asian man wearing a brown leather jacket and jeans came in and took a seat next to me.

"Max?"

What the fuck. Was I that easy to spot?

"How did you know?"

"Bob described you."

My pizza arrived. I ignored it.

"Really? What did Bob say?"

"Said you were kind of gnarly. Short hair, thousand yard stare."

"I better start wearing shades."

He smiled. "Bob said you were stand up."

"I try."

His pizza came out of the heater. Vegetarian like mine. We ate in silence for a few minutes. Pizza and coke, a cornerstone of the American diet.

Finally he said, "What did you want to talk about?"

"A recent murder. Jem Ming. I'm assuming the crime scene on Lombard is still fresh."

"Yeah, except for the body. I caught the case with my partner. What do you know about it?"

"Nothing yet. I need access to the crime scene."

He sat back and lifted his eyebrows as if I'd suggested borrowing his gun.

"Seriously?"

"Serious as a serial killer."

That got his attention.

"Okay, Max, this is bullshit…"

"The girl on Lombard, was she strangled?"

Alvin's mild manner hardened. "What makes you ask that?"

"Cause of death wasn't in the papers."

"Autopsy's not in yet."

"But…"

"But what?"

"You think she was strangled."

He stood up, half his pizza uneaten.

"Tell Bob I'm sorry."

"Please, finish your lunch and I'll explain."

I detailed the evidence I had, including the killings in other precincts and their obvious similarities.

He studied me curiously, like a scientist inspecting a new species. He did have an academic look with his long black hair and boyish features. Despite his being a cop there was a certain frankness in his gaze.

"What's your interest in this?"

"I've been hired by family members. Look I understand nobody wants the FBI fucking everything up. But this guy is on number eleven by my count."

Mentioning the FBI was as much a warning as it was showing empathy.

Alvin heaved a long sigh and looked away. "Look, Max, I came to this same conclusion many weeks ago. I brought it up a number of times. Even tried to put it in a report. It was quashed and I was on the shit list. Our Captain doesn't want to rock the political boat. Elections coming up soon."

"I just need one visit to the crime scene while it's fresh. I promise to share whatever I come up with."

Alvin finished his pizza, chewing thoughtfully.

"I'm doing this for Bob Lowell," he said finally, "I owe him." He met me eye to eye to make sure I understood. "But I'll be right there with you."

"Agreed, when?"

"Tonight. Seven sharp." He took a card from his pocket and wrote on the back. "Meet me there but don't park your car in the lot."

***

I arrived on two wheels. I chained the bike to a parking meter and walked the rest of the way. The address Detective Lee gave me was the Sunset Motel, known to cater to one hour guests. I arrived ten minutes early and Lee was already in the parking lot.

He was sitting in his unmarked Ford, talking on his smart phone.

I hoped it wasn't about me.

"You're early, good," he said when he saw me. "My daughter," he added as he pocketed the phone, "she needs help with her homework."

From his brisk manner I got the idea he wanted to dispatch this favor as quickly as possible. I couldn't blame him. It was late and he had a family. For an empty moment I wondered what it would be like to have a daughter.

I followed Lee to a second floor room next to the soda and ice machines. The door was draped with police tape. Lee removed the tape and we went inside.

The cramped room was a shambles. I took out my phone and began taking photographs. Lee watched me, reciting details as we went from area to area. Overturned furniture, small mirror on the floor with the usual trace amounts of white powder.

"Jem Ming, twenty two, we don't know if it's her real name yet. Believed strangled still to be confirmed by autopsy. Lots of prints, no clues."

"What about DNA?"

"Mostly all the Vics are clean—I checked with forensics. That includes the Richmond murders. Except for the one in the Tenderloin. We recovered DNA from a wine glass and a trace of semen on an item of lingerie. Otherwise nothing to connect the homicides."

It wasn't a big room but the girl's struggle to live had displaced lamps, pillows, and chairs. Even the shower curtain was ripped from its rod. Outside the bathroom was a single black shoe with extremely high sequined heels. I snapped a close up and looked around.

"Where's the other shoe?"

"What other shoe?"

"There's only one shoe here."

"The other one must be around."

"I don't see it."

I scanned the room again. "My best guess is that she was killed in the bathroom and the murderer dragged her onto the bed and posed the body."

"How do you know that, Max?"

His steely tone told me he was reaching for his cuffs.

"I've seen some of the crime photos. They've all been posed. Is it okay if I look under the shower curtain?"

"You have gloves?"

"How about a clothes hanger?"

I took a wire hanger and carefully lifted the floral shower curtain. I flashed back to Peter Ng's plastic covered corpse.

At the base of the tub was the other shoe. I put the hanger aside and took a close up. The sequined spike heel was stained with a dark red spot.

"Check this out," I said, moving aside.

Lee knelt down to examine the shoe. "Might be blood maybe."

"Might be the killer's DNA maybe."

"You think?"

"She struggles, runs into the bathroom, tries to fight him off with the heel of her shoe, draws blood, he strangles her, she yanks down the curtain, her other shoe comes off when he drags her into the bedroom."

Lee sighed. "We'll see. Right now I'll have to bag the damn shoe and book it as evidence. If that's blood on the heel....well shit…"

"You find something?"

"Don't know yet."

He took out a pocket knife, opened it, and used the blade to lift up the loose inner sole of the shoe. He pulled back the thin strip of leather. Underneath were three hundred dollar bills folded flat.

When Lee unfolded the bills with his knife I saw the business card tucked inside.

"You guys didn't lift this curtain yesterday?"

It was a reasonable question but it seemed to annoy Lee.

"My partner went over the scene after the body went to the coroner. I had to go to county and interview a perp in a separate case."

"Who's your partner, Vance or Riggs?"

He squinted at me. "Marty Riggs. Sometimes it's Vance. Sometimes they work together. We rotate."

"How do they feel about your serial killer theory?"

"They agree with Captain Barnes."

He deftly lifted the card with the blade and kept it balanced there while he read the print. "Oracle Escorts," he muttered.

I knew the name. It was the other service the killer used besides the Green Star.

Then Lee did something that impressed me.

He flipped the card over and it landed on the flat blade. There was a phone number written on the back and the initials D.S.

"Nice move," I said, reaching for my notebook.

He gave me a lopsided grin. "My father was a chef. I could flip omelets when I was seven."

I wrote the number down and stood up.

"How does this compare with the Katherine Chow crime scene?"

"You saw the files."

"You were there."

Lee got to his feet and held out his hand. "I'm going to need that number you wrote down. It's police evidence."

"I thought we were going to share…"

"*You* were going to share. I let you into the crime scene as we agreed and yes, you helped discover what may be a key piece of evidence. But it belongs to the SFPD."

I tore out the page with the number and gave it to him. I had it memorized anyway.

"You're the boss."

Lee nodded. "That officially concludes my favor. Now I have to drop off the shoe at the precinct and get home in time to see my daughter. Luckily I came prepared."

He took two plastic baggies from his pocket and carefully put the blood stained shoe in one bag and the hundred dollar bills in the other. The card went into his pocket.

"We're done here, Max. Say hello to Bob for me tomorrow night."

***

As I bicycled home I realized I had a lot of research work waiting for me. I needed to cross check Oracle and Green Star with the victims. I also had to run down R.J.'s phone number. Which meant hacking the client lists of both services.

I picked up a rotisserie chicken and a six pack and settled down in front of the computer.

At three a.m. I went to bed frustrated. Even cross referencing I couldn't find a match.

On impulse I called the number. It was no longer in use.

I was back to square one.

When I awoke I took advantage of the clear weather to bicycle over to the Embarcadero and hop a ferry back to Sausalito. I didn't go directly to my safe house in Corte Madera but veered off to visit my pal Len Zane.

***

Len is a master mechanic and his shop sits across highway 101 behind a discount gas station and a warehouse. At the moment Len was putting the finishing touches on my '94 Mercury Sable. By no means a glamorous ride even when new, Mercury discontinued manufacture years ago.

However the Green Ghost as I call it, has a number of features which suit my lifestyle: two roomy stash panels, a radar detector and police scanner, race car suspension, and a motor which will push the needle well past 170. And most importantly—it's totally anonymous.

The entire package had been handcrafted and maintained by Len. At present the Green Ghost was in for a tune up. Which is a two day operation for Len who takes meticulous pride in his work.

Len was also my weed dealer and his slow smile of greeting hinted that his grower pals had brought in a good harvest.

Long, lean, and lanky Len could have easily been a film cowboy. His steed of choice was a BMW motorcycle and he kept a small stable of hot bikes for personal use.

He wiped his hands on a rag as I dismounted my bicycle.

"I left you a surprise in your stash box," he said.

"Might get crowded in there."

He paused. "How so?"

"I'm looking for a personal weapon."

"What's wrong with the nine you got mounted overhead?"

The Green Ghost has two secret compartments. A small one under the dash where I store my boo and sometimes a .38, and one overhead large enough to house a dictionary or a kilo, or the Sig Sauer 9mm that sleeps there.

"It's a favor for a friend."

"Favors like that can backfire."

"Which is why I came here."

He nodded thoughtfully. "Better step into my office."

Len's office was two easy chairs at the rear of the garage with a small table between. On the table was an ashtray and a deck of rolling papers.

Without fanfare he took a baggie of weed from his denim shirt pocket and rolled a modestly substantial J.

For a few puffs we were silent but as the grass began to light up the darkened corners of my brain I decided to check my local standing in the community.

"I heard the Vandals still have a price on my head."

"Kind of makes you feel important don't it?"

I looked up. Len was smiling. He plucked the joint from my fingers.

"Wouldn't worry about it. You took out most of the vets. New guys have no idea what you look like."

He leaned back and exhaled.

"But these days the Vandals are back up to speed, pun intended. Still movin' meth, horse, and whores."

By then Len's grass had eased the tension knotting my body and I was able to separate actual problems from potential disasters.

"So you think the bounty is nothing to worry about?"

"It's horseshit. The Vandal's way of saving face."

"Speaking of saving face I do need a piece. Nothing too heavy. Maybe a Beretta forty five."

"I've got a Glock 30S—ten in the clip one in the spout. But I hate to part with it. You sure about this friend of yours?"

"Wouldn't be here otherwise. Look if it's a hassle I can drive to Reno."

Len drew himself up. "Did I say it was a hassle? Just would be a shame to waste this piece on your run of the mill asshole."

I put my hands up in surrender. "Take my word for it. There's no shame in this deal."

Len is extremely judgmental in his choice of associates so I had to tread softly.

He took a last meditative drag on the J and pointed it in my
direction.

"Won't be cheap."

"Never is."

"Including the tune-up, the oh-zee, and an extra clip we're
talking three grand."

I counted out Shark Boy's money and Len went into the
interior of his garage.

Five minutes later I drove out in the Green Ghost with my
bike in the back seat and my new Glock and an ounce of weed
under the dashboard.

The Mercury purred like a Cheetah sniffing prey and ready
to sprint but I took it slow and patient.

I parked about a block from my house and pedaled the rest
of the way taking only the weed and Shark Boy's retainer.

Len's potent J had left me energized and as soon as I entered the in-law unit behind my landlord Organic Phil's home, I
got to work. After stashing the money in a small safe behind a
wall panel, I switched on all three of my computers and started
cross checking the information I had gathered.

A few minutes later it hit me.

Fuck it.

I was spinning my wheels.

I switched off the computers, turned on the FM radio, and
zoned out on jazz and blues on my favorite station KPOO.
Len's grass eased me into a meditative state and when I got up
to make myself a sandwich I had sorted out my priorities.

Number one was tomorrow's meet with New World.

After one of the best tuna sandwiches I ever devoured
I started assembling the equipment I'd need. Two tiny audio
recording devices and a trio of nano-cameras.

That done I turned my attention to giving New World
Developers a thorough scrutiny.

The first interesting fact I discovered was that the late Peter Ng's security firm XTech had been acquired by New World three years previously. The sale price had been fifteen million.

So Ng hadn't been hurting for money. He had other reasons for leaning on Jimmy. Maybe he did it to keep his hand in, I mused, former intimidator keeping his edge. I still liked my first theory: Ng intended to kill Jimmy himself because didn't want a witness.

And obviously he was doing it on behalf of New World Developers.

However Jimmy and I were the only two who knew that. And tomorrow we would meet the man who called the shots.

Getting a line on CEO Taylor Kingston proved difficult. There was no photograph, bio, Wikipedia info, or Facebook, Twitter, LinkedIn presence. That alone made him highly suspicious.

Like me.

Which made me rethink the equipment I intended to deploy. Since it was all practically microscopic I decided to take a couple of extra gadgets.

I kept poking around but found few cyber prints left by Taylor Kingston. Finally I shut it down, turned on the TV, and vegged out on Len's excellent weed.

Chapter 8

"You can't give the public what they don't want."
— Guy Kibbe, Footlight Parade

Crossing the Golden Gate Bridge I was uncomfortably aware of all the hardware in my car. Certainly my Sig was well concealed but the very fact that I might have to use it weighed on my thoughts as I paid the toll in cash.

Cash because the bridge Fast Pass is connected to a credit card, one's time of crossing is recorded. These records have already been used in evidence in various court cases especially divorce proceedings, to establish a defendants movements such as an afternoon visit to the mistress, or whatever. In my case I made it a rule to keep my electronic footprints as dim as possible. Example: all of my computer resources are in the name of an alternate identity whose address is a postal box.

It is almost impossible to avoid the authorities these days. And I'm not just talking law enforcement. The corporations have become a law unto themselves, exerting their money and technology to control every aspect of our lives.

Soon Apple will put Big Brother on every wrist. If you don't believe me just ask the NSA.

Paranoid? As William Burroughs used to say, paranoia is having all the facts. Fact: those smart TV's report back to their masters. Fact: if you have a credit card, computer, mobile phone, or even a relatively new car you are on their radar. Not to mention cameras everywhere from the gas station to deep space.

Therefore once I found a secure spot to park I carefully transferred the Glock from the panel under my dash to my black leather briefcase.

I was wearing a dark blue blazer, gray flannel trousers, blue shirt, and maroon tie for the meeting with Taylor Kingston.

The briefcase completed the look. It also served as support for my private arsenal of surveillance devices.

***

"You look like a damn lawyer," Jimmy said when I walked into his shop.

"Criminal lawyer maybe. Anybody in back?"

Jimmy shook his head.

"Ready for this meeting?"

He shrugged. "Haven't you noticed? I'm wearing a tie."

True. San Francisco's dress code is slightly to the right of sloppy. Doctor Chu's usual work clothes were Dockers and a sport shirt but today he was wearing blue pinstripe trousers, a white shirt, and a blue tie. He reached behind the counter and lifted a pin striped suit jacket.

"I'm good to go."

"Let's take the scenic route."

He paused, jacket half on. "How do you mean?"

"Your tunnel. I'd rather keep Shark Boy off our tail. Besides which I have an illegal weapon for your protection."

Jimmy seemed touched. "Thank yo Max. I owe…"

"I hope you never have to use it. But there's an extra clip in case."

Jimmy locked the door and pulled the shade. We went into the back room where I gave Jimmy the Glock. After admiring the pistol for a few minutes he reluctantly stashed it.

"Nice balance."

I nodded. "At close range it's very effective."

It was cool and damp in the underground tunnel that connected Jimmy's shop to the storeroom. Occasionally I could hear the rumble of overhead traffic and wondered if the old ceiling would withstand an earthquake.

We climbed a makeshift ramp that led to Jimmy's musty storeroom.

Jimmy unlocked the door a crack and checked the street.

"You go first, Max. Turn right and wait for me on Broadway. I'll lock up and meet you there."

A bit elaborate but in a vacuum-packed community like Chinatown every step is noted and scrutinized. Street gossip gave Shark Boy a reliable surveillance system.

As I waited for Jimmy I mentally browsed the spyware I'd brought along and tried to figure out where to plant each item.

A cab came by and I flagged it. I took my time opening the door so Jimmy could catch up.

"This is convenient," he said.

Reflexively I checked to see if the driver was Chinese. He was Russian.

Jimmy gave him the address and the cab deposited us in front of one Market Plaza, a trio of skyscrapers on the Embarcadero. New World Developers occupied the top three floors of the Spear Building.

Security was tight. The desk guard called upstairs and after we were cleared he walked us to the elevator and unlocked it.

"Penthouse floor," he said. I thought I detected a note of respect. On the way up I made a show of polishing my glasses while scanning the elevator car for cameras.

I saw one overhead.

No matter. My glasses housed a nano-camera.

Everybody was watching everybody.

Best I could do was try to keep the score even.

"Any ideas?" Jimmy whispered, as if that made a difference.

"He called you. Let's hear what he has to say." I rolled my eyes upward.

Jimmy got it. He nodded and remained silent for the next forty odd floors.

The doors opened on a white reception room. The large picture window facing the elevator offered the visitor a dizzying

view of the Bay Bridge and beyond to the Berkeley Hills. A
male receptionist sat behind a white desk to the right of the
doors. The only other furniture was a black leather couch.

The receptionist greeted us with a wary smile. He was
young, perhaps twenty-eight, with short blond hair and alert
blue eyes.

"Mr. Chu? We weren't expecting your friend."

"Mr. LeBlue is my counselor," Jimmy said without
hesitation.

He pointed at the couch. "Please take a seat while I call."

That suited me fine. As soon as we sat down I pinned a tiny
camera into the leather backrest.

The camera was connected to a relay imbedded in my briefcase which in turn connected to my laptop in North Beach.
Until they found it I would have a peek at Taylor Kingston's
other guests.

The camera in my glasses worked on a similar relay. My audio devices left the strongest trail because they connected to a
smart phone registered to the same dummy ID as my computer
system.

The receptionist came towards us, holding a baton and a
straw basket. He was taller than me with wider shoulders and
no visible body fat. Probably a black belt in some obscure martial art.

"Please stand gentlemen."

He had us dump our keys and phones in the basket airport
style while he went over us with his baton.

He paused at the brief case, baton hovering.

"I'm sorry, sir, you'll have to leave the briefcase outside."

I smiled. "No problem."

After the electronic pat down we followed the receptionist
to his desk. He punched some numbers on the keyboard and
the wall behind him slid open.

Dramatic.

Like a pair of bumpkins in a palace we slowly walked into a spectacular salon walled by glass on three sides. I couldn't help gawking and nearly didn't see the Asian woman seated behind a thick glass desk.

Even slightly distorted under the glass her legs were long and slim. Her sleeveless white sheath dress flowed into an ivory neck and her flawless features were framed by straight white blond hair. When she stood to greet us she moved with athletic grace.

"How do you do, Doctor Chu. Taylor Kingston—I'm so pleased we can finally meet."

She shook Jimmy's surprised hand.

Then she turned an regarded me with eyes that matched the color of her dark jade necklace, . "And you, Mr. LeBlue, I understand you are Doctor Chu's counsel."

She extended a hand as smooth as water.

"Advisor. I'm not a lawyer," I said, with all the gravity I could muster.

She held my hand for a long second. Jimmy glanced at me.

"Nice place," I managed.

Her shrug spoke volumes. "It's a little impersonal for my taste, but impressive. Please, gentleman, sit down. Would you like something to drink? Tea, coffee, perhaps something stronger."

"What are you having?" I found myself saying.

Again Jimmy glanced at me. I was close to flirting with the woman who probably sent Ng to kill him.

"I prefer tea," she said

"That's fine."

"Good for me," Jimmy murmured.

A black leather couch and two matching armchairs were grouped around a long glass table facing the window. Tall stalks of flowering red gladiolas rose from a crystal vase at the far end of the table.

I watched Taylor Kingston in stunned silence as she said something into her phone.

Call me sexist but I hadn't been expecting the ruthless CEO of New World Developers to be a woman. And not one so beautiful.

Both Jimmy and I took the couch and waited for her to finish her call.

On the other side of the huge window San Francisco Bay lay at our feet like a sparkling blue carpet that stretched from the Port of Oakland to the Golden Gate Bridge and far beyond.

Impressive indeed.

Between the view and the impact of meeting Taylor Kingston I almost forgot why I came.

Before she hung up I pinned a tiny microphone, no bigger than a needle, into the black leather cushion behind me.

I polished my glasses and made sure the camera was on. As I replaced them the door opened behind me and I glimpsed the reflection of the receptionist wheeling a cart inside.

Our hostess came to join him. At that moment my little camera picked up the two of them together. I hoped it was working.

"Here we are. Sorry to keep you waiting. Thank you, Mark."

As he left Ms. Kington served tea with old school ceremony that suggested time abroad. More English than Asian, right down to the Wedgewood and tiny cookies that passed for crumpets. I was curious but realized I had said enough.

"Here you are, Doctor Chu," she said passing the cup and saucer. "Being a healer I'm sure you appreciate the benefits of tea."

Her melodic voice carried a trace of London. Despite my efforts to remain totally unmoved by her classic grace I was fascinated. As she handed me the cup and saucer her green eyes lingered on mine.

"Let's get to it shall we?" she said, settling down in an easy chair, "I think we all know why we're here."

Jimmy was remarkably cool.

"To be frank, Ms. Kingston, I came as a matter of courtesy. I believe you already know my position."

"Yes of course. However you don't know my position."

Jimmy leaned back. "Which is?"

So far Jimmy was looking like a crack negotiator: calm, unhurried, no bullshit. I was beginning to feel superfluous. To keep myself relevant I tried to find a spot to plant a camera and another mic. It was difficult because my attention didn't stray far from our hostess.

"I propose a partnership. New World is willing to give you three million dollars in exchange for a half interest in your building."

It was a curve ball that took Jimmy off balance. He glanced at me then recovered.

"Well that is certainly worth thinking about."

She stood up. Against the dramatic backdrop of San Francisco Bay viewed from the forty-third floor Taylor Kingston seemed like an ivory Nefertiti. Her white dress clung to her supple, long limbed body and her eyes were like hard, bright emeralds.

Suddenly I saw a woman who might have a man killed.

"Of course, Doctor. But please don't have me wait too long for your decision. We have a timetable."

"A timetable for what, Ms. Kingston?"

My question landed like a day-old fish.

She gave me a sideways glance and the temperature dropped below freezing. Her icy malice drilled into me.

"We're a development company, Mr. LeBlue," she said, voice slow and patient as if instructing a child. "This involves contracts, penalties for unfulfilled commitments, and large scale investments. New World would like to renovate sections of the city which have remained in a dangerous state of disrepair for over a hundred years."

"And Doctor Chu's clinic…?"

Her pink mouth curved in a sly smile and she morphed from scary to playful in an instant.

"That remains to be seen doesn't it? His decision."

"I mean what do you intend to do with your half of the building should he decide to take your offer?"

"There'll be provisions that insure Doctor Chu will still control what becomes of the building. You see, gentleman, Doctor Chu's reputation in the community is a valuable asset. And we are willing to pay full value."

It sounded too good to be true.

"How long does Doctor Chu have to make his decision?"

"Would a week be long enough?"

I looked at Jimmy and sipped my tea. It was excellent. Strong, warm, and fragrant, like our hostess. Her icy demeanor had melted and she waited politely for Jimmy to respond. Despite my reservations I couldn't help being drawn to her.

"A week is reasonable," Jimmy said, setting his cup down.

Taylor Kingston stood up and half turned in a clear indication that as far as she was concerned our meeting had ceased to exist. And us along with it.

"Alright then, gentleman, a week it is," she said in a clipped martial tone. "Mark will show you to the elevator."

She pressed a button on her phone. The door opened and the receptionist stepped inside. He waited at the door and led the way as we filed out.

I made note of the fact that the elevator required a key to operate and moved closer to allow the camera in my glasses to record the type of lock. Jimmy and I didn't speak on the way down but his taut expression said volumes. When we reached the street the dam broke.

"Jesus, Max, what the hell do you call that?"

"A business meeting."

"Business?"

"She made you an offer you can't refuse," I said echoing Shark Boy. Except I wasn't laughing.

"She's threatening to take my clinic, my family, and the whole damned community."

"We knew that going in. Now we know what you're worth to her."

I took a deep breath. The breeze blowing off the bay smelled fresh and real, unlike the conditioned air on the top floor.

"How would you handle her?"

"With extreme caution. But we do have an ace up our sleeve. Three in fact. I planted a few bugs around her glass fortress."

The stress webbing Jimmy's face dissolved and he grinned. "Max you're a genius."

"Actually I'm a sneak. I'll let you know after I get home and check what we pick up."

***

It was minimal TV.

It could have been a Warhol home movie, with long hours of nothing happening at all except for Mark on the phone, Mark at the computer, Mark leaving the computer to go in and out of the glass sanctum. Nobody else in, nobody out.

One good shot of Mark and Taylor Kingston together. That was it.

The inner camera I'd planted was worse.

In my haste I had jammed it at such an angle that all it picked up was a view of Taylor Kingston from her black stilettos to her knees. And the microphone was garbled. All in all a second rate job.

Disgusted I left the desk and poured myself a scotch. I kept looking over my shoulder at the two computer screens. They may as well have been blank. As I reached for my cigarettes I glimpsed something move into the reception area.

I hurried back to the desk and started recording. A man had emerged from the elevator and was walking to Mark's desk. I couldn't quite make out the visitor but I saw Mark jump to his feet and usher the man inside.

Obviously well known. But not to me. The figure was grainy and the pixels broke up when I tried to enlarge the image.

Mark came out and made a phone call.

Cursing aloud I turned to the second screen. All I could see in the other room were legs and shoes. I turned up the volume but the conversation was more static than words.

Then something happened that restored my faith in sin.

Shins, shoes, and stilettos had intertwined and were shuffling back and forth. The raspy audio picked up something that sounded like music and I realized Taylor Kingston was dancing with her visitor.

Or something.

The shuffling continued then stopped as the man's shoes moved out of the frame. The stilettos stayed and a few moments later a white dress dropped around Ms. Kingston's shapely ankles.

The stilettos stepped out of the dress and off the screen leaving me gritting my teeth in frustration. There was no way I could use any of it. I didn't even know the identity of the guy who persuaded Taylor Kingston to display her considerable assets.

I swallowed my scotch and lit a cigarette, resigned to futility. A few puffs later things changed.

Taylor Kingston flowed back onscreen like a water nymph descending to the bottom of a lake as she eased her naked body onto the carpet. She was followed by an equally nude but far less graceful male who lowered himself one shaky knee at a time until his slack features could be seen,

Receding hair and sunken chest, plump belly, perspiration running down his face—even without his custom suit and signature fedora I recognized Martin Yen, the fucking Mayor of San Francisco.

Literally.

Chapter 10

S hark Boy decided to go big.

"Put a couple of thirties on here."

"That makes it three-sixty."

"I can count, Tommy—do it."

"You never go over your body weight before," Tommy Ho grumbled. He racked a pair of thirty-pound plates on either side of the already stacked barbell.

"Spot me."

Albert Chan's huge hands gripped the bar. At six four, three hundred pounds he was all sculpted muscle with massive shoulders and chest tapering down to abs like coiled steel springs. Added to this was his speed honed by years of martial arts training. Nobody wanted to fuck with Shark Boy. Not even Tommy who had seven hits to his credit.

"Five reps."

Tommy stood ready behind the bench as Chan slowly pressed the huge weight once, twice…on the third rep he began to tire. Four was smooth but strained. On the fifth rep he wavered. Tommy reached out to assist.

"No dammit!"

The veins in Chan's neck swelled, flushing his skin. With an animal howl he heaved the weight above his chest.

"Five," he groaned triumphantly.

Tommy helped Chan guide the barbell back to the rack.

"You want protein drink?"

"No. Drop back to three hundred."

Watching Chan do ten easy reps, as if three hundred pounds was a warm-up, Tommy's admiration was tinged with fear. He had his own side operation and if Shark Boy found out, he'd kill him with his bare hands. Tommy had seen Chan crush Sam Hung's rib cage a few years back.

"Protein and a towel."

After refueling Chan liked to hit the heavy bag. He used hands, elbows, knees, feet…they need to get a fresh bag every month. Most they had to dump, thick leather hides split open by Chan's relentless attack. The rest were donated to various youth clubs.

On occasion Tommy would spar with Chan, careful to rely on good quick defense and an excellent mid-air kick. Mostly he danced away. Even a playful swat from Shark Boy could land him in the emergency ward.

Chapter 11

"**Y**ou're shitting me, right?"

Robert Lowell, Captain in the Petaluma PD, is a square-jawed, no-nonsense peace officer. Tough but fair. As American as a cowboy on a white horse. A cross between George Clooney and Tom Brady.

And if it comes down to life or death there's nobody else I would rather have on my team.

At the moment he was staring at me, half-smiling as if he knew I was putting him on and shaking his head because he knew I wasn't.

Over a tequila or two I had recounted my escapades with Shark Boy, my inquiries into the Chinatown murders, and my parallel ventures on behalf of Jimmy Chu vs. New World Developers. Naturally I left out the part about Jimmy shooting Peter Ng and me helping dump the body.

Bob seemed intrigued by my description of Taylor Kingston but he was completely blown away when I told him what my tiny misplaced camera managed to record.

"The mayor…?"

"In all his glory."

"I guess it's not illegal."

"But most likely unethical. New World is moving in on San Francisco and they need the blessing of City Hall. Illegal bribes, contracts, who the fuck knows."

"What do you plan to do with the video?"

"Nothing. I'm not a blackmail expert like Rupert Murdock. It's Jimmy's insurance policy if and when they put pressure on him."

"And these serial murders?"

"One step at a time. Thank Detective Lee for the favor but I could use a short sit down to compare evidence."

"Alvin likes you but he thinks you're a wild card."

"Tell him he's a great judge of character."

Bob grinned. Then he got serious.

"News up north is that the Vandals are back into human trafficking."

"Anything to do with what's happening down here?"

"Maybe. Two girls escaped from the gang in Santa Rosa. Both of them are Asian via Salvador."

"Cops interview them?"

"Yes but they didn't speak English that well. They took the cops back to the scene but by then the Vandals were long gone."

"Where are the girls now?"

"They were released."

A group of people at the next table burst into laughter. Tony Nik's is dark and narrow but the crowd is local and the bartenders friendly. We were at a table in the rear and our conversation was hard to hear over the noise and music.

Which suited me fine.

I had adopted a defensive posture considering I seemed to be in everybody's crosshairs. Certainly Taylor Kingston and the Mayor would be eager to join the shooting party.

"The girls who escaped. Do you think you can locate them?"

"I can try."

"I'm thinking there might be a Chinatown connection."

"Okay, Max, but what makes you think that?"

"This Shark Boy character knew the Vandals have a bounty on my head. Maybe it's a stretch but why would he know that?"

Bob drained his drink and shrugged, "Since we broke them the Vandals went back to selling guns and meth. They're probably branching into human trafficking. But the Chinatown connection is kind of thin."

"Maybe. But Shark Boy also knew I found a kidnapped girl. Which is why he recruited me."

"Okay I have friends in the Santa Rosa PD. I'll ask around."

"I owe you."

"You don't owe me a damn thing. By the way I ran into Craig Manson, Detective Lieutenant Manson I should say. He's head honcho in Fairfax now. But you know it's a one cop town."

Craig Manson had joined Lowell and me on an unofficial strike mission on Vandal headquarters to free my lady love Nina and her cousin.

We also blew up their meth lab and drove their operation way out of town. Their leader Shane Hazer had escaped and was rumored to be holed up in Montreal but I had no doubt he'd be back someday to exact revenge.

During the shoot-out Manson had suffered a serious gunshot wound to his leg and still had a pronounced limp.

"Give him my best next time you see him. He's a hell of a lawman."

"I'll tell him you said that." Lowell raised his glass. "Craig really looks up to you."

Show me a hero and I'll write you a tragedy said F. Scott Fitzgerald. He should know.

It made me uncomfortable that Craig looked up to me. It should have been the other way around. Despite having a family to think about, not to mention his own ass, the kid didn't back down when the bullets started flying.

I was so engrossed in my own legend that I didn't notice the black car trailing me as I walked home. But when the car turned into a driveway about a hundred feet in front of me I took it as a hint to get focused.

By now I knew the routine.

Cinematic but corny.

On cue the smiling blond bodyguard left the car and opened the rear door with mock ceremony. Albert Chan was waiting inside.

I eased beside him, taking care to avoid physical contact.

He stared straight ahead. "I thought I paid you to find this fucking killer."

His quiet tone resonated with menace. I was impressed.

"Did you expect results in three days?"

He turned to look at me. His cherubic features had morphed into a steel battle helmet.

"I expect you to respect the families of these poor girls. I hear complaints about your methods."

That explained a lot. And raised a big red flag.

"By some remote chance do any of these family members owe you money?"

It was like striking a match in a dynamite factory. The two bodyguards in front stiffened and Shark Boy seemed to swell up, looming over me like a massive storm cloud. I braced myself.

His grim features broke into a grudging smile of approval.

"You're good, Max. Yes, some of the families borrowed money from my Tong. What's that got to do with the murders?"

"Still remains to be seen. Meanwhile, Albert, let me do my job. What do you know about the Green Star escort service?"

"Only that they rep some of the girls who were killed. You think there's a connection?"

"Maybe. Now if you have no further information, I'll be on my way."

"I'll drop you off."

"Thanks I need the air."

The huge man studied me for a moment, eyes glinting in the semi darkness.

"You know who you're dealing with right?"

"Yeah, a micro manager who expects instant results. Jesus, man, lighten up. I've got work to do."

"You'll be hearing from me."

"I'm looking forward to it."

Again I took the long way back to my pad but I was kidding myself. Shark Boy might not have known my precise location but he had me down to five square blocks.

It was his hood. I just lived there.

***

The first thing I did when I arrived was check my surveillance cameras.

The mayor's departure through the reception area was fuzzy but I had him cold in living close up, cavorting with the decadent Taylor Kingston.

Later I saw Ms. Kingston get on the elevator with her assistant Mark and for the next few hours there was no activity. Then it happened.

A security guard walking through the reception area with a walkie-talkie activated some sort of electronic squawk. Within a half hour Mark was back dressed in gym clothes and in the company of two men in black suits armed with hand-held detecting equipment.

Shortly after that my little electronic stake-out shut down.

Just as well. The footage I'd collected was like being handed a nuclear device. I couldn't put it down and I had to be goddamned careful what I did with it.

Then it came to me. I put it in storage for the time being. In fact I put the mayor's erotic interlude with the CEO of New World Developers in five different safe sites. All ready to detonate at the touch of the right button.

However I would have to live long enough to drop that finger.

That aside I decided to do a deep search on the latest victim of the Chinatown strangler Jem Ming.

First thing I discovered was that I had been careless. I had assumed the action stopped with the escort services. But that was just the first layer.

Peeling it back I discovered Jem Ming had a sophisticated one-lady operation. She was featured along with three other attractive ladies on a site called *High Class Sluts*. For a healthy fee one could book live dates same as the Green Star. But the next layer was innovative.

It was Jem Ming's personal website. For an even healthier fee one could book screen to screen sex sessions via Skype. The site included a photo album of Jem in various costumes: nurse, policewoman, schoolteacher, schoolgirl, lingerie model, dominatrix.

Jem as lingerie model caught my attention. Each of the victims had been wearing stockings and high heels. But their killer had been up close and personal, not separated by miles of fiber optical cable.

I went back and checked *High Class Sluts* searching for the management. I found that there were forty ladies featured on the site's roster.

Three of them, Vera Wu, Katherine Chow (Kate Sweet), and Jem had been victims of my strangler. Too much of a coincidence.

After finagling my way past a stiff firewall I found the name Brenda Fury, purportedly the manager. I didn't buy it and tunneled deeper until I found the name of the person who owned and maintained *High Class Sluts*, Media Horizons, the registered owner of which was one Susan Wagner.

By the time I retired for the night I had a complete file on Ms. Wagner's personal and professional life. Indeed in many ways they were intertwined since she went from prostitute with one arrest no conviction to Macy's saleslady, back to prostitute with two arrests no convictions, to successful media madam with forty young ladies to choose from.

Make that thirty seven.

I was still counting when I fell asleep.

I was up at six and rolled around on the floor, stretching and loosening stiff muscles. The ache in my ribs was still there reminding me not to get drunk and play Galahad with other people's girlfriends. On the other hand Leslie did seem grateful for the rescue.

Reasonably warmed up I went out for an early run around the hood. The empty streets were carpeted by a cool, thick mist and as I ran past Washington Square Park a ghostly army of Chinese men and women stood in the fog silently practicing Tai Chi in slow motion curves.

The run took me up and down some carefully chosen hills to Aquatic Park where the Dolphin Club swimmers were out there in the harsh, frigid water. Like me.

Back at my place, showered and alert, I scanned the computer for news before going out for a luxurious breakfast at Mama's. That was as good as I would feel that day.

It started with a text message from Jimmy. He and Nina were the only ones who knew the number of my pre-paid phone which was changed monthly.

Need Help.

The two words set my heart pumping and I hurried across Broadway into Chinatown. When I got to Jimmy's shop I saw the ambulance outside and the paramedics inside. A pair of uniformed cops kept onlookers at bay but two or three tourists had their phones raised in the international salute to calloused indifference.

I maintained a discreet distance until they wheeled out a stretcher bearing a Chinese male. Even though his head was bandaged I could see it wasn't Jimmy.

On impulse I walked quickly to the next block and knocked on the door of Jimmy's storage room. A few moments later the door opened.

"What took you so long?" Jimmy said.

"I had to make sure the guy with the head wound in your shop wasn't you."

"My brother-in-law, he's been working with me while he's in school."

"What happened?"

"I was in back checking stock, Bryan was up front, two men came in and just started beating him up. I couldn't get to my gun so I called 911 and took the tunnel over here. Did he look okay, was he conscious?"

Jimmy was hyped on adrenaline, talking fast, sweating…I gave him the same advice he often gave me.

"Take deep breaths, sit down somewhere."

"But Bryan…"

"We'll catch up to him at the hospital. Right now you've got to get yourself centered. Then we'll walk back to your shop. If anyone asks we met for a coffee at Trieste."

"Okay, Max, what then?"

He sounded better already.

"Then you check the shop for damage, take your gun with you, and lock up. From there we'll go to the hospital. When we know Bryan's condition you can call your wife."

Jimmy managed a weak smile between breaths.

"Alright, give me a minute."

A few items had been overturned in the front room and Jimmy's heat lamp was smashed in the clinic as well as some bottles but obviously the intruders were intent on bodily harm, no matter whose body they found.

Fortunately the Glock was where Jimmy had stashed it and after he locked up the shop we went to the emergency ward at St Francis hospital.

We waited an hour or so before a harried young doctor informed us that Bryan Luen suffered a broken arm, two cracked ribs, and a concussion. He was resting comfortably and would be there for at least four days.

Jimmy called his wife and assured her Bryan would recover.

"There's nothing you can do, honey, I'm here and I can't see him. He's under sedation and not allowed visitors. I'm waiting for the doctor now. I think if we come in the morning it'll be better."

Jimmy shut his phone and put it in his pocket.

"Why the hell would somebody do this?"

I put a finger to my lips and extracted the phone. Then I removed the chip and other vital parts.

"It's my fault."

That surprised Jimmy. He shook his head. "C'mon, Max, that's…"

"The cameras I planted?"

"Yeah so?"

"One of them caught Taylor Kingston fucking Mayor Yen."

After Jimmy recovered I gave him a run through of what I'd recorded and how the devices were discovered.

"The mic I planted caused feedback in the security guard's mobile. Very soon after that they called in the bomb squad and they took us out of the picture, pardon the pun. Funny thing though."

"The pun wasn't that funny."

"If I hadn't planted the camera in the wrong spot it never would have picked up what actually happened after drinks with Martin Yen."

"One way to do business."

"Time honored."

"So what now?"

"You're wife and…"

"I'm way ahead, Max. I'm sending them to visit relatives back east. I'll work something out with their school."

"You should go with them."

"It's me they want, Max."

"Then find a safe house. I'll get you a pre-paid phone. Most likely yours is already bugged. Computer too."

"Seriously?"

"If they knew what we have you'd be dead. Bryan too. You know what they say."

"No what?"

"You can't fight city hall."

Chapter 12

The tall Asian woman's moves were efficient and very fast. She spun and caught her opponent with a spinning back fist to his chest and ducked under a clumsy roundhouse that would have dropped her to the mat.

Shark Boy laughed. The back fist might have hurt most men but his pectoral muscles were like metal plates. But he had to admit the bitch was very quick. He dropped his hands trying to lure her in. She stepped in, tapped him twice on the jaw, and hopped well away from his kick. It was frustrating but he liked it. It kept him in shape and in balance. As a result he was becoming faster himself.

At the end of their session he was drenched in sweat. She on the other hand, except for the damp gloss on her skin, was barely perspiring. Even her hair had remained in place.

Chan bowed. "Thank you. I always learn from you."

She bowed back deeper. "You honor me."

"Join me for a relaxing sauna while we discuss business."

The sauna was part of his private gym which included a weight room, dojo, treadmills, and a Jacuzzi. Chan visited the facility daily.

After they were settled on the cedar wood benches Chan got to the point.

"The profits from our escort services are up five percent but still down ten percent from last year," he said with a trace of annoyance. "Funny thing is our population, tourism—all those figures are up."

"The young techies moving into the city use their dating aps. We've changed our marketing to higher end clients which accounts for the increase. But we have competition from independents. One in particular is using some of our girls."

Predictably the news stoked Shark Boy's aggressive nature. He didn't like anyone poaching his property. She was counting on his reaction. And she had guessed right.

Chan slammed the bench hard enough to shake the small room. "Godamnit they're like hyenas at a kill. Everywhere! Get rid of them!"

"As you say. But I can't do it alone."

He took a deep breath and calmed down. "Use Tommy. He's efficient."

A wave of exultation washed away her tension. It was perfect. She would erase one of the last links to her betrayal, and Chan could never trace anything back to her. Yet there was still a piece unresolved.

"Philly told me he received a visit from somebody investigating Lily Chung's death. He said the man roughed him up. Do you know anything about it?"

"It wasn't any of the people on my payroll."

"It could be this man you hired…that you won't tell me about."

"Need to know, darling. If it was my man then he's doing his job isn't he?"

The woman let it rest. She had gotten what she needed to execute her plan.

The sauna had heated up and they were both perspiring heavily. Chan had a towel draped on his lap and used it to wipe his face and chest leaving him naked. She saw him looking at her a certain way and let her own towel slip down exposing one breast.

Shark Boy made it a strict rule to never mix sex and business, but with her black hair tumbling over smooth, glistening shoulders, her alert, pink tipped breast and long, sweat oiled thighs, she was too erotic to resist. He felt himself become hard.

As he neared she smiled and slowly removed the towel.

***

She celebrated with a cappuccino at a North Beach café. Until today Shark Boy didn't know Tommy Ho was working with her. Now she had Albert's go ahead. Which erased her crime.

It was perfect. She phoned him right away.

"Tommy?"

"Yes."

"Are you still tailing that son of a bitch?"

"Better. Plant a bug. We're on him like hot sauce on eggroll."

"Very good. Albert wants you to do something for me."

"Albert?" he said warily. "You sure?"

"Absolutely. Don't worry, I have his okay. Meet me at the store and I'll fill in the details."

While finishing her coffee she went over the fine points of her plan. This Max must be eliminated—for the greater good.

Chapter 13

"Time can be vicious when you take it for granted." — Warren Beatty, *Bugsy*

The deadline on Taylor Kingston's offer was five days off so I concentrated attention on my serial killer.

Truth be told I still did not have the slightest idea how to deploy the explosive footage without putting Jimmy in some serious gunsights. There were lots of powerful people involved in the deconstruction of San Francisco. Big time sports, big banks, hedge funds, multinational construction corporations, city contractors, real estate moguls, tech czars; all with a good motive to whack Dr. Jimmy Chu.

As for me, what's another hit man more or less?

Susan Wagner appeared to be a soft target.

An independent operator she owned and maintained the website. Sort of a visual parking lot for young females. No doubt she charged a monthly fee plus commissions.

Since she had lost almost ten percent of her stable it was reasonable to assume she would be cooperative.

Reason had little to do with it.

At first glance Susan Wagner put me down as a cross between a child molester and an IRS agent. The second glance was worse.

When I told her I was there on behalf of Jem Ming's family she pegged me as a liar.

"Really Mister…who did you say, Vance?" she snapped, repeating the name printed on my phony business card with undisguised contempt. "Tell me who exactly hired you. Jem's sister or her brother?"

I knew it was a trick question so I punted.

"Her father asked me to look into it."

"Bullshit. Her father couldn't even come to the funeral. Now if you don't leave I'll have to call security."

I looked at her for a moment. Her brassy blond hair had an executive cut, her red blazer was tailored, and her black pants fell over expensive shoes. Despite plastic surgery her face showed signs of wear and her gray eyes were hard.

Her office was on the third floor and there was a security guard in the lobby. So I thanked her and left. However I didn't leave empty handed.

Until then I didn't know that Susan and Jem were pals.

When I got home I put both their files side by side and compared their progress in the sex trade. It was clear they met while both were working at Macy's. Also clear was that Susan Wagner had already been arrested for solicitation before Macy's but charges were dropped.

A few months after Susan registered with the Green Star Jem followed suit. Shortly after Susan started up *High Class Sluts* Jem came aboard. So Susan more than anyone would know the identity of Jem's last trick.

Which meant I would have to figure out a new approach.

The most obvious was to hack into the site's financial transactions: credit card accounts, client information, it would all be there. But it couldn't tell me client preferences such as who preferred their ladies in lingerie.

And who liked to strangle them.

I hacked in anyway, printed out her client list, and put it aside.

Then I dug around for some sort of appointment record. I found credit card records in one file and a calendar on another. The calendar was a simple record of which girls were working on what day.

Jem's escort appointment was right there on the day she was killed. But it didn't have a name or a credit card record.

Which meant the bastard paid cash. Hence the hundreds under Jem's heel.

Pure speculation but it was all I had to go on.

Along with the certainty that Susan Wagner could ID Jem's killer.

Therefore Philip Vance, the phony name on my phony business card, would have to lean on her a bit. Nasty work but at least Max wouldn't have to do it.

It was boring process. Phil looked up Susan's home address and staked the place out.

Susan was doing very well for herself. She occupied the top floor of a two unit Edwardian on Russian Hill which she owned, and rented out the lower flat. The place had a two car garage and a view of the bay.

It was located just a block away from some good cafes and food shops on Polk. I picked up a large coffee and a pastry and settled down on a nearby garden wall.

There was nothing unusual about someone pausing for a coffee break in that neighborhood which was dotted with small parks and outdoor benches.

I kept my eyes on my phone, occasionally glancing at Susan Wagner's residence. It was about six p.m. and I figured she would either be going out after work or having food delivered. Now I was aware it was possible Susan might have gone out directly after leaving her office, or she could be cooking at home, or she was still at her place of business.

The latter I cleared with a phone call. Susan wasn't at the office. Thus she was somewhere else. Some Sherlock.

Halfway through my coffee I got lucky. Susan's garage door slid open and a silver Mercedes convertible slowly backed out, giving me time to ID Susan at the wheel and get to my trusty bicycle.

Tailing a car in San Francisco is much more efficient on two wheels. For one thing you are reasonably anonymous, for another you can weasel in and out of traffic. This comes in handy on Valencia Street in the Mission District where bikes, pedestrians, and cars compete for space in two narrow lanes both ways. This slows down the cars and makes us cyclists a faceless annoyance to everybody. All of which made it easy to follow Susan's Mercedes.

My guess was that she was headed to one of the hip restaurants that dubbed the former lowly Mission the Gourmet Ghetto. The Latino barrios have gentrified into techie enclaves pushing out low rent tenants and the colorful shops and small businesses that once flourished here like a tangle of wildflowers. Boz Skaggs said it beautifully in his lament to the lost hood *Last Tango on Sixteenth Street.*

Sure enough Susan made a right turn on Eighteenth Street which suggested she was probably headed for Delfina's, a five star Italian joint with an eight week waiting list for reservations.

The Mercedes slowed down and seemed to be nosing around for a parking spot so I took a position where I could watch the restaurant.

Five minutes later I spotted her.

One thing about Susan she knew how to dress. Her black silk suit was tailored just right with pants cuff falling over black and silver stilettos, and a red and black pattered scarf knotted stylishly around her neck.

She stopped when she saw me approach then tried to duck inside Delfina's but I was two steps ahead and blocked her path.

I produced a print-out of her business calendar.

"You booked Jem Ming on her last date," I said without preamble. "Tell me who the john was or I hand a copy of this to a homicide detective."

I was half-bluffing. She probably knew more cops than I did.

To her credit Susan didn't crack. She studied the print-out then started to give it back.

"Keep it. I've got more."

"Okay. I have the information at my apartment. Meet me there in three hours. I assume you know where I live."

Oh yeah, she was cool.

A man in my position doesn't want a scene no matter how strong his evidence. Fortunately she didn't know that.

To pass the time I lingered to see who Susan was meeting for dinner. I walked to Guerrero Street and found a second hand store left over from the Mission's bohemian era. There I found a gray straw fedora, dark glasses, and a sleeveless denim jacket which I threw over my leather jacket.

Thus transformed I lurked near Dolores Park waiting for Susan to finish dining. Considering Susan's svelte figure I figured sixty, maybe ninety minutes to complete dinner, wine to check. From experience I knew the food is superb but people are waiting for your table.

At the fifty minute mark I began drifting closer to the Delfina's. I made a pass and paused at the restaurant's pizza dispensary next door.

At the sixty three minute mark Susan and her dining companion exited the restaurant. She didn't notice the dude in the fedora taking photos of her and the pale, portly man at her side.

I followed at a discreet distance and saw the man escort Susan to her car. I decided to tail him for a while but as soon as Susan drove off the man hailed a passing cab.

This left me one more card to play.

I stuffed my new vest and hat between two fence slats and sauntered into the restaurant iPhone at ready. When I got the host's attention I showed him the photo I'd shot of Susan and her friend.

"Wasn't that Ridley Scott, the film director?"

He knew the name but even film buffs don't know what Ridley looks like. The host was a nice looking young man with a narrow black suit and one of those fade haircuts. My own hair fades on its own.

He looked at the photo and gave me a condescending smile.

"I love his films but I don't think so. In fact…" he turned and scanned the open reservation ledger nearby, "…that man's name is Dr. Wayne Gacy.

Of course it was a phony, I noted, thanking the host. When I got back to the spot where I'd stashed my disguise the denim jacket was there but my fedora was gone.

I'd gotten fond of that hat.

***

Aware that my appointment with Susan could be a set up I cycled to where my car was parked, put the bike in the trunk, and drove to her apartment. I parked in a Walgreen's lot and walked the rest of the way, my Sig Sauer tucked inside the briefcase I had fished out of the trunk.

Susan Wagner had a separate entrance to her flat. But as I started to ring the bell I noticed her garage door was only partially shut. The Mercedes was parked inside and I wondered if Susan had left the door open for me. If she did it was likely a trap.

So I slipped the Sig out of my briefcase and ducked under the half closed door.

I stood for a moment making sure I was alone in the darkened garage. As my eyes adjusted to the light I checked for a security camera.

There were two, positioned to catch someone opening the car door on either side. I slid along the wall and reached out for the camera on the driver's side to disable it. But it was already out of its socket.

Poor maintenance? Not likely.

The second camera was located near a door that led to Susan's flat. I wondered why it was pointed at the car and not the door. When I touched it I knew why. Disabled as well.

That was my cue to wipe down anything I might have touched and split. However I was there on a need to know basis—and Susan knew what I needed to know.

The stairs were carpeted which muffled my footsteps. The door to the apartment was closed but when I gave the knob a discreet turn it was unlocked. I took a deep breath and stepped briskly inside, gun dowsing for intruders (such as myself) or a waiting assassin.

The landing was clear and the apartment completely silent.

The lights were on and I had to pass the living room no matter which direction I took. Using the classic move I'd lifted from cop TV shows I hit the wall with one shoulder and rotated inside, sweeping the area with the Sig.

Nobody.

I was left with three choices: kitchen, bedroom, or bathroom. Actually there were five: two bedrooms each with its own bath. The smaller one was unoccupied. I found Susan in the master bedroom. She was sprawled face up on the floor floating on a large pool of oily blood.

Her throat had been cut.

I'd encountered my share of dead bodies but there's something particularly gruesome about a corpse whose jugular has been slashed. The harsh slice usually leaves a gaping red wound, like a horrific grin.

Then there's the overflow of blood reminiscent of the killing floor of a slaughterhouse, as if Susan Wagner was just another slab of prime rib.

Unwilling to go nearer lest I leave a footprint I turned to leave. Then I glimpsed something that stopped me cold.

A gray fedora sat at the edge of the dark red lake.

The same fucking hat I had purchased in the Mission three hours before.

Chapter 14

Christine was excited.

She was going on a plane to visit her family in Boston. She had never been farther than Disneyland before. Her parents had taken her to Paris for a week but that didn't count. She was too young and didn't really remember much of it except that it was a lot colder than San Francisco.

All afternoon in class she kept glancing at the clock. Her mother would be picking her up at four and they would shop for some last minute stuff. Best of all her parents had gotten permission to let her out of school two weeks early.

She kept glancing at the clock but the hands never seemed to move.

"Miss Chu!"

Christine turned and saw her teacher Miss Kwok glaring at her.

"Today's lesson is here on the blackboard, *not* on the wall."

"Yes, Miss Kwok."

"Now then, do you know the answer to the first equation I took the time to write on the blackboard?"

Christine peered at the blackboard. She wished she hadn't put her glasses away.

The problem on the board read: $3X15-5=?$

"I'll give you a hint," Miss Kwok said, "the answer is the same number of minutes you'll be in detention if you don't answer this correctly in thirty seconds."

Christine heard a few kids in the class giggle and felt her cheeks redden.

She peered at the board.

"Uh...fifty?"

Again she heard giggles and knew it was the wrong answer. She looked at Miss Kwok.

"I don't have my glasses."

Miss Ming was stern as ever.

"We'll discuss this during your detention period—and the next one who laughs will join you."

The class suddenly went still. Everyone knew Miss Kwok meant business.

Christine tried to pay attention but she was miserable. She had planned to go shopping after school. She had her eye on a cool pair of Nikes and a Warrior jacket. She was a huge Steph Curry fan. It was practically her whole new wardrobe for Boston. Now she'd have to go home right away. Her mother had given her a strict timetable. And like most of the girls she knew Christine never disobeyed her parents. In fact her mom would be very upset if she found out about her detention.

So Christine retrieved her glasses and waited it out. She was facing forty minutes of detention. And Miss Kwok would make sure she served every minute.

There was a copy of *The Hunger Games* in her backpack that she had brought along for the flight. At least she could spend the time reading. If she got caught she could claim it was for the book report Miss Kwok had assigned the class. Technically she wouldn't be there on the day it was due.

But Christine was sure Miss Kwok would demand the report as soon she came back.

When the final bell rang Christine dutifully remained in her seat and opened her book. However Miss Kwok handed her a number of math problems instead. It didn't take her very long to solve the problems. Christine had always been a good student, especially in math.

But Miss Kwok had caught her daydreaming and Christine's arch rival in class, Cindy Sing, had seized the opportunity to embarrass her.

They were neck and neck for top honors in class and Christine resolved to bear down on the books and secure first place when she returned from Boston.

She started dreaming about Boston again until a sharp voice cut in.

"Miss Chu, have you completed your assignment?"

"Yes, Miss Kwok."

"Bring your work up here please."

Christine waited at the side of the desk while Miss Kwok checked the results of her solutions.

"Yes, these are all correct but your handwriting is sloppy. Please return to your desk and copy the equations legibly."

Christine took a deep breath and hurried back to her desk glancing at the clock. It was nearly three forty, with luck she'd still be on time to go shopping with her mom.

Very carefully she copied the equations clearly and in less than six minutes she was ready.

She raised her hand, waiting anxiously for Miss Kwok to notice her. Finally she looked up.

"Yes?"

"I'm finished."

"You mean you completed your assignment don't you?"

"Yes, I completed my assignment."

Miss Kwok was always a stickler for that sort of formality. Christine believed she enjoyed lording it over everyone. She waited patiently for the teacher to review her work and was relieved to see a hint of a smile when Miss Kwok looked up.

"Well done, Christine. I suppose you may go now. But don't forget to study while you're away."

"Thank you, Miss Kwok, I won't."

Exhilaration hummed through her body as she gathered her things and left the building. Her mother wasn't there. Impatiently Christine checked the time. Three forty three, seven minutes early.

"Miss Chu?"

Christine looked up and saw a stocky man in a black suit and tie smiling at her.

He had perfect white teeth and held a sign with her name on it.

"Your parents have been delayed. They sent a car to take you home," he gestured at a town car waiting at the curb,

Christine thought a moment. "Can we stop along the way? I have to do some shopping."

The driver's smile widened and he opened the car door.

"Of course, Miss, wherever you like."

Chapter 15

"When they come they'll come at what you love."
— Michael Corleone, *Godfather III*

Pausing only to grab the goddamned fedora I bolted for the stairs then skidded to a halt. Susan Wagner's killer had taken the trouble to plant the hat with my DNA all over the headband. Which meant, a: he knew who I was and b: he knew I'd be coming.

No doubt he'd already dropped his dime and the police would be arriving any moment.

There's an old Chinese proverb 'avoid the authorities' which I try like hell to live by. So I hurried into the kitchen frantically searching for an alternate exit.

A door at the end of the pantry led to a small outside deck and a stairway to a garden below. A fence separated the garden from the neighboring plot.

I went downstairs slowly and quietly as if I was enjoying the air. Actually I was sweating as I strolled through the garden and by the time I reached the fence my fedora was soaked. I stood for a moment checking the area. Beyond the fence was another garden and I could make out a path on one side of a neighboring home that led to the street.

Just as I hopped the fence the darkness behind me was illuminated by lights and I heard the low squeal of brakes. I hurried to the street before people started looking out their window or worse, videoing my exit on their smart phones.

The path led to a street just around the corner from the excitement. I was tempted to double back and check it out but there was always the danger that Alvin Lee my new friend on the SFPD was on the scene and might question my presence. So I just kept walking.

After circling the block I picked up the Green Ghost and drove back to Marin taking extra measures to make certain I wasn't followed, including going the wrong way on a one-way street.

Once I was over the bridge I took a series of back roads before arriving at the in-law cottage I rented from Organic Phil. The place was dark so I turned off my headlights and parked behind the house.

The interior of my place is high tech low comfort.

Not to say I don't have the basics: double bed, couch, TV, audio, easy chair, kitchen table.

However when it comes to work I have state-of-the-planet equipment and a well-padded chair on rollers. I also have back-up systems at Eli's place and of course the almighty Cloud.

As soon as I arrived I poured a healthy scotch, lit up a J, turned on Aretha Franklin, and sank down in the easy chair.

The planted fedora spooked me. It meant I had been tracked every step of the way by the person who killed Susan Wagner.

Where did he pick up my trail?

How much did he know about me?

Questions flurried through my weary brain like frightened birds.

They all flew away when the Preacher showed up. The Preacher didn't do frightened. In fact he was pissed.

Thing is, anger isn't much good in an empty room. All it did was cloud my judgement and skew my logic. However one thing was certain. I had to hunt down the bastard before he killed me.

Or worse—hurt Nina.

Between my suppressed rage and concern for Nina's safety it took a lot more scotch to finally get to sleep.

I awoke at dawn with a slight hangover and a knot in my stomach. After downing lots of water I opened the fridge. Despite my Spartan lifestyle I keep the larder stocked.

I fished out a half cantaloupe, a mango, and a papaya. I sliced them up and tossed them into the blender along with some fresh orange juice, apple juice, and protein powder.

The frothy mix went a long way to refreshing my parched brain. I hit the computer and searched for news of Susan Wagner's murder. At the same time I dialed Nina's number.

"Max, what's up?"

"Need to see you."

"I thought we agreed…"

"Things have changed."

She was quiet for a moment.

"I'll be here all morning."

There was nothing about the killing on local media. I rummaged around until I found my sweeper, a device I use to check the house for bugs. I took it outside and carefully went over my car.

No reaction.

But when I ran it over my trunk area the sweeper gave a faint squeak. I opened the trunk and the squeak got louder.

The son of a bitch had put a tiny tracking device under my bicycle's saddle.

Rather than remove it I put a number of essentials, including the Sig in my backpack, and cycled over to the ferry landing.

The sky was overcast and the water choppy, dampening the charm of the short voyage. When the ferry docked I checked out the bicycles parked nearby. Hoping I would not be mistaken for a thief I detached the mini tracker from beneath my seat and attached it to a nearby bike. While working I noticed the thing was a Ridley Noah which retails for at least eight grand. Another sign of the San Francisco times.

As I saddled up to leave I saw a tall, burly dude of perhaps forty wearing red, white, and green racing shorts bearing down on me, coffee cup raised like a stop sign. I figured him for the owner of the excessively expensive two wheeler and cut him some slack. I rolled to a stop, smiling innocently.

The man paused, glared at my bike to make sure of its modest price range then marched past me to retrieve his luxury toy. From his girth I guessed he used it once a week at most. Let my stalker deal with him.

I met Nina at a café on Valencia. Even at that early hour she looked radiant.

"You look like shit, Max."

"You mean sick?"

"I mean crazy. You have that same stare I remember from that time when you…" she shrugged "…I need some coffee."

"What time, Nina?"

She coolly met my crazy stare. "When you killed the man holding me hostage."

"I'm glad you remember that time."

She reached across the table and took my hand. "Tell me, Max."

Her touch unleashed a flood of emotion.

"Baby, trust me, there's some heavy hitters on my ass which means sooner or later they'll come for you. I need you to disappear. Right now. Today."

"What about you?"

"Once you're safe they won't be able to get to me."

"Where am I supposed to go?"

"I'll buy you a ticket to Mexico. When this is over I'll join you."

"Today you say?"

"I'll even help you pack."

Nina cocked her head and smiled. "Better make that a late flight."

***

The moment Nina left for the Zejuataneo I missed her.

The knowledge that I did the right thing did nothing to fill the emptiness. However The Preacher crept back into that void.

I was angry.

Angry I had to send Nina away.

Angry someone was nibbling at my cloak of invisibility—everyone in fact.

Angry I was beholden to Shark Boy.

Angry someone was killing call girls with impunity.

And angry at a corrupt mayor who enabled hedge funds and developers to pull off a cynical land grab that would leave many thousands—including Jimmy—displaced.

Me, I was permanently displaced.

On the theory that my flat in Marin might be compromised, and the hope that my pad in North Beach wasn't, I made my way to Chinatown looking over my shoulder at every turn. Jimmy was busy with a client so I opted to grab a snack at a local bakery.

While enjoying a fragrant coffee and fresh coconut bun I spotted a familiar figure through the plate glass window. A slender Asian man with bleached blond hair. I recognized him as Shark Boy's enforcer. I watched him duck into an alley next to a shaded newsstand across the street.

Having suffered the indignity of being stalked by everyone in town including bleach boy I decided to do some following of my own. However when I crossed the street I discovered the alley was an empty dead end. Resisting the temptation to write it off as a metaphor for my life I walked further down the alley and heard two things.

The sensuous whine of Chinese music drifted from the top half of the window of a basement dwelling. I also heard a series of clicks, like chips on a poker table or dominoes. A second later I realized they were probably Mah Jong tiles. Bleach boy had ducked into a neighborhood gambling joint somewhere below the sidewalk.

Since the alley was a dead end I went back for another round of coffee and waited for him to come out. The coconut buns were fresh out of the oven and I was on my second when my quarry emerged from the alley.

His blond hair made it easy to keep track of him in the crowd of strollers. He made periodic stops at various stores, staying no longer than ten minutes. After his fourth stop he veered off the main drag into a wide, quiet, alley strung with red paper lanterns and entered a three story building with a classic Chinese façade. The sign above the door read Wu Sing Ki Neighborhood Benevolent Association. A Tong.

Curious. It had been my impression that the young man with the blond pompadour worked for Albert Chan, and the Sun See Huang Tong.

He lingered inside so I wandered over to one of the stone benches nearby, sat down, and fired up a cigarette. I also readied my phone's camera and when my blond pal walked out I got a clear shot of him beneath the sign.

Unless I intended to muscle the guy there was no sense continuing my tail so when he sauntered into a seafood restaurant I peeled off and went back to Jimmy's neighborhood clinic.

***

When I arrived Jimmy was behind the counter filling a customer's prescription. An herbal healer, he weighed out various roots and what looked like tree twigs, wrapped each separately, then instructed the white-haired woman how to use them. I stood by, dipping into the Goji berry bin while waiting.

As the woman left Jimmy gave me a questioning look.

"Deadline in a few days," he said, voice tight.

"When I screen our video for Taylor Kingston she'll back off."

He nodded but I could see he wasn't convinced.

"Family get off okay?"

"Today is Christine's last school session. She and Linda fly to Boston tonight."

"How about a late lunch?"

Jimmy locked up and we walked to an Italian restaurant on the corner of Broadway and Columbus called E Tutto Qua. The booths along the side afford a good view of the street, which suited a man with my elevated threat level.

Over pizza and wine I told Jimmy about the tracking device on my bike but I left out the part about Susan Wagner's murder. Still it was clear.

The man who followed me to the Mission and snatched my fedora also cut Susan's throat then planted the hat.

"You think Taylor Kingston is having you followed?" Jimmy said between bites.

"Could be Shark Boy. Or both."

"What will you do?"

"Ted Williams."

"Who?"

"The great hitter. He averaged over .400 one year. He wrote a book on how to hit a baseball."

"So?"

"The first rule in his book is… wait for a good pitch to hit."

Jimmy smiled. "Are you sure you're not Asian?"

His phone rang. Jimmy moved to take it.

One look at the screen and his smile collapsed into a sinkhole between stunned disbelief and sheer horror.

"Daddy…" was all I heard. It was enough.

I couldn't see but I knew the ten year old girl on the screen was Jimmy's daughter. I caught a glimpse of her tied to a chair and blindfolded.

Then the phone went blank.

There was nothing else. However the message was clear.

"Christine…" Jimmy's voice seemed to crawl from the bottom of hell.

My brain was racing. The Preacher had just kicked into high gear: cold, fast, and fucking furious.

"Go stay with your wife," I said.

Jimmy looked at me blankly, still seeing the image of his daughter blindfolded.

I kept my voice low and calm. "Go stay with your wife, I'll take care of this."

He nodded without seeming to hear.

I leaned closer. "I'm going to get Christine back understand?"

Jimmy looked up and seemed to see me for the first time. Whatever he saw made him shrink back a little. "Yeah, I understand, Max."

"Stay with your wife," I repeated.

I put Jimmy in a cab, went back to the North Beach pad, and loaded up my laptop. Then I called Taylor Kingston.

Her boy Mark answered.

"This is Mr. LeBlue. Tell Miss Kingston we are ready to settle this matter. I'll be there in an hour."

"Miss Kingston can't…"

"Trust me, Mark. Miss Kingston will want to see me."

"I'm sorry that's…"

I hung up.

Propelled by rage I took a cab to New World's glass tower on the Embarcadero. If I had taken my car I would have been tempted to take my Sig Sauer for a stroll.

Except that Mark and a security guard or two would surely pat me down. They might even do it in the lobby before escorting me upstairs.

Sure enough Mark was there with a beefy man wearing a blue uniform and an unhappy expression.

Mark smiled apologetically.

"Nothing personal. Just routine security."

A suicide bomber would have gotten less personal scrutiny.

I was patted, poked, probed, and scrubbed with a handheld detector. All the while Mark kept smiling as if he were fitting me for a tight suit.

Finally he escorted me to the elevator. All the way up I struggled to maintain my composure. To Mark's credit he didn't try to make small talk or stare me down. He kept his eyes on the floor numbers racing past the screen and his body relaxed.

As for me, I looked straight ahead, jaw clenched.

I marched stiffly behind Mark through the sterile hall. He stayed on his phone until we reached the door of Taylor Kingston's office. The door opened and I strode past him, my blood steaming.

When I saw her I cooled down a notch. She was dressed in a red suit and black heels. The deep neckline outlined her breasts and a pearl necklace nestled happily between. She seemed taller than I remembered. Her emerald eyes fixed on me like a stalking cat. She knew I wasn't there to strike a deal.

She folded her arms and waited.

I glanced back and saw Mark hovering at the door.

"You don't want him here for this."

Her eyes held mine then flicked away.

"Alright, Mark," she said with a trace of contempt. She was expecting the usual threat.

When the door closed I went to her glass desk and opened my Mac.

"Sending strong arm boys to rough up Chu was nasty but you crossed the line, bitch."

"Watch your words."

"Watch this."

I jabbed the play button and spun the laptop around to face her.

For a second her expression wavered as she recognized herself and Mr. Mayor rolling naked on the carpet not far from where we were standing. Then an invisible veil dropped over her face.

Her features showed no emotion, in fact they showed very little signs of life. Her voice too was flat and toneless.

"What do you want?"

"Chu's daughter. Right now or I press send."

"I have no idea what you're talking about."

"You deny sending thugs to Chu's clinic and kidnapping his daughter?"

She paused. "Yes I admit we sent contractors to influence Doctor Chu's decision but we had nothing—repeat—nothing to do with Doctor Chu's daughter."

The Preacher gave her a microscopic scan and knew she was telling the truth—and lying at the same time. About what he couldn't tell but he knew she was telling the truth about Jimmy's little girl. He kept me from posting the video to the mailing list I'd prepared.

"I don't have time to argue the point. Back off from Chu or this goes global. If I find you lied about his daughter you will regret it."

"Like Peter Ng?"

The question blindsided me. She was good.

"I don't know the name."

This time it was Lady Kingston putting me under the microscope. It made no difference. I held the ultimate weapon.

I snapped the Mac shut and turned for the door.

"I'm afraid I can't let you leave with that."

I looked at her. Taylor Kingston stood framed by a magnificent view, silver blond hair gleaming in the sun and her face smooth as polished marble. She wasn't kidding.

"Really? Jack my laptop? You think that will solve anything?"

Too many questions.

She had already pressed a button on her desk phone. Within seconds the door opened and Mark came in, smiling as usual. He was trailed by a beefy security guard.

"Take the laptop and escort him out."

Judging from her crisp tone she had great confidence in Mark.

The Preacher didn't give a shit. At long last he got the chance to step out and even the scales.

Mark approached fast and focused just like he'd practiced.

The Preacher was way ahead.

When Mark grabbed his wrist I whipped the laptop around and nailed him smack on his chiseled cheekbone.

Mark dropped to one knee and stayed there.

The security guard tried to block the exit but the Preacher was having none of it.

Without breaking stride I drove the point of my shoe into his shin just below the kneecap. As the guard doubled up in pain I swatted him with an elbow and moved past.

I was trembling with adrenaline all the way down. When the elevator doors slid open I half expected more security guards but the lobby was clear.

Still unsteady I took a few deep breaths when I stepped outside. I continued on foot, just me and the Preacher. As I walked the realization set in.

The Preacher enjoyed immunity but I now had yet another lethal enemy. However at that moment there were more urgent matters on the table besides my own sorry ass.

Somewhere along the way I hopped a Pacific line bus. I must have looked intense because the passengers kept edging away. I hopped off at Kearny and Columbus and made a bee line for Specs bar. Two drinks and one cigarette later I was calm enough to think.

I didn't have much time for contemplation. Jimmy's little girl was still out there.

I phoned Jimmy for an update.

"Max, they called."

"What do they want?"

"Money. Three hundred thousand."

"When?"

"Tomorrow night. They'll tell me where."

"I'm going to need your phone."

"What?"

"Trust me, I'll return it in a few hours."

"Suppose they call me back?"

"Then I'll nail their location instantly. The other way takes a few hours."

There was a long silence. "Where are you?"

While waiting I had another scotch and went over what I needed to do.

Jimmy was late. I was on the verge of ordering another round when he walked in.

"Linda's barely keeping herself together," he said when he joined me, "I gave her a sedative."

"You can go back right away."

"Actually I have another errand."

"Errand?"

He signaled the bartender. "The ransom money. I'm putting it together."

"I didn't know the banks were still open."

"Chinese bank. Twenty-four hour service."

Thinking of the work ahead I declined another drink. While I waited for him to knock down his cognac I saw the strain on his face and backed off further questions. Jimmy was barely keeping it together himself.

***

When I returned to my pad my flat mate Sanjin was in the kitchen cooking. He had returned from his four day conference. Eli too. Was due back in a week. Since they left I'd become personally involved in two murders, and a kidnapping.

"Are you hungry? Curried rice and tofu." My Marin landlord Organic Phil would have been proud.

"Not now thanks, I've got a rush project."

Rush was the wrong word. For the next few hours I labored over the short video on Jimmy's phone. I transferred it to my computer and went over the images frame by frame.

There weren't many frames and on a larger screen the pixels were fuzzy. Fortunately the video was in HD which gave me a few shreds to work with. By reducing the images I got a clearer shot. But enlarging the image would blur out the background.

Although the room behind Christine was bare I could faintly make out something over her shoulder. It could have been a poster or errant light. It was the best I could wring out of my Mac.

A knock at my half-open door roused me from the screen. "Yeah what?"

Sanjin shyly poked his head inside. "Would you like some tea? You've been working for almost three hours."

I took a deep breath. "Probably a good idea. I didn't realize…"

"When you're deep into work, time is like a riptide. Before you know it you are way out at sea."

I followed him into the kitchen. "Perfect description of my situation. Out at sea without a paddle."

"What are you working on?"

There was a pot of tea and a couple of peanut butter and jelly sandwiches on the table. I sat down a helped myself to both.

"Imaging project," I told him, trying to be polite.

"I might be able to help you with that."

"How so?"

"I've been working with the Astronomy Lab at Berkeley and they gave me some new imaging hardware. We use it to enhance images from deep space."

Suddenly I had a problem. If I accepted Sanjin's generous offer he would see the horrific image I was trying to enhance. And subsequently what I was doing with it.

If I didn't I would have to return to phone to Jimmy and admit defeat. And a ten year old girl would remain at the mercy of her captors.

No choice actually.

"You're going to have to trust me on this. And I need to know I can trust you."

"About what, Max?"

"I have a short video of a girl who has been kidnapped which was sent to her father's phone. I'm hoping I can find something that will help me locate her. But you can't tell anyone about this, agreed?"

"Oh my God of course. I'm glad to help. Bring the video in here."

On entering Sanjin's room I was immediately impressed by his new computer setup. Three large screens, double keyboard, scanners, enhancing consoles, a far cry from his old Mac pro.

"Where did Berkeley get this stuff?"

"NASA," he said settling down at the desk and lighting up the screens.

Sanjin winced when he saw the image.

"Dear Lord that poor child." His fingers moved rapidly over the keyboard. Then he paused.

"Max?"

"Yeah?"

"Are you some kind of private eye?"

"Uh yes, but it's mainly computer work. This is my first case of this sort."

"Shouldn't the FBI be doing this?"

"My client doesn't want his daughter endangered."

"Of course." He returned to the keyboard.

Sanjin was good. In about ninety seconds the image was up, crisp and clear in all its horrible detail.

"This is dreadful," Sanjin said, "but there's nothing in the room."

"Behind the girl's left shoulder. There's a window."

"Half a window."

"Can we zoom in on that half window?"

"No problem."

"What's that outside the window? That red blur."

Sanjin zoomed in on the window and brought the slightly blurred pixels into focus. "It looks like a lantern." he murmured.

Indeed it was. A red lantern.

And I knew where I'd seen one last.

Chapter 16

"It always seems impossible until it's done."
– Nelson Mandela

I texted Jimmy to meet me at the City Lights Bookstore. They house their genre fiction in the basement and it's quite private.

Jimmy was breathless when he came down the stairs. He'd obviously ran the distance from his apartment in Chinatown.

"Did they call?"

"No, thank god. If I had answered things might have gone sideways. Were you able to come up with the cash?"

"Yes."

"Where did you get it?"

He heaved a sigh. "Shark Boy."

I let that sit for a moment. "Here's your phone. Let me know right away when they contact you."

"Yes of course. Did you…?"

"What?"

"Did you find anything on the video?"

"Just that Christine is scared."

Bad choice. Jimmy's expression seemed to collapse. Then he reset himself.

"Yeah. I'd better get back to Linda."

I knew what would happen if I told him what I'd seen in the video. He'd go storming into the Wu Sing Ki Tong with his new Glock blazing. Better the Preacher handle it. He was a better shot.

The first thing I did was to go where my car was parked and retrieve my Sig Sauer p229. I made sure it was locked and the extended magazine loaded with thirteen 9mm rounds. I shoved the gun behind the belt at the small of my back and took my utility knife from the glove compartment and secured it in my sock.

The Preacher was ready to roll.

Better slow down I told myself. My adrenaline was creeping into the red zone. The Preacher couldn't afford to peak too soon. Neither could Christine.

So I took a slow walk down Jackson Street and when I crossed Grant began cutting through the alleys until I reached the one with the red lanterns.

Along the way I picked up take out coffee and a coconut bun. When I reached the building that housed the Wu Sing Ki Tong I took a seat on a concrete bench a short distance away and waited for Jimmy to call.

The coffee and bun had been a good idea. An hour later my phone buzzed.

"They called with instructions."

"What about Christine?"

"They said money first."

Which meant Christine never.

My path was clear.

At the moment the area nearby was deserted so I took a minute to make sure my Sig had a round in the chamber. Then I took the safety off and tried to restrain the Preacher until there was some sort of plan.

Turned out the plan came to us.

Blond pompadour a beacon in the dim evening light, Shark Boy's hired gun hurried into view.

Still sitting on the bench I half turned away and waited for him to pass.

When he went by I spun, jumped up, and pressed the Sig into the back of his neck. "Slow down, blondie."

He actually relaxed when he recognized my voice.

"You know wat's going to happen to you?"

"I know your brains will be decorating the sidewalk if you don't do exactly as I say."

He shrugged. "What?"

"You will escort me inside the fancy building here and if you say one word in Chinese I'll kill you. Understand?"

"You can go in but you'll never get out."

"In that case neither will you."

But I was worried.

There was a good chance I was wrong about where Christine was being held. And by who.

However there was no turning back. So I prodded him forward with my Sig until we reached the door to the Wu Sing Ki tong.

"English only," I reminded, noting the speaker next to the buzzer.

A voice rasped in Chinese.

"Tommy." The blond man said.

The door buzzed open.

Like a boxer responding to the bell the Preacher emerged, eager for battle.

"How many?" I said.

The blond man hesitated. "Three maybe four."

Counting Tommy that made five. No more than two rounds each the Preacher calculated, which would leave three bullets for stragglers. Way back at the rear of his skull a small voice reminded that if he was wrong about this everybody, including Christine, was seriously fucked.

But the voice was drowned out by a tidal wave of adrenaline as we entered a narrow hall.

A short, five step stairway led to a closed door.

I pushed Tommy and he slowly started climbing.

At the top I reached around Tommy and turned the door handle. It was unlocked.

There were three men inside a very large room. A pudgy man with glasses and a red shirt sat behind a heavy, carved wood desk and two younger men across the large room lounged on a sofa watching soccer on a big screen TV.

We entered slowly, Tommy walking stiffly in front of me so that they couldn't see the Sig pressed into the base of his skull.

Through a single window on the far wall I glimpsed the red lanterns outside.

The three men seemed curious but not suspicious.

For a moment we all looked at each other.

Then the Preacher blinked.

I shoved Tommy into the room and showed them the gun.

"I want the girl—now!"

Tommy yelled something in Chinese and the two guys at the TV hopped off the couch with remarkable ease and circled me, knees slightly bent in a classic martial arts crouch. Tommy had recovered his balance and adopted a similar stance. All three men appeared to be in excellent condition: light on their feet, flexible.

"Yiiiii!"

Fists flailing Tommy stepped and leaped—one pointed shoe snapping out like a switchblade slashing at my head.

Hitting a moving target is dicey, especially when it's flying straight at you. Tommy's first step registered in my peripheral vision which gave me a nanosecond to duck back, swing the Ruger a quarter arc and fired.

A chunk of raw flesh splattered the wall. Tommy spun in mid-air and dropped like a sack of grain, its contents spilling over the floor.

The other two froze, their hands half-lifted, eyes wide with shock. One gave me a weak, placating smile revealing perfect white teeth. I wasn't impressed. The man behind the desk hadn't moved but he was sweating profusely.

My ears were ringing from the blast and I wondered if it had drawn attention. To make sure I waved the gun at the two men who were still in a rigid crouch and gestured for them to get down on the floor.

"Face down—now!"

They warily complied unsure if I intended to execute them.

I turned to the man behind the desk. "Where's the girl?"

"Please, nobody here. Look, look, please…" He pointed to a red door at the side of the room.

There were two options: shoot the three of them and search the place unencumbered, or herd them all ahead of me.

I suppressed the Preacher's opinion and waved the sweaty guy up from behind his desk. He complied slowly and shuffled to the door. As he moved I noted he was paunchy but had heavy shoulders and thick forearms. Good to know should it come to hand-to-hand combat.

When he reached the door I told him to stop. "Open the door slow and step back."

He opened it and I checked inside. Another stairway.

Reluctantly I got the other two on their feet and with Paunchy leading the way we all filed upstairs.

The space on the second floor included a modern kitchen, a living area, bathroom, and two small bedrooms one of which had bunk beds. However they were all completely empty.

I told the paunchy dude to sit down against the wall and the other two to lie on the floor face down. Then I rooted around the kitchen drawers and found a roll of duct tape. One by one I bound the hands and feet of the men on the floor. When that was done I motioned the paunchy man to get to his feet.

"Where's the girl?"

It was a desperate question and he knew it. The place was empty, one man was dead, and unless I executed the other three my likeness would be all over America's Most Wanted.

He shook his head vigorously. "Please. Nobody here. Take money…"

I was starting to believe him.

I had killed a man for no reason.

A chaotic sinkhole yawned open in my belly tipping my balance and for an ugly moment I considered taking a last dive— until I remembered Jimmy's tunnel.

"Downstairs."

The paunchy man flinched. Beads of sweat ran down his neck as I prodded him to the lower room. I glanced back and saw the two men on the floor writhing back and forth. As we left I wondered how long the duct tape would hold.

Tommy was still there, bleeding from a hole in the middle of his chest.

I told paunchy to stop and circled the room until I found the spent shell casing. In the process I moved a rug aside with my foot.

My hostage appeared to be terrified. He clasped his hands in supplication. "Please don't shoot. Nobody here."

He was good but I'd spotted something when I moved the rug. A large square, cut into the center of the floor. Looking close I saw a small dent in one side of the square. I bent to test it and sure enough it lifted.

Paunchy tensed, eyeing the door leading outside. He was a half second from bolting.

"You move, you're dead."

He stiffened and stayed put.

"Over here."

I thought he was going to faint. Hand trembling he lifted the trap door.

Sure enough there was a stairway.

"Inside—go."

Paunchy took a deep breath and laboriously lowered himself down the steep stairs. It was dark so I turned on my phone's flashlight. There were seventeen steps. I had counted five steps leading to the first floor which meant we were twelve steps under the sidewalk. It was damp and the dense, stale air carried the heavy funk of two hundred years without a breeze.

The stairs led to a short tunnel. At the end of the passage were two doors.

I herded Paunchy to the left one.

"Open it."

He pushed open the door then stood aside to let me pass.

Nice try Paunchy but I didn't bite. Never get too close to a hostage.

"Inside."

With a sigh of disappointment he stepped into the room. Holding the phone aloft, I swept the light back and forth.

It was a store room housing a jumble of gambling equipment: roulette wheel, poker table, faded felt crap table, all covered with a thick layer of dust.

Paunchy shrugged. "Nothing…" He backed out and started up the stairs.

"Stop. Other door."

I sensed him gathering himself for a move and lowered the phone.

"Don't make me put a bullet in you."

He exhaled slowly and fumbled with the handle. He was shaking again and dark sweat stains mapped his red shirt. He half turned to peer at me through fogged glass.

"Please don't shoot."

To calm him down I prodded him with the gun.

"Open the door."

When it opened I saw why he was so scared.

The room was bare except for a shaded lamp that rested on a small table. In the dim light I saw a little girl in a disheveled school uniform seated on a straight-backed arm chair. Christine was bound hand and foot and her body sagged to one side. Her eyes were closed and her mouth was open.

For a bad moment I thought she was dead.

Then her head lifted and she looked at me as if I had come straight out of her nightmare and shrieked.

"It's okay, it's okay," I said, my voice hoarse. "I'm getting you out of here now."

Paunchy was fearfully inching toward the open door.

"You—behind the chair."

Paunchy moved behind Christine.

I snapped the sweaty bastard's picture with my phone then slipped the utility knife from my sock and cut Christine free.

When I looked up Paunchy had once again drifted towards the open door.

I took two quick steps and walloped him hard with my gun. The barrel caught him across the jaw and he fell like a stunned steer. The only reason I didn't smoke the bastard was the time it would have taken to retrieve the casing.

Aware the pair I had left on the second floor might have managed to free themselves I picked Christine up and quickly climbed the seventeen steps to the first floor then down five more to the street. When we got outside I realized I was still holding my gun. Fortunately there was no one in the alley. I put Christine down.

She was still wobbly and crying softly.

I knelt and put my arm around her. "It's okay, Christine, you're safe. We're going to call your daddy now."

While she sobbed into the phone I stayed crouched beside her watching the building we had just left, the Sig between my knees.

Anyone who came out the door was a dead man, spent casings be damned.

***

Good luck finding a cab in Chinatown. However the bus line on Sacramento runs every four minutes or so and I carried Christine to the nearest stop.

More than a few passengers seemed surprised to see a rough looking Caucasian with a tearful, obviously distressed Asian child but my glare shielded us from further scrutiny during the short ride.

Still I had no doubt at least three people had dialed 911 by the time we got off at Hyde Street.

Jimmy and Linda were waiting in a car. The moment we stepped off the bus Linda emerged from the back seat and swept Christine in her arms. Jimmy followed.

The only person not crying was me. I just wanted to get the hell out of there before someone actually responded to those 911 calls.

Chapter 17

*"One's destination is never a place, but a new
way of seeing things."* — Henry Miller

To work off the residue of adrenaline washing through my limbs I bicycled across the Golden Gate Bridge all the way to my place in Corte Madera. As soon as I got home I poured a tall glass of scotch and rolled a fat joint. Then I turned on KPOO my favorite FM station and sat on the couch listening to rhythm and blues which—if you think about it—is an apt description of existence.

I didn't bother turning on the lights until my glass was empty and I had to get more scotch. The fine weed had gone a long way to restoring some balance to my psyche and the scotch blanketed my frenzied emotions enabling me to put things in some sort of perspective.

Tommy was the only one who could identify me and he was dead. However the others would certainly be looking for me around town. And they had plenty of company.

No doubt Taylor Kingston had already embarked on a mission to destroy me. Susan Wagner's killer knew who I was and would definitely try again. Shark Boy would be inquiring about Tommy, and the Vandals had a standing bounty on my head.

I had morphed from invisible man to shoot on sight.

I spent the next ten minutes or so sending the photo of Paunchy standing behind Christine bound to a chair, to Detective Alvin Lee.

After navigating labyrinthine portals from Sweden to Hong Kong to Iceland, Alaska and back to Hong Kong, the photo was routed through Honolulu before arriving on Detective Lee's computer.

At the very least Paunchy could be charged as a sexual predator. Unless of course the Tongs had Alvin on the pad.

The adrenaline had drained leaving me wrung dry and exhausted, I went back to the couch for a nightcap and awoke at dawn still on the couch, the radio playing blues. I left the radio on and went to bed.

Much later I got up with a soggy brain and sore limbs. After a long shower and good breakfast I put on fresh clothes, stuffed my backpack, and started driving north to Tahoe.

***

The Green Ghost was in good form. I cranked up KPOO on the FM and grooved on the blues until the signal faded somewhere near Vacaville.

Despite Len's custom sound system the further I got from San Francisco the harder it became to get a clear station. I was reaching for my old iPod when the national news came over the speaker.

I settled back. Time I caught up on hard news and what was happening in the real world.

Right. What I heard was far from real, and as soft as toilet tissue.

The big news centered on the latest mindless obscenity by Donald Trump. For months he'd been polluting the campaign with his toxic rhetoric. It was clear he held truth, valor, and honor in contempt, and saw decent human values as a sign of weakness. Yet there he was, browbeating everyone in range, denigrating women, demonizing minorities—even strong arming critics on camera—without any fear of having his media spigot turned off.

The blond toad is the inevitable spawn of our culture of celebrity.

In the end it's all about the ratings. Which means money.

Brave young men gave their lives to preserve our freedoms for what? So smug bigots like Trump can spout their venom, incite hate and division in America—all enabled by so-called news shows to generate higher revenues for their car commercials.

And here's the saddest one of all—our vets died so we can have fucking store sales on Memorial Day.

Salute that, young soldier.

I had hoped the long drive would help me decompress maybe even unwind a bit in the crisp forest air but the news of the day stoked my smoldering rage and I couldn't wait to find what I needed.

My radar detector buzzed and I realized that anger had pushed me way past the speed limit and I cooled it the rest of the way.

Half of Lake Tahoe is in California the other half in Nevada which has gambling, a liberal firearms policy, and mom and pop gun shows. Meaning you can buy a weapon without a background check or even an ID so long as you have cash.

Checking local computer listings I found three trade shows within miles of the Nevada border. One was held in a school gym and billed itself as a hunter's expo but very few deer require the AK47s or sub-sonic carbines I saw on sale. Or the automatic shotguns displayed beside a couple of the long-barreled magnums like Dirty Harry used to carry.

Actually I was looking for something similar, however these were too much hardware for my purposes. Although glamourous the S&W Magnums were difficult to conceal, heavy and unwieldy.

I didn't need glamourous, I needed compact and deadly.

It wasn't a total loss.

I found a Kevlar vest that didn't look like a sailor's lifejacket and fit okay under the leather jacket I was wearing. Hopefully it would be thick enough to stop a bullet.

The next show was in a tent and had a variety of collectible weapons all of them high end. This one called itself a Military Swap Meet and for the most part it was. Here and there you'd see an UZI or Kalashnikov among the Mausers, Colts, and Civil War revolvers. Lots of memorabilia from World War II—all in all a legitimate event for enthusiasts.

The third show I visited was more like a tailgate party in a parking lot.

There was barbecue, beer, and country rock whanging from improvised speakers. The array of vendors also had improvised displays, either on folding tables or tailgates of their RVs.

There too, one could find early Mausers and Colts, but for the most part it was automatic weapons from Glocks to assault rifles. And one dude had exactly what I'd been looking for.

I was eating a barbecued chicken sandwich and holding a cup of warm beer when I saw it.

Displayed on a green felt card table was a Taurus 460 .45 revolver with a four inch barrel.

It was love at first sight.

Then I noticed the man behind the table watching me. He was a rangy dude sporting a white ponytail and turquoise necklace.

He nodded at me. "You can set the beer down if you like."

The dealer's wares were all lined up on a poker table which had cup holders.

I nodded back politely, dropped my beer in the nearest holder, and reached for the Taurus. The rubber grip seemed to meld with my hand. The heft and balance were perfect.

"Brand new right out of the box," the man said.

I carefully set the Taurus down and took a thoughtful bite of my sandwich. The best thing about this outdoor event was that I could be reasonably sure there were no security cameras. Still it might seem suspicious if I didn't haggle.

"What about ammo?"

The man smiled. "Comes with a ten round carton."

"Forty five caliber?"

"'Course. High velocity."

I took another bite of my sandwich and pretended to inspect a nearby Colt .38.

"How much is this one?"

"One seventy-five. It's a single owner weapon, used."

"What about the Taurus?"

My little charade didn't fool the dealer. He knew he had me. "That's eight hundred including ammo and the box. Like I said, it's new."

I picked up the cup and sipped my beer.

"How about six fifty?"

The dealer grinned. "How about eight hundred?"

"Seven?"

"Seven fifty, best I can do."

I sighed. "Okay I'll take it."

All that to just blend in.

Later while parked in a secluded area I stashed the Taurus in the compartment under the dash. The short nosed .45 was a tight fit. I had to put the extra bullets in the overhead compartment where the Sig resided.

My new revolver only had five rounds but it would stop a charging grizzly and didn't leave spent casings.

In an effort to ease the tension webbing my body I stopped in the CalNeva hotel (where Sinatra in his heyday married Mia Farrow) and sat in for a few hands of poker. Normally I find the game engrossing but the heavy Asian presence in the Casino make it difficult to concentrate on my cards. I kept wondering if Shark Boy or Kingston Taylor had representatives in the house. Maybe even my industrious serial killer had found a way to track me.

After dropping a quick two hundred bucks I left the casino and opened the panel beneath the dash. The sight of my new .45. eased my paranoia. Despite losing at poker it had been a successful trip.

Resupplied but far from reassured I drove back to Marin. This time I skipped the damned news and snapped in the iPod.

Santana's album *Supernatural* flowed out of the speakers. I sang along with Rob Thomas on *Smooth* and cranked up the sound for the next forty miles ever mindful of the radar detector.

Refreshed I dialed up Thelonious Monk. His album *Brilliant Corners* is inspiring background for me when I'm trying to figure things out. Somewhere in the middle of *I Surrender Dear* it occurred to me that I had overlooked a couple of key fragments of evidence.

I floated into Marin on the wings of *Bemsha Swing* eager to get to my computer. I had forgotten to check Susan Wagner's last supper companion Dr. Wayne Gacy.

I immediately recognized the reference to the infamous serial killer from Chicago who strangled thirty-three victims. Certain it was a phony as I had previously thought, I started a deep search anyway. I also had the phone number Detective Lee and I had found in Jem Ming's shoe.

That nudged me in another possible direction. But first I delved into Dr. Gacy.

Hacking is painstaking work in that you have to delete any trace of your footprint which is becoming more difficult by the hour. However hackers have much in common with safe crackers, prison escapees, and Wall Street pirates.

Human beings are blessed with the peculiar knack for finding the flaw in any given system, no matter how sophisticated.

No doubt it's part of our survival arsenal ingrained since the first monkey stole an egg from a snake.

Figuring Gacy might be an add-on I launched a search for every doctor in the bay area named Wayne. While the computer processed the information I turned on the FM and poured a small scotch. I chased it with a big glass of water and rolled a J, one eye on the screen.

I was hallway down the joint when the names appeared. Four in San Francisco, two in Oakland, six in Berkeley and— get this—thirty-two in Marin County. Of course it figured since Marin is Wayne Dyer country—self-development heaven.

A closer look showed twenty-two Dr. Waynes were therapists of one sort or another—mostly PhDs with a massage table. Three of the actual MDs were pediatricians and the other seven specialized in sports medicine. Lots of work there.

I was trying to figure out how to winnow down the Waynes to viable suspects when it occurred to me that Wayne might be as phony as Gacy and would lead me down a useless rabbit hole.

I decided to take a gun break.

The Taurus came encased in a handsome dark wood box lined in green felt. As I removed the weapon I made a note to get rid of the box.

Revolvers are dependable. This one had a solid rubber grip, smooth trigger action, and was easy to conceal. Well worth the trip north.

Perhaps it was the pride of ownership or the weed or the James Cotton Blues Band on KPOO but I made an intuitive hop—if not quite a leap. What if I took the seven digit number we discovered in Jem Ming's heel then affixed area codes of the entire region to the number we found in Jem's shoe…and hoped the computer could come up with a match? A long shot but all I had.

It took a bit of time to process, meanwhile I toasted an old bagel, found some smoked salmon in the fridge, and uncapped a root beer. I needed to cultivate a healthier lifestyle. Too many people had me in their sights.

Less drinking, more ducking.

I was thinking about the bag of trail mix in my cupboard when I heard a familiar sound.

Quiet.

The whirring had stopped. I checked the computer screen and to my total surprise it was there.

***

Right under the name and address of a Doctor Wayne Sutter, MD, DDS in Berkeley was the number with a 925 area code. Which was not in Berkeley. On closer inspection I found he was part of a trio of physicians who had a clinic called University Medical and the 925 number was his mobile.

It explained why the number hadn't registered the first time I had made a cursory search. 925 was a bit out of the loop serving bedroom communities like Walnut Creek and Danville.

Fine. I'd managed to connect Jem's phone number to a person.

Now I had to prove Dr. Wayne Sutter was the man who killed ten escorts, cut Susan Wagner's throat—and did a neat job of trying to pin it on me.

More than likely he was working with someone. How else could he have known about the hat? I'd bought the damned thing while he was dining with Susan.

Attaching a name to the number made me feel better and I called Jimmy to make sure everybody had got out of town safely.

"Max, I don't know what to say."

"Then don't say it. Did you return the money?"

"I never got it. Chan kept delaying the meet. Almost like he was toying with me."

"Chan?"

"Shark Boy."

"Right. Just as well. Now he can't claim Vig on the cash."

"We'll see."

"I hope you're staying at a safe house."

"Don't worry I'm covered."

"Let's meet tomorrow away from North Beach. How about Jane's on Fillmore at eleven?"

"See you then."

Once the turf of the legendary Fillmore Slim—a fabled African American hood replete with jazz clubs, soul food, and high style shops—Fillmore street has morphed into precious boutiques, pricey bistros, and new age bakeries like Jane's that offer solid coffee and fresh baked pastry along with slimming salads for the well-to-do ladies who lunch, and there were plenty. The place was immensely popular with the smart set. A perfect hiding place for a fashion victim like myself.

Jimmy was late but I managed to slip behind a table a step ahead of the thirty something matron who spotted it too late. I endured her entitled glare secure in the knowledge that it had been a fair contest.

Another of a book's many fine qualities is its usefulness in staking a claim to a table while standing in line to order. Today I had brought along *Nine Dragons*, a compelling Michael Connelly novel.

I was reading it as I sipped my coffee when Jimmy finally appeared.

"I wanted to make sure I wasn't followed," he explained, leaning over to whisper.

"Grab some coffee and we'll talk."

He came back with a mug of tea and two blueberry muffins.

"I hope one of these is mine," I said, half joking.

He pushed the plate in front of me. "The whole store is yours if you want, Max. I can't ever repay you."

"Tell you what, let's save the congratulations until the game is over. We have pissed off some serious people."

Jimmy thoughtfully stirred his tea. "I don't get it. The Wu Sing Ki have never been involved in anything past small time gambling but so is everybody else in Chinatown. Why would they suddenly get into kidnapping and target Christine?"

"Tommy is one of Shark Boy's bag men."

"He's more than that. Word is Tommy Ho assassinated one of our prominent business men two years ago. His specialty is strong arm extortion. "

I felt better but not much.

"Albert will know it's me from the description. I hope you're staying at a safe location."

Jimmy shrugged. "Safe enough. So what's our next move?"

"Your next move is to lay low. Christine's safe, the heat's off your property so it's best you take a vacation."

"No way, Max. So long as you're out there, I'm out there with you."

His stony expression told me I'd be wasting my time trying to convince him otherwise.

I sighed and watched the ladies leaning over their half-eaten specials deep into gossip and shopping tips and wished I could simplify my life into something less lethal—like running a tourist bar in Mexico with Nina.

"Your call," I said, "But there'll be more blood before any of this is over."

He nodded gravely.

Much against my better judgement I pulled out my mobile phone.

"Before I show you this I want you to swear you'll do nothing. Understand that going off half-cocked will get us both killed. And then Christine will have no one to protect her."

Again Jimmy gave me the grave nod.

When I showed Jimmy the photo I'd taken of Christine's captor it was clear he was having trouble keeping his promise. His body stiffened and he half rose from his chair, his eyes bright with killer rage.

"Easy. Stay frosty. Do you know the guy?"

"Of course. Everybody knows the scumbag. His name is Victor Kang. He's the banker for the Wu Sing Ki."

"Banker?"

"They lend money to people with no credit."

"What happens if they can't pay?"

Jimmy took a deep breath. He was making a massive effort to stay calm but there was still death in his eyes.

"They pay…one way or another."

"If it makes you feel any better I probably fractured his jaw."

A quick grin flashed across his grim expression.

"Matter of fact it makes me feel a lot better."

"Are you leaving?"

We both looked up and saw a female survivor of at least two cosmetic surgeries smiling at us like an entitled bird sizing up a worm. When she saw Jimmy's death stare she backed away without waiting for an answer. I don't suppose my own scowl was any comfort.

***

The place had filled rapidly so we didn't linger much longer. Before leaving we agreed that Jimmy would discreetly follow up on the photo of Victor Kang I had sent to Alvin Lee and prod him to investigate if he hadn't already.

"Be damned careful how you make contact. There's a murder charge attached to that picture."

As we walked out there was a scramble for our table

Chapter 18

"Brevity is the soul of lingerie."
— Dorothy Parker

The weight of everything I had done finally crushed my inner defenses. I scuttled my afternoon plans and drove back to Marin.

I had killed a man.

Not my first but it still ripped a chunk from my emaciated soul.

Despite the bright sun and turquoise sky over the flat green bay all I saw were dirty gray clouds and polluted waters. From habit I parked a couple of blocks away and plodded to my in-law apartment behind Organic Phil's house. Once inside I dropped onto my couch. On days like this I count mistakes instead of sheep.

I recognized the symptoms. Back in the day my remedy was booze and coke—a chemical lobotomy.

It took a great effort to roll my ass off the couch onto the floor. I had to work up enough energy to take off my clothes. Once down to my shorts I did some stretches. When I felt loose I got up and boiled some water for tea. In the meantime I rolled a J.

I like my tea strong, three bags worth of black. As I smoked the J, I switched on some music. I sat on the floor, drank my tea, and tried to empty my head of thought, like they teach you in Yoga.

It proved useless, something akin to pushing back the tide with a broom. Over time however, I was able to sort thought from misery—and began to tick off my priorities.

Number one was nailing Susan Wagner's killer. Which would solve at least three of my problems.

That left only Taylor Kingston, the Wu Sing Ki Tong, The Vandals, and perhaps Shark Boy to worry about.

The moment my contract was fulfilled I'd leave them all in the dust.

That was my flight plan.

If I dropped out of sight now Jimmy would pay the price. Even with the video shielding him from Taylor Kingston, his family was vulnerable.

Just as I settled behind the Mac for a detailed search on Doctor Wayne my burner vibrated. Only two people had the number.

My chest swelled when I heard Nina's voice.

"Max, I miss you."

"Me too, baby."

"You sound weird is something wrong?"

"Is something right?"

"I can't do this, Max."

"Do what?"

"Let's face it, the separation isn't working out."

"Please, Nina. Right now you'd be honey to a lot of killer bees."

"I can't stand the thought of you facing all this alone."

"I'll be there soon."

"Max?"

"Yeah?"

"If you're not here a week from now I'm coming to get you."

The phone went dead.

Women.

Now I had a fucking deadline.

San Francisco is a small city. No way I'd expose Nina to the four man cage fight I was currently trapped in.

On the other hand, her voice, the fact that she actually cared scattered my depression like a cleansing wind.

Feeling better I attacked the Doctor Wayne project with renewed purpose. Turned out he had a wife Marilyn and two kids: Bruce, age seven, Candi age two. The girl's name was the only thorn in the rosy picture of suburban bliss. Who names their new born after a stripper?

Peeling back the petals I found Marilyn was Sutter's second wife. They had been married in Dallas about a year after the death of his first wife.

Shortly after that he moved to Lafayette, California and set up shop in Berkeley. Their wedding picture showed a pale, stocky man of forty, slightly balding, nest to an attractive woman with big Texas hair. Perhaps it was the hair but Marilyn seemed taller by a couple of inches.

There was some controversy when his first wife died. Her parents wanted an autopsy but the body had already been cremated. Cause of death had been ruled heart failure.

Doctor Wayne Sutter graduated from Harvard Medical School, spent a year in residence at a cosmetic surgery clinic, then went on to The University of Pennsylvania for a degree in oral surgery. After that he moved to Dallas, married Connie Buchanan, and, judging from his tax records, built a prosperous practice specializing in cosmetic dentistry. Four years later his wife died. A year later Sutter remarried and nine months later sold his house and practice and relocated out here with his new wife Marilyn and son. Candi was born in San Francisco.

Apparently Doctor Sutter had done very well since coming west. His million dollar mortgage was nearly paid off, his personal income was well past a seven figures, and he employed a nanny, a cook, and a handyman.

The secret was that University Medical was a one-stop makeover clinic.

Face lift, body implants, a People magazine smile—just roll on through like a car wash—emerging shiny and detailed as they hand you the keys to your brand new image.

Along with a massive bill.

They even had apartments for short term rentals during recovery.

Making an appointment for an up-close look at Sutter wasn't likely. My image was beyond repair. And considering he might have set me up for Susan Wagner's murder he probably knew my face.

Two things I knew for sure. The phone number was a match as was the first name.

Anorexic evidence.

Jem Ming could have been a patient at the clinic. And California was teeming with Waynes. The initials on the card we found in Jem's heel read D.S. Doctor Sutter? Dentist?

On impulse I checked the names of the other two physicians at the clinic. One was Doctor David Sarnoff, cosmetic surgeon.

My link to Sutter was melting away by the second. All I had was Wayne. And there was no evidence Sutter was the same man who dined with Susan Wagner the night her throat was slashed.

Still, I got a match on the phone number based on Wayne.

I decided to keep Doctor Sutter under surveillance for a few days.

The blueberry muffin Jimmy gave me at Janes was all I had eaten that day. As I grilled a small steak I began to feel a real yearning to crawl out of my self-imposed isolation and raise a family with Nina some place where I didn't have to look over my shoulder.

Yeah, like in heaven.

After dinner I watched the Golden State Warriors play inspired basketball then turned off the TV and read *Nine Dragons* until I fell out.

***

I must have been exhausted because it was nearly ten when sunlight prodded me awake.

Too late for Doctor Sutter so I spent the rest of the morning sifting through what little evidence I'd gathered at the motel room where Jem was strangled. The name Oracle Escorts and the pictures I'd taken at the scene.

What struck me was the similarity in footwear displayed in the crime scene photos of three of the other killings. The stiletto heels were excessive, even by today's standards.

There were high heels aplenty for sale on the internet but it stood to reason that if a lady had to walk on erotic stilts for professional reasons she would want to test drive them. So I googled Yelp for a list of local shops.

Two were within walking distance of my North Beach pad which also made them likely candidates for the Chinatown customers. My day's agenda was shaping up.

After texting Jimmy to meet me in a neutral zone I drove into San Francisco. Normally I would have taken the bike but I felt insecure without the solace of the two loaded pistols in my car.

Clement Street where I was meeting Jimmy is little Asia. Every culture from Chinese to Vietnamese, to Thai, to Filipino has taken root there.

And they all drive

Luck was on my side. After circling the block only twice, I slipped into a parking space a short walk from the Vietnamese café I had chosen for the meet. Reason one: it served strong coffee, and two: it was well out of range of whoever might be gunning for us.

Jimmy was seated in the rear when I entered. His expression had lost its murderous edge but clearly something was wrong.

"What's up? You look worried."

He shrugged. "I'm more than just worried, Max."

"Did you contact Detective Lee?"

"Not yet."

"Why not?"

"They found Victor Kang at the Wu Sing Ki Tong. Somebody shot him."

"Dead?"

He nodded mournfully. "Max, this is getting way out of hand."

"It was out of hand from the jump."

"So what do we do?"

"You stay low. I'm going to contact a friend."

Jimmy started to protest but the waitress came over. I ordered coffee and a Vietnamese pork sandwich. My idea of a healthy lunch.

"My friend is in law enforcement," I said in an effort to calm Jimmy down. I couldn't say too much without compromising Lowell.

Then it hit me. "What about Tommy Ho?"

"What about him?"

"When I left the place he was a corpse."

Jimmy exhaled and sat back. "Sorry, Max, I should have remembered."

"If I could forget it I would too, believe me."

He glanced around to make sure we wouldn't be overheard and lowered his voice. "Ever since…" He leaned closer. "… ever since I shot…"

I lifted my hand and nodded. "I know."

"It's hard for me to not think about it."

"You were protecting yourself and your family. You need to remember that."

"I try but… Is it like that for you or…?"

"Yeah Jimmy, that's what it's like."

"But you were rescuing Christine."

I shrugged. "Yeah true."

Fortunately the waitress arrived with our food preventing us from being drawn into a philosophical black hole from which nothing could emerge.

Yes I suffered profound consequences from killing another human being.

Would I do it again?

I bought the Taurus .45 didn't I?

Too many sociopaths, psychopaths, and just plain ice-cold predators had me on their menu.

Sorry.

***

Given the news of the day I decided to give North Beach a wide berth. For the time being The Green Ghost would be my rolling headquarters.

For reasons of safety I didn't ask Jimmy where he was staying. He agreed to stay off his mobile phone and keep in touch with the pre-paid burner I gave him.

It was still well before rush hour so I drove out to Berkeley. I wanted to scope out Doctor Wayne's environment.

When traffic is light the drive over the Bay Bridge has its attractions: the graceful suspension span is one, but I'd always been fascinated by the steel loading cranes lined along the Oakland port. They resembled the exoskeletons of prehistoric creatures and it's rumored they inspired George Lucas' robotic dinosaurs in Star Wars.

Approaching my exit I passed a lake complete with a rowing club, ducks, and various forms of wildlife, which belied the heavy freeway traffic ten feet away.

University Avenue reflected Berkeley's diversity. Used books, Indian saris, hookahs, art supplies, second-hand furniture, hip-hop fashion, collector's comics, American pies, Japanese sushi, Italian sausage, thrift stores: all available in the rows of casually shabby shops and restaurants lining both sides of the Avenue. As I progressed towards the hills the landscape became modestly upscale by increments.

To my right was Shattuck Avenue a busy shopping center and theater district however I was headed for the more sedate end of the Berkeley campus.

The University Medical Clinic was nestled on a tree-shaded street not far from Berkeley's graduate school of journalism, North Gate Hall—an Asian inspired, wood shingled building designed by John Galen Howard.

Doctor Wayne's Clinic was not so much beautiful as it was functional. The stolid three-story building seemed out of place amid the quaint stores and coffee shops on the crooked street facing the campus.

From the outside it was nothing special. A box with windows. There was a parking area behind the clinic big enough for the three Mercedes sedans, A BMW sports coupe, a Land Rover, and a Lexus. From my research I knew that the black Mercedes 63S belonged to Doctor Wayne. I was tempted to toss the car but it wasn't the time or place. Security cameras were everywhere.

Instead I walked over to the apartment complex the Clinic used for out-of-town patients. It was only a block away and seemed pleasant enough. Shaped like an inverted U with two apartments on each side of a wide space divided by a narrow flower garden, the building's dark wood shingles, and simple design seemed vaguely Japanese and echoed Berkeley's North Hall.

I took a break in a coffee shop across the street that afforded me a view of both the apartment complex and the clinic. The shop also sold books.

I bought a copy of *The Ultimate Good Luck* by Richard Ford and spent a quiet forty_minutes with my coffee, my new book and my suspicions._

Surveillance is ninety percent boredom and ten percent indigestion. Nothing came of my impromptu stake out so I strolled back in time to avoid a ticket from the parking cop writing her way towards my car and headed home.

Route 580 to Marin is peppered with interesting sidelights. There's Golden Gate Fields the race track on the bay, and as you approach the Richmond Bridge double rows of huge gasoline storage tanks—colored rust brown to blend in with the hillside—loom over the freeway…leaking into the earth. These belong to the oil refineries that rule Contra Costa County like a third world country.

The bridge itself is a rickety affair, two lanes on each side often planked over and in constant disrepair. Driving across I could see the oil slick seeping from the tankers moored to crude concrete terminals. The shiny green coating on the water was also littered with floating debris. No sign of the EPA.

Meanwhile the residents of sunny Marin, separated from this industrial waste by San Quentin Prison and a mere mile or so of lovely trees and flowers, wonder why they have such a high incidence of breast cancer. Many of Marin's better restaurants even carry warning signs to that effect. Go figure.

As I left the bridge I could see the rear of San Quentin where the guards have a shooting range, hopefully where a stray round won't puncture a passing motorist.

Five minutes later I was driving through an idyllic picture of American life. White cottages, rose gardens, blond women driving to the mall, the clear blue bay—as if the other side of the bridge was a grimy mirage.

A parking space opened up a few blocks from my pad so I left the car and walked the rest of the way. I took the Taurus with me. The streets are usually deserted except for runners and cyclists so I was actually taking a chance walking with a gun in my pocket. Marin cops are notoriously strict and have little action beyond rousting juvies and writing DUIs.

However the Taurus wouldn't do much good concealed in my car. And at the moment I wasn't sure how close that GPS tracker on my bike had pinpointed my location.

Paranoid? Oh yeah.

Once home I googled the news on Victor Kang's murder. The local papers reported Victor Kang treasurer of the Wu Sing Ki Benevolent Association had been found shot to death in the Association's headquarters. Acting on a tip, police had gone to the Wu Sing Ki address. They found the door open and found Kang's body. Police had not ruled out suicide.

I hacked into the SFPD's computers for a more detailed report.

The homicide report was slightly more informative. The building was empty when police entered. They found Kang's body on the second floor slumped over a desk. Autopsy determined he had been shot twice in the chest and once in the head. A classic hit.

Difficult to classify three taps as a suicide.

There was no mention of Tommy Ho anywhere. There was also no mention of a phone among Kang's personal effects recovered at the scene.

My first take was that Shark Boy had discovered that Tommy Ho had double-crossed him by hooking up with Kang to abduct Christine. He killed Kang and made sure Tommy Cho's body disappeared to avoid any connection to the Sun see Hung. He also took Kang's phone because it contained a record of recent contact with him.

At the moment it was the only theory that made sense.

But that was for the SFPD to figure out. I still had a serial killer on my agenda.

It was early enough to drive back to San Francisco before rush hour. To prevent any sort of fuck up I walked to my car, drove it back to my in-law unit behind the main house, and replaced the Taurus in the panel beneath my dash. Sure enough as I pulled out of the driveway a police cruiser sailed slowly by.

***

Parking spaces in the city are easier to find between five and six when the offices empty and people go back to somewhere they can afford. I found a spot near Tommy's Joint and stopped in for one of their signature platters: turkey, mashed potatoes, and coleslaw. The pub also stocks over forty brands of tequila. Instead I polished off my meal with their fragrant coffee.

Fortified and sober I fed the parking meter and walked to my first stop.

The sign outside of Foot Worship billed the shop as the '*Ultimate Fetish Footwear Experience*'. It was actually two stores, the mezzanine floor housing *Felicity's Fetiche* a boutique which provided 'apparel for the uninhibited'.

Visible on the upper floor was a wall to wall rainbow of role playing costumes from Little Bo Peep to Night Nurse as well as edgy street clothes.

I went upstairs and inspected their extensive line-up of footwear.

While certainly provocative and eye-catching, the vast array of transparent heels, lace up boots, and exaggerated platforms weren't quite the hard core models the victims had been wearing when they'd been strangled.

Downstairs at Felicity's was more to my point. It seemed to cater to the professionals. The merchandise was cleverly displayed on mannequins assuming various roles. My favorites were a pair of female fire fighters in high heeled boots and thong panties.

"May I help you?"

A tall, skinny young man wearing rose-tinted glasses and a purple sweatshirt smiled expectantly at me.

"Just browsing. My girlfriend wants to get a pair of very high heeled shoes. Are these as high as they go?"

"Do you mean price or style?"

"Well both I guess. I'll be paying for it."

He waved an airy hand. "Of course. I think you'll find our shoes moderately priced. The heel style is another matter. Not every woman can handle these new stepladders." He paused to give me a proud glance, "that's my name for them."

I smiled appreciatively.

"A lot of our customers are exotic dancers. So is she blonde?"

That one flew by me. "Is who blond?"

"Your girlfriend."

"Uh, she's Latina. Why?"

He lowered his voice. "I only ask that because many of our tall blond girls have…*issues* navigating. I mean on skis or boards no problem, but heels…?" His vice dropped to a whisper. "… *Klutz city.*"

I pretended to look interested. "You seem to have made a study of this."

He waved airily at the displays around him. "Well I am a professional in the erotic fashion business," again his voice dropped, "which is growing by the way. And I've found certain common traits depending on…cultural factors."

Now I was interested. "Really? Sounds fascinating. What did you find?"

He beamed as if accepting an award

"Asian women know how to wear clothes, especially high heels. By comparison California blondes are more comfortable in flip flops. High heels make them dizzy so they always look as if they're teetering on the edge of a cliff. Latin ladies can go either way but most seem to be dancing the tango whatever footwear they choose. Asian females--no problem. And as for our black beauties they pair three hundred dollar platforms with a sweater from Target and create a whole new style… But the absolute best on those skyscraper stilettos are *Trannies*… Don't you agree?"

I couldn't say.

Edified but not satisfied I reluctantly headed for the next stop in my list. As it happed it was located in the heart of North Beach. The one place I had hoped to avoid.

Chapter 19

"The rose goes in the front big guy."
— Kevin Costner, *Bull Durham*

On Grant Street just off Columbus Avenue, Original Sin was within a stoned throw of four of my favorite North Beach haunts. I knew it wasn't wise to go there. Then again wisdom doesn't seem to be my strong suit.

Billed as 'The Hot Shop' its pink façade stood tucked between two restaurants. The interior was deeper than it seemed from outside. The sales desk was at the far end of the store. In between was a pastel gauntlet of lace and lingerie. The racks and shelves overflowed with frilly erotic gear and a musky scent hung over the room. It hit me as soon as I walked in. I paused for a few moments and spotted what I was looking for.

To my left was a display of outrageously surreal, absurdly high, stilettos and platforms that defied the wearer to walk two steps without toppling.

Some resembled giant steel claws, others had animal skin motifs, there were complicated straps and platforms built like transparent Frankenstein boots, one cute number had heels made from brass knuckles.

Erotic? Eye of the beholder.

I was examining the superstructure of the steel claw model when I saw a familiar shape at the far rear of the store. Familiar but unfamiliar in that I couldn't place the shape.

"May I help you or are you just browsing?"

I turned and saw a truly stunning young female smiling at me. I had been so intent on the figure in the rear I hadn't noticed her approaching me. Some investigator.

Briefly unsettled I gathered myself. "Well I was interested in your line of shoes. The designs are quite original."

Her smile became playful. "We are called *Original* Sin."

What is it about beautiful women that make a man feel foolish no matter what he says? Fortunately I had my investigation to lean on.

"You must have special customers."

"We do cater to exotic dancers of both sexes," she confided, "but you'd be surprised at how many housewives and husbands shop here. At least seventy percent of our volume. So—which are you?"

"I'm not a housewife."

"So you're a husband."

"No, I'm not married."

She seemed pleased which for some reason made me feel good. Now let me be clear, I admire the ladies as much or more than the next man. But Nina was hands down the best thing that had happened to me since puberty

However the lady asking the questions was an eleven plus. As much as her beauty was the sheer impact of her presence. Tall, classic proportions, intelligent amber eyes flecked with gold, lustrous black hair with Betty Page bangs, long legs, sensual grace, husky musical voice, the inner luminosity film directors worship—and it was shining at me.

"Are you looking at shoes for…someone?"

"Uh actually, I'm researching erotic fashion for a film we're shooting."

"The smile faded a bit. "Porn?"

"Not at all. It's more of a thriller. Set here in San Francisco. Pretty big budget."

Most people have a certain reverence for Hollywood so the cover story went over easily. What the hell, Tinsel Town is full of liars.

She seemed impressed. "We do have a showroom for our special order clients," she said thoughtfully, "not too far from here."

"Sounds like a place I should visit. Do I need an appointment?"

"Well," she glanced over her shoulder towards the rear of the store, "give me a minute okay?"

She flowed away like water and I found myself looking forward to her return. It didn't take long. Watching her drift back between the racks was almost hypnotic. An added attraction was the gaudy jungle of erotica which stirred deep currents.

She dangled a key chain.

"Shall we go?"

Like Pavlov's dog I followed.

***

It was dinner hour and North Beach was bustling. My lovely shop girl led me fifty feet to Fresno Alley which was home to *The Saloon*, an unrepentant blue collar bar which dispensed hard blues and straight whiskey. As we passed, the place was gearing up for the night and there were a few reprobates smoking outside and a grizzled bouncer at the door.

Halfway up the alley was a bright pink building with green trim around the windows and front door.

We hadn't spoken as we walked but just before she put the key in the lock she turned.

"You haven't told me your name."

Of course I lied. "Jake, Jake Victor."

She smiled playfully. "Mother told me never trust a man with two first names."

"How many names do you have?"

This little byplay would hardly win awards but I was well off my game. I noticed the smokers in front of The Saloon were also fascinated by the Asian knockout in the simple black dress.

"Mai Sun," she said, almost shyly. "Come."

I followed her up a long narrow stairway to the second floor. At the top was a pink door edged in green, same motif as the exterior. Fresno Alley is shabby as was the aging building and bare, narrow staircase but the space I entered was surprisingly plush.

A blue wall-to-wall rug covered the floor and there was a small bar and espresso machine in one corner. A low glass table and a few black leather chairs completed the area. The rest of the room was decorated with big ticket erotica: leather lingerie, whips, paddles, masks—all very well crafted and with prices to match. Two mannequins—one male, one female—were outfitted in leather and lace: he in a flashy motorcycle jacket and leather pants and she in a red leather corset, thigh length stockings, mile high heels, and leather hat complete with black net veil.

"Everything is made from the very best materials," Mai said. She stayed close as she walked me around and her jasmine scent made it hard to focus.

"Over here are some of our custom boots," she was saying as we paused before glass display shelves. "We can design and make anything you wish."

The boots ranged from knee-high to mid-thigh, many with intricate lace systems. A couple had impossible heels and, like everything else in the show room, were very expensive, starting at three grand per pair.

I noticed a pink door next to a large mirror on the far wall.

"This is exactly what we're looking for," I said, "uh, is there any more in there?"

She smiled and started walking slowly towards the door, her scented shoulder very close to mine. My blood was pumping noticeably and my skin was heating up. As we approached the door I caught a glimpse of the two of us. We made a nice couple.

"Over here is our model room," Mai said, "twice a year we have a fashion show." She glanced at me playfully. "Like Victoria's Secret."

She opened the door. "Give me a minute to straighten up in here."

While waiting I studied my reflection.

It was a bit hardcore. More Brooklyn than Hollywood. Definitely low budget.

"Come in, Jake."

I paused at the doorway.

Mai's simple black dress had been replaced by a crimson robe which hung partially open revealing alert breasts, long black stockings, and a red thong. Behind her was a blue couch as wide as a bed.

She lifted a remote. "We can adjust the mood during a show, even play music."

To prove it she lowered the lights and soft jazz came from speakers around the room.

Her playful smile became wicked.

"Do you like what you see?"

I was breathing too heavy to answer. Her eyes locked on mine and drew me toward her.

Chapter 20

The tall Asian woman with the bee-hive hair couldn't believe her luck.

She waited to make sure she hadn't been seen before she called.

"What?"

"You need to send someone to Fresno."

"When?"

"Right now."

"Why?"

"The man we've been looking for is there."

"You're certain?"

"Affirmative. I recognized him from a previous encounter."

"How long will he be at the house?"

"I've made sure he'll be…occupied."

"Sit tight. They'll be there in ten minutes."

I'll be gone in five, she thought, ending the call.

She didn't need to be around any longer than necessary. For all she knew she might be included in the assassination package. Her protector was ruthless.

She hoped Mai Sun would survive unhurt.

It would be a shame to lose an asset like her beautiful assistant. Mai had been schooled since she arrived from Hong Kong at sixteen. Just as she had been.

However there was no emotion attached to the potential loss. Mai Sun was an earner, nothing more. Nothing personal.

She gathered her things and left without locking the shop. While looking for a cab she called her silent partner.

"It's me."

"Why are you calling me here?"

"Trust me. It's important."

"Alright, alright, what is it? I have a…"

"Our problem is about to be removed from the equation."

The man paused. "I see. Are you sure of your… calculations?"

"Oh yes. My professor is on his way."

He chuckled. "I hope he's a good teacher."

"The best." She flagged a cab and eased inside.

"Does he know about us?"

"If he did we'd already have been…expelled."

She was smiling but his tone shifted. He sounded both anxious and expectant.

She knew what that meant.

"I need to see you."

"Let's wait until exams are over."

She directed the driver to Clement Street where she kept a safe house in her sister's name. Before going inside she shopped for staples and took food out from a local restaurant.

It was best she wasn't seen anywhere for a few days. She only hoped the assassins didn't damage the showroom.

Chapter 21

"My name is Addison DeWitt.
I am nobody's fool, least of all yours."
— George Sanders, *All About Eve*

I blinked.

An exquisite female stood a few feet away, her crimson robe barely concealing her considerable assets. Mai smiled at me provocatively.

And I was definitely provoked.

I stepped back and took a deep breath to gather myself.

I glimpsed my reflection and blinked again.

The man in the mirror was nobody's idea of love at first sight.

A spurt of reality cut free the web around my brain and two thoughts came tumbling out like dice. One: I'd seen enough interrogation rooms to recognize a two-way mirror. Two: this was a set up.

Snake eyes. I turned and made for the door.

Too late. Three men were at the base of the stairs.

I reached for the Taurus.

Shit.

It was safe in my car.

I slammed the door and pushed the useless lock button. Frantically I glanced around, grabbed a nearby chair, and jammed it under the knob buying myself about thirty seconds. I headed for the inner room and paused. Two-way mirror meant cameras. Without thinking further I snatched the veiled hat from the mannequin and clamped it on my head.

Barely shielded from the waiting cameras I bounded through the door and caught up with Mai who tried to lock herself in a restroom. Roughly I wrestled her outside and put her in a choke hold.

"Back exit."

She pointed to the bar. Behind it was a door.

"Smart girl."

Something crashed behind me.

I pushed her to the floor and ran for the door. Fifty-fifty it was another restroom. Yanking it open I saw a steep stairway and scrambled down three steps at a time. As I hit bottom I shouldered the door.

I bounced back.

Feverishly I rattled the knob and pulled. It opened and I leaped outside a nanosecond before the stairway exploded with bullets and shattered wood.

I looked around. I was back on Fresno—a dead-end alley.

Ahead of me The Saloon was in full swing with hard blues blaring and people spilling into the street. I ran straight for them figuring my pursuers wouldn't shoot.

"Hey, Mary!" someone yelled.

A few feet later I realized I was still wearing the fucking veiled hat. Tossing it aside I sprinted for the safety of busy Columbus Avenue.

Did I say safety?

Glancing back I saw two young Asians hot on my ass. I stepped it up a gear, keeping my eyes on the traffic lights which tick off the seconds before they change.

At the last possible moment I charged across the intersection narrowly avoiding an SUV. My hunters were forced to hang back but it was a temporary victory. They were still in sight.

And they had mobile phones.

I kept galloping madly, dodging traffic and people, but as I neared Washington Square Park, an ominous sound pulled me up.

Motorcycles, first one then the other. Not Harleys but the high whine of crotch rockets like Kawasakis or Suzukis. I ducked into the back entrance of Café Roma and sat near the window. Sure enough two Asian dudes on street bikes were crisscrossing the hood.

I retired to the restroom in the basement and collapsed there. My recent embrace of a healthy routine had come a day late and a few dollars short. My shirt was drenched limp and my lungs were begging me to surrender.

I took off the shirt and splashed cold water on my face and arms. Then I patted myself dry with the shirt and tossed it in the trash.

My black T didn't show the sweat stains. I folded my jacket inside out and draped it over my arm. A new look.

As I came up the stairs I could hear the constant buzz of motorcycles outside. I peeked through the window and saw they were working both sides of Columbus Avenue. I decided to have a beer and sit it out.

Fortunately there was an Italian soccer game on the overhead TV and a small crowd of aficionados had gathered around affording me ample cover.

Two beers and three goals later I ventured outside.

No doubt my stalkers were still combing the streets but I had a plan. Trying to hail a cab was chancy and would expose me. But I knew a bus passed the Roma Café before it turned the corner and stopped in front of Washington Square Park. So I kept an eye on the back window and as soon as the bus appeared I hurried out the front door, walked quickly across the street, and hopped on the bus when it arrived.

It deposited me well out of range and I took a cab back to where I'd parked the Green Ghost. Once behind the wheel with the Taurus below the dash and the Sig in the panel above my head I was able to heave a deep sigh of relief.

Followed by a long, miserable groan.

My carefully constructed fortress of invisibility had collapsed. If I had any sense I would have realized it was over when Shark Boy pressed me into service. Now things had deteriorated past all repair.

Not only was I known to Jimmy Chu's mailman, Shark Boy, a serial strangler, Susan Wagner's killer, a local homicide detective, various Tongs—apparently my face was also familiar to people I didn't know at *Original Sin*. People who wanted me badly enough to have their beautiful manager—or whatever she was—lure me to a place where I could be slaughtered.

And Mr. Brain-Follows-Dick went right along.

A lamb at a barbecue.

I drove across the Golden Gate Bridge to Marin, careful to stay under the speed limit and looking forward to a good night's sleep.

No such luck.

Because I was wary of carrying a weapon on the street I pulled the Mercury into the parking spot behind the main house. It couldn't be seen and I could safely transfer the Taurus to my house.

Paranoid? And then some.

As I entered my flat I heard a too familiar sound. The angry buzz of a street bike. Make that two.

I locked the door and sat in a chair with the lights out and my .45 at ready while the whining engines grew louder then receded like grimy waves.

That damned GPS tracker had given them an approximate location. At least I hoped it was just approximate.

Or maybe it was just a couple of local kids having fun.

Still wondering I fell asleep in the chair.

***

The tall Asian woman's bee hive bobbed with indignation.

"*Your* people failed," she said.

"I don't see it that way."

"Oh no? How…"

"Mai failed. My men were there. He knew."

The woman tensed, "Not from Mai. I can assure you…"

"I'm willing to give her the benefit of the doubt."

"Of course she's…"

"However she'll have to go back online."

"What do you mean?"

"What the hell do you think I mean? Mai is going to have to work her way back into my good graces. Which means she'll be part of our escort stable."

"But she's…"

"As I said I'm giving her the benefit of the doubt. She's a bright girl and can be useful. Otherwise… I'd be forced to sell her."

The woman sucked in her breath.

"Of course."

After ending the call she sat still for a few moments until she regained her composure.

To be sold was worse than a death sentence.

You're fortunate he did not turn his anger on you, she reminded. Mai would have to take care of herself.

Later her phone buzzed. She knew who it was.

Although tempted to let the call go into voicemail she answered.

"Yes."

"We need to meet."

She recognized the tone, the fervent urgency beneath his hushed words.

"Not now. There's an ongoing problem."

"What about the money?"

"Money is not the problem."

"I still need to talk to you."

His voice was close to a whine.

"I told you we must wait. It's too soon."

"Please I must meet with you."

Her stomach clenched. She knew what that meant. While their association was profitable, lately she found it extremely distasteful. And she was far from a shrinking violet.

"Wait a few days," she said, "things will be back to our…
routine."

"I'm not sure I can wait."

This time the whine had a threatening edge.

She got the message. "Give me time to get things together."

"When?" he asked with a note of triumph.

His adolescent arrogance inflamed her anger.

"The day after tomorrow. Is that soon enough?" she said
calmly.

Seething, she put the phone aside. He had made her wealthy
but now he had become a liability. His addiction was out of
control. If her sideline were to be uncovered she'd be killed or
worse. Not even prison would be a refuge.

Very soon her silent partner would have to be silenced.

Still angry, she made another call.

"Fredo, it's me. Have you made any progress?"

"We've been all over Corte Madera, even Mill Valley. Last
known coordinates. No sign."

"We?"

"I had to call in help. It's a two man job. Don't worry, he
doesn't know anything."

"I'm not worried—but you should be."

Furious, she ended the call.

***

Shark Boy had to admit he made a mistake.

Max turned out to be a serious pain in the ass. A wild card
vigilante disrupting his carefully structured organization. Now
his deal with New World was in serious jeopardy.

Time to go to the mattresses, he thought, lifting a phrase from
his favorite movie. He often bragged that the director of
The Godfather owned a building only six blocks from his own
headquarters.

At first he considered a simple assassination. Perhaps
Doctor Chu as well. *No profit in that,* he noted, *the bastard has*

already cost me money. Chan decided to set up a meet with Duke. They had business to discuss anyway. As usual finding an obscure venue was always a problem. These fucking bikers were millionaires but they looked like the violent criminals they were. They also attracted negative attention.

In the end he agreed to meet them at the Ferry Building. On the other side was the promenade along the water where strollers passed by the hundreds. Nothing unusual about a businessman taking a break to watch the ferry come in and have a brief conversation with a couple of passersby. And he intended to be as brief as possible.

Duke was late which annoyed him. He brought along his hulking buddy which further annoyed Chan.

"Let's get to it. I'm busy."

"Sorry, Mr. Chan. Traffic."

"Whatever."

The hulk glared. His long blond hair looked unwashed and his eyes were bright with meth.

"The shipment is ready," Chan said, looking out at the water.

"Where?"

"El Salvador. Small port called El Cuco. Your captain knows the way."

Duke lit a cigarette. "How much cargo?"

"Ten boys. Five toys." In their code 'boy' referred to heroin, 'toy' to sex slaves.

"How much?"

Chan rang it up like a grocery bill. "Five hundred K for the boys, two fifty for the toys. Seven fifty total. Three fifty in advance. Payment due tomorrow in the usual manner. Are we clear?"

The blond man seemed offended. "Tomorrow? When is this fucking ship supposed to sail?" His voice started to rise, attracting people nearby.

Chan maintained a tight smile. "The ferry? I don't know when it departs."

"Yo, Thor," Duke put in quietly, "relax, no worries. We're goin' on this cruise together, man."

"You might be glad you waited," Chan said, eyes fixed on Thor. "I'll have that man you want so badly—and his lady friend. Care to make me an offer?"

Duke didn't hesitate. "Four hundred thou for both."

"Good. I'll contact you. Until then." Abruptly Chan left the railing and walked back into the bustling corridors of the Ferry Building and browsed the stalls and shops stocked with fresh produce and gourmet food. He stopped to buy a loaf of walnut bread, some Italian olives, and a sirloin steak before calling his driver.

After dinner he contacted Fredo, his new captain after Tommy's death. Fredo had yet to prove himself. In Chan's view he didn't have Tommy's killer instinct. But he was good with numbers.

"Fredo? Any line on that guy?"

"Not yet, I been checking around. He lives somewhere on Chestnut maybe."

"I can't use maybe. Cover the block twenty-four seven. Two mem. If anything moves call me—understand?"

"Got it."

Later, over a snifter of fine cognac, Shark Boy wondered how much Max would be worth to Taylor Kingston.

Chapter 22

I woke up with a gun in my hand and a stiff neck from sleeping upright.

A little stretching and a hot shower loosened my muscles and I blended up some fruit juice. It was a bright, cheery Marin morning but my paranoia lingered like a vulture smelling death.

My life has been carefully constructed so it can be dismantled on short notice. Laptops, hard drives, adapters, scanners: all of my equipment can be folded up, packed in two suitcases, and carted to the next oasis,

Personal effects? A few books, clothes, CDs, weapons… minimal bordering on vacant.

Depressed I began gathering the essentials. By the time I dumped everything into the car my depression had morphed into cold rage.

I realized I had no fixed destination. My North Beach pad was too close to the eye of the storm. Which reminded me. Eli was due to return from London. I decided to check in.

"Max," he said enthusiastically, "I had a great trip in London. I stayed at the Saville Club."

"Can't wait to hear all about it. Look I need to go away for a few days myself. If you have a computer problem I'll fix it long distance."

"Yeah fine. You know what? I think I'm being followed by the CIA."

That came out of nowhere.

I said, "Where did that come from?"

"Well you know I've been working on this formula on gravity waves. That's why they asked me to the conference in London," he added proudly.

"That's great, Eli, but how does the CIA fit in?"

"So okay, my formula—which isn't quite finished yet by the way—could have applications for space travel and…" he lowered his voice "…anti-gravity weapons."

I was used to Eli's flights of conjecture and, to be sure, he was a legit physicist but sometimes he could be a tad dramatic.

"What makes you think the CIA is following you?"

"Since I've been back I've seen this black Mercedes parked on the corner. With two guys sitting in it."

Instantly I went into paranoia mode.

"Did you get a look at them?"

"No, are you kidding? I walked in the other direction."

"Did they follow you?"

"No. But they were there when I got back. Two days now they've been around."

"These guys, were they Asian?"

"I couldn't tell. Oh my God you think the Chinese government is sending agents too…?"

"I think you should calm down. If secret agents wanted you they'd have you by now. I'll call tomorrow. If you see them again let me know."

I already knew.

The bastards had a bead on my North Beach flat.

Which made it unanimous. I finished packing my gear with renewed determination if not a destination.

Before I left I called Jimmy.

"Max, where have you been?"

"Did something happen?"

"No. But I'm going a little screwy holed up here. I've been thinking of going back to my clinic."

"Last thing you want to do, Jimmy. They've turned up the heat. I think they've got my place in North Beach staked out. I'm moving to a neutral location. When I find one I'll call and we…"

"You don't have a place to stay?"

"Like I said they're watching my neighborhood. It's just temporary."

I neglected to mention my Marin pad. Need to know.

"Max, you can stay here with me."

He took my silence for reluctance, which it was.

"Really, Max. There's plenty of room. Great neighborhood. All the conveniences, cable TV, Wi-Fi…"

That convinced me.

"Last chance to change your mind. I'm a lousy roommate."

***

As it turned out Jimmy didn't have to deal with my gnarly character.

The house was so big we never had to see each other. It even had a two-car garage with a space for the Green Ghost next to a slick Mercedes SL550.

In less than two hours I was plugged in and battle ready.

"I'm housesitting while my friends are in China. I'm taking care of their cat and their plants."

"Where's the cat?"

"She's around here somewhere. She shows up when she's hungry. Her name's Florence and she's cranky."

That made two of us. Despite the deluxe surroundings I was acutely aware that I was the target of three sets of hunters. It was like being a chicken on an alligator farm. One hop out of the coop and you're somebody's lunch.

"So what's our plan, Max?"

Good question, I'd been wondering the same thing.

Without divulging my personal history I went over our enemies list. I reminded Jimmy that the people who killed Victor Kang were still out there and looking for us.

Next up was Taylor Kingston and her wrecking crew. She had already admitted she sent the goons who sent Jimmy's cousin to the hospital.

And then there was the person who had slit Susan Wagner's throat. Possibly the same dude who was busy strangling escorts.

Jimmy took it all in without a word. Then he leaned back and took a long breath. "Well you were running down these high heel shoes right? Obviously the killer has a lingerie fetish. And obviously…" he drummed his fingers on the counter "…the Susan Wagner murder, the person who followed you to the Mission, the guys who came after you from that store Original Sin…they're all connected. This serial killer has a *team*."

"Great. Add them to the list."

"What if we both focus on the killer? I mean you neutralized Taylor Kingston for the moment. And if Shark Boy hired you to find this strangler that should keep him off your ass."

"You would think so. But he's a hands on kind of gangster. And killing Tommy Ho might not sit well with him."

"If Tommy Ho was in business with Victor Kang and double-crossing Shark Boy then you did him a favor."

"I don't think he'll see it that way. He lost money on the deal. The vig on that money you didn't borrow."

I sipped my herb tea and looked around. The sunlit kitchen seemed a planet removed from earthly conflict with its fresh yellow walls, airy view, marble counters, and well-stocked refrigerator. Nothing like a little luxury. I had been there three hours and was already used to it.

"For all we know Shark Boy could have set the whole thing up himself," I mused. "Think about it. He gets his money back but you keep paying interest."

I shouldn't have said that.

Jimmy's expression shifted into I'm-about-to-do-something-crazy mode.

"You think the bastard might have kidnapped Christine?"

"Whoa, step back, Jimmy, this is all just conjecture."

"We'll see. Meanwhile I'll pay a visit to Original Sin and see what's up. Maybe I can get a few shots with my phone."

"Come on, man, that's just nuts. You're a neighborhood boy. Somebody is certain to recognize you."

Jimmy's slow smile was both sly and nasty.

"Maybe, maybe not. Wait here, I'll be back."

While waiting I took my tea into the den and switched on the big screen TV. I thought I'd catch up on some news but every channel was clogged with talking heads endlessly parsing the latest absurdity by Trump and his coven. Finally I found BBC and got a fix on the fix our planet is in. Overpopulation, war, global warming, Sudanese refugees, Syrian refugees, suicide bombers, corporate pollution, the Ebola virus, the Zika virus, ISIS beheadings, Cartel beheadings, police executing black teens, random school massacres—and that's just today.

No wonder God hates us.

In desperation I turned to ESPN trying to regain a sense of purity through the Zen of basketball. But when Jimmy reappeared I laughed for the first time in weeks.

***

Top to bottom he was clad in an Oakland Athletics ball cap, orange tinted sunglasses, a Hawaiian shirt, a vest with multi pockets, Bermuda shorts that dangled past his knees like striped curtains, white socks, and belted sandals. As a capper he had a camera hanging from his neck and a guide book in his hand.

"How do I look?" he said proudly.

"Like a mugger's dream."

"Do you still think I'll be recognized?"

"Not at first sight. Okay—I take it back. But don't make anything obvious. You're a horny tourist taking a few shots of the merchandise."

Jimmy grinned. "No shit, Sherlock."

"Don't hang out too long. Their salesgirl will make you forget why you're there."

"The lady who led you to slaughter?"

He had me there.

"Just watch your ass."

***

Aware he had a family to take care of, Jimmy Chu took every precaution. His taxi dropped him at the corner of Kearny and Broadway where he joined the constant stream of Asian tourists gawking at the gaudy strip clubs as they wandered towards Chinatown. Along the way he caught a reflection of himself in a mirrored door and was surprised by the odd figure who glanced back at him.

It made him feel better. He wasn't used to this detective business.

Better get used to it fast, he told himself, *you are in the mix, like it or not.*

On the surface he was trying to help Max but the reality was they had been in this mess together since he shot Peter Ng. And he could never repay Max for bringing his baby girl home safe.

He took his time, pausing once in a while to snap a photo. He did the same when he reached *Original Sin.* He snapped the lingerie and leather display in the window then walked inside.

***

After some browsing he chose a leopard bra and garter belt and walked to the counter in the rear. Along the way he paused to snap a photo with his mobile phone. Then he approached the girl at the counter.

She was a pretty Chinese girl with bleached blond hair. Pretty but not the stunning brunette Max had described. However he did glimpse a woman in the office behind her.

"Is it possible to get a selfie with you," he asked in Chinese, while she rang up his purchase. "I want to show them in Hong Kong."

"Why not?" she said without enthusiasm.

Jimmy positioned himself so he could include whoever was in the office on the first shot and moved slightly to get a better angle on the second.

"Thank you," he said with a slight bow as he paid.

***

The woman with the bee hive hair stepped out of her office.

"Who was that?" she said, staring at the untidy figure leaving the shop.

"Just a tourist."

"Didn't you notice?"

"What?"

"He spoke Chinese with a Chinatown accent."

"Are you sure?"

The woman didn't answer. She walked to the door and followed the man who had just left the shop.

***

Jimmy knew he had fucked up.

That bit about Hong Kong was unnecessary and stupid.

He also had the feeling he was being tailed. He stayed calm and strolled over to Tony's Pizza for a slice. While seated at an outside table he took the opportunity to check the street. The only person who seemed out of place was a tall Asian woman with upswept hair. She was wearing a black sheath dress with a deep slit to the thigh and was walking on the other side of the street headed toward Washington Square Park. On impulse he snapped her picture while pretending to make a call.

Most likely she was too far away, he thought. Over sausage pizza and a coke he perused his guide book as most tourists did while taking a break at an outdoor table. He kept an eye peeled for anything suspicious but it was a normal sunny day in North Beach. Still reading the guide book he left his table and walked a few blocks where he caught a cab. He had the driver drop him a couple of blocks from his new home and took a circuitous route back feeling proud of his two hours work.

***

I stared hard at the pictures on Jimmy's phone.

There were three shots, none of them clear. Two were of Jimmy with the new sales clerk. In both was a blurred shape behind them in the rear office that he vaguely recalled from his visit.

The third photo too was of a distant shape in silhouette, a female with upswept hair.

Slowly, like a telescope trying to locate a distant star, my memory came into focus.

The woman at the Green Star escort service: tall, dark, razor sharp—Ky Sin.

"This is the bitch who set me up."

"Are you sure?"

"She recognized me from a previous visit."

"At that store?"

"Green Star Escort Agency. She seemed to be in charge."

Jimmy was still wearing his undercover gear minus the cap and shades. He peered at the photo skeptically. "Not much to see."

I had to agree but it was the same silhouette with bee hive hair I had glimpsed at *Original Sin*.

"I'm certain," I said, "has to be her."

Jimmy seemed crestfallen. "In that case she must have followed me when I left the store."

"Why would she do that?"

"I said something in Chinese about showing the selfies back in Hong Kong."

"What's wrong with that?"

"I speak Chinese with a local accent."

We let that settle for a moment.

"I *felt* somebody was tailing me," Jimmy said finally, "so I took my time, stopped for an outdoor pizza, read my guide book, all the tourist things."

"Think she bought it?"

Jimmy shrugged. "I think so. Anyway I didn't come directly here."

"Good," I said but I resolved to keep sleeping with my Taurus.

Chapter 23

"A smart guy gives advice—a genius takes it."
— Moe Klein, *Demon Pope*

I was homeless but not mansionless.

Sunlight slashed through the slits in the window blinds switching on the yellow walls like neon. My room had high ceilings, a comfortable double bed, writing desk, mirrored dresser, and adjoining bath.

I took a long steam shower and used a thick beach towel to dry. When I came downstairs the scent of fresh coffee wafted into the carpeted hall. Jimmy was already in the large kitchen with its view of the bay, busily scrambling eggs. At his feet was a fluffy white cat with a black eye patch happily gobbling up the contents of his bowl.

If I wasn't being hunted by half the state it would have been a perfect morning.

After breakfast I fetched my computer and pulled up the information I'd culled on Doctor Wayne Sutter.

"Forget about Lady Sin for a while and let's concentrate on this dude," I said,

"Who is he?"

"My only suspect. Do you have the keys to the Mercedes?"

"Yes. Why?"

"There's a fifty-fifty chance he could recognize me. However, you arrive at his clinic in your snazzy Mercedes dressed a bit more upscale than you are now." He was wearing the striped shorts from his reconnaissance mission and an Alcatraz T-shirt.

"What am I supposed to do at his clinic?"

"Make an appointment for a consultation."

"Then what?"

"Then try to get a sense of who he is without getting too pushy."

Jimmy shrugged. "I can do that."

***

Tempted as I was to try out the deluxe roadster I resisted the urge to ask for two reasons. One: I had brought along a weapon. Two: Jimmy was terrified he might scratch a fender.

"My friend Gary is very proud of this car," Jimmy said as we slowly rolled down the street. "I'm surprised he left me the keys."

"Maybe he's not as proud of it as you think."

"Max, believe me, I've known Gary since we were kids. He grew up reading car magazines. This SS550 is Gary's dream. He had to wait five months for it and he's always talking about how great it is. One day he made me put my backpack in the trunk so it wouldn't scratch his upholstery."

"Now I believe you," I said, adjusting the leather seat to recline.

The Mercedes was smoother than my custom Mercury. The Green Ghost had a tendency to growl while the black roadster never rose above a whisper. This was partially due to Jimmy's cautious driving style. Each new turn was an adventure.

In time we arrived at the Berkeley clinic. Jimmy had dressed for the occasion: black blazer, gray trousers, light gray sweater, Gucci loafers. California formal.

Jimmy dropped me at a nearby café and parked the 550 in the clinic's parking lot.

I had brought along a copy of *The Ultimate Good Luck* by Richard Ford and happily lost myself in fictional *noir* as opposed to the real life death struggle I was currently engaged in. But Ford's novel of double-cross, murder, and failed love was much too close to my own life. So I dropped it in favor of

People magazine and perused Kim Kardashian's enormous ass which apparently she insists on flashing at a moment's notice.

A full media moon.

In fairness Kim's oversized booty did divert my thoughts from the perils of my present situation.

I had nearly finished my second coffee when Jimmy came into the café. As we had agreed he took a seat at another table and phoned me.

Paranoid? Absolutely.

"How was the consultation?"

"Not bad. Doctor Sutter was right on time for our appointment. With good reason."

"How so?"

"The rough estimate for a facelift and skin peel is thirty-seven thousand. That's not including all the side fees including anesthesia." He paused, "Do you think I have a double chin?"

"Only from the neck up. Okay, we know he's expensive. What's your take on him up close and personal?"

"Well he could use a chin lift himself. He's got a soft stomach, very pale skin…"

"Anything else?"

"No uh, oh yeah he perspires a lot. Had two big boxes of tissues handy. Other than that he's all business. Not much small talk."

That started me thinking if the SFPD had any DNA evidence in their murder books. Next time Jimmy might grab one of the used tissues.

"That's good. Did you manage to take a photo?"

"Not necessary. There's a recent picture of him in the pamphlet he gave me. He's sending me an official estimate by email."

Even better, I could reverse engineer into his personal files.

"Great, mission accomplished. I'll meet you down on Shattuck."

I left the café and strolled down to Shattuck Avenue, one of the main drags in the college town and a few seconds later the 550 slowly rolled down the hill like a shiny black turtle. Jimmy was hunched over the wheel ever alert to any threat to Gary's prize Mercedes.

I slipped inside and settled down for the long ride across the Bay Bridge. The spectacular western span that connects Treasure Island to San Francisco designed by Donald McDonald had become a proud landmark.

And I had the opportunity to inspect every bolt as Jimmy crawled resolutely onward ignoring the impatient motorists behind him.

***

I decided to inspect Doctor Wayne's pamphlet instead. The large photo showed an older, plumper version of the groom in the wedding picture I'd pulled up on my computer. There was something else too but I couldn't really place it. I put it down to my own projection.

"So what now, surveillance?"

I put the pamphlet in my side pocket. "Not physical. Electronic maybe. I have Doctor Wayne's mobile number and the number Ky Sin gave me. It might be possible to hack into one or the other."

"You can do that?"

"A few years ago in the UK Rupert Murdoch's merry band of blackmailers were tuned in on everybody who was anybody. They hacked into mobile phones, computers, the works. They destroyed marriages, careers, reputations, the whole nine until they got nailed."

"What happened?"

"The usual. Lots of publicity. Public trials. Slap on the wrist. Murdoch's now even richer and married to Mick Jagger's ex-wife."

"How do you know this stuff?"

"I just read it in People."

Jimmy stopped at a yellow light, infuriating the driver behind us, and fiddled with the controls. "Hey, let's try out the Japanese massage. It's built into the seats."

Seconds later I felt a warm gentle pressure move across my lower spine and another between my shoulders.

"Wow," Jimmy said, "this is luxury."

I had to agree. The warm pressure hit my back in places I didn't know needed a massage. As I started to relax I noticed a silver car in the side mirror sliding up alongside us. It was the driver Jimmy had slowed down at the past stoplight.

Typically he gave me the finger even though I wasn't at the wheel. He was an Asian dude and I thought he looked familiar until he grimaced.

Then I knew he looked familiar.

It was the dude with the perfect teeth I had left tied up at the Wu Sing Ki Tong. He recognized me at the same time and twisted away. A second later I realized he was reaching for his gun.

"Move—He made us!"

Jimmy looked at me blankly. "What…?"

My window exploded in a hailstorm of glass.

I ducked and pushed Jimmy's foot down hard on the accelerator. The 550 sprang ahead like an uncaged cat. At the same time I grabbed for the .45 at the small of my back. As my fingers closed around the grip a bullet punctured the door.

"Oh shit!"

Jimmy's foot kicked at my hand still jammed on the accelerator searching for the brake. Before he found it the 550 rammed the car in front of us.

"Noooo…" Jimmy's wail cut through the sudden silence. Gun ready I lifted my head in time to see the silver car make a squealing right turn and speed away.

I looked around. We were in the middle of the intersection. The Toyota we crunched belonged to an irate, overweight woman who was struggling to get out of her car. The light was red and counting down nine seconds giving us a clear shot out of there.

"Turn left and drive—Go damnit *go!*"

Maybe it was the raw urgency in my voice or maybe it was the .45 I was waving but Jimmy jerked the wheel left and hauled ass across the intersection before the woman could extract herself from her car.

"Oh my God I'm bleeding all over the seat," Jimmy said after we covered a few blocks.

"Forget the fucking seat are you hit?"

"I think so."

"Pull over up ahead. Let's take a look."

"The cops…"

"This won't take long pull over."

Jimmy found a spot partially blocking a driveway and I ran around to the driver's side. When I saw where he was bleeding my adrenaline level dropped a notch.

The bullet had grazed his arm above the tricep. Minor but still could cause shock. After helping Jimmy into the back seat I took the wheel.

"We can't go to a hospital. We'll be arrested," Jimmy said. "Shit when Gary sees his car he'll shoot me himself."

I kept driving thinking hard. Jimmy was right but we had no choice.

I might have left Jimmy to take the rap on this one. Being shot by hijackers definitely certified his need to get to an emergency room.

Or…

"Relax, Jimmy I have an idea that gets everybody off the hook."

***

In less than ten minutes we arrived in front of St. Francis Hospital on Hyde Street.

"Can you make it inside on your own?"

"Yeah sure, Max, thanks."

"Good. Remember, give me five minutes before you report the Mercedes was stolen and you were shot in the process."

"I'll stall as long as I can but they'll probably phone it in for me."

"Even better. I know exactly where to park Gary's car."

It took about five minutes to get to Sixth Street between Market and Mission where I found a parking spot, wiped my fingerprints, and walked away from the car. I glanced back. One window was shattered, the front end badly crumpled, and the interior leather drenched with blood. My jeans too were stained with Jimmy's blood but that was little cause for attention on that particular street. I had easily found parking because civilians were reluctant to park there. The hood crawled with criminals of various persuasion from MS13 to Asian Crips.

Looking around at the gangbangers, jailhouse lawyers, and sullen women lounging in groups in front of SRO hotels and liquor stores I suspected Gary's custom Mercedes had a short expiration date.

In contrast walking around stately Pacific Heights with blood splattered jeans and a .45 tucked in your waistband is decidedly frowned upon. So I took a cab to the door of my new home and hurried inside.

Jimmy arrived about four hours later his arm in a temporary sling. By then I had partially hacked into Ky Sin's phone. Doctor Sutter's was more difficult. Apparently he was extremely cautious and had installed firewalls but I was confident I could drill through in time.

"How are you feeling?"

"A little woozy. They gave me painkillers."

"How about the cops?"

"They took my statement in the emergency room. They said it might be the same guys who got into a hit and run earlier."

"Smart cops."

"I still feel bad about the car."

"Insurance will cover it and if it doesn't I'll make up the difference."

"Where are you getting all this money?"

"Shark Boy, who else? He's giving me twenty-five grand if I find the killer."

"And if you don't?"

I shrugged. It wasn't an option.

Jimmy went to bed but I continued probing Ky Sin's phone. It proved to be a lost cause. I had to go to the mattresses.

The Sting Ray.

Sometime during the night Florence came to join me in bed.

I was starting to like that cat.

Chapter 24

"It seems the faster we're carried the less time we have."
— Orson Welles, *The Magnificent Ambersons*

The Green Ghost may not be pretty but I'll stack it up against anything on the freeway. After my brief, messy fling with the SL550 my souped-up ride felt like a real road warrior.

Even Jimmy sitting shotgun was impressed.

We were on our way to a store in Oakland that sold sophisticated surveillance equipment and the Stingray was as sophisticated as you can get.

"How long have you had this Mercury? It's got power when you pass other cars."

"I bought it used and built it up here and there. Especially the engine."

Not to mention the two secret panels, the police scanner, radar detector, and computer.

"They stopped making Mercury. This thing will be a classic."

That's what worried me. The more classic it became, the more visible.

"This device you're buying. It's really that good?"

He shifted uncomfortably. He'd left the sling at home but his arm still hurt. I knew, I'd been there.

"So good the ACLU has a court case pending against the manufacturer."

"What does it do?"

"Nothing much. Just enable me to monitor Doctor Sutter's private calls, read his texts, hear his voice mails…in other words his phone will be my phone. Police use it against protesters like Move On and Black Lives Matter."

Technically: The Stingray simulates cell phone towers in order to trick any nearby mobile phone into connecting to them. This records locations, numbers of ingoing and outgoing calls, as well as intercepting the content of voice and text communications. It also opens up emails.

Privacy? Gone with the smoking section on TWA.

Jimmy rubbed his wounded arm.

"That thing's scary actually."

"Which is why the ACLU brought their case against the manufacturer. Anybody with a thousand dollars and some know how can invade anybody's life. Even the President's. Something to think about."

And now that I was thinking about it, my next target would be Shark Boy's mobile.

As soon as I bought the damned thing I took it out of the box and made sure it was ready to sting Doctor Wayne.

It wasn't difficult. Jimmy drove to the clinic in Berkeley and parked in their lot behind the building. Then Jimmy called Sutter's mobile while I operated the Stingray.

Yes. The device captured three phones, among them Doctor Wayne's.

I was in the house.

Jimmy drove to the city while I sat in back with my arm around the Stingray like some triumphant trophy hunter embracing his kill.

For the next few hours I scoured Sutter's phone and found a number of calls and texts to Ky Sin. The more recent texts seemed urgent. The responses seemed cold.

Most importantly I had established a connection between Doctor Sutter and the woman who had tried to kill me. More digging turned up the Ace. Calls and texts between Sutter and Susan Wagner, murdered less than a week ago.

All of this required me to unlock deleted material which took hours of concentration. The Stingray could open the door but I still had to search for the safe and figure out the combination. At the end of it I was ready for a scotch and a toke or two.

Unfortunately my evidence couldn't be used to arrest anybody, having been illegally obtained. Which meant I practically had to catch Doctor Wayne in the act.

The next morning I was awakened by my new toy.

I had programmed the Stingray to buzz when Sutter made or received a call. Sure enough he had texted Ky Sin.

Mst cu wo dly

Must see you without delay—in words you don't have to pay for. Charging customers by the letter to send texts has effectively corrupted civilized language.

Some twenty minutes later the Stingray buzzed again.

Tmro 1

Tomorrow at one. Obviously somewhere they'd met before. A place I didn't know.

***

Later that morning Jimmy and I drove out to the Wig Factory in the Mission District. Another of those old time eccentric shops that flourished in San Francisco pre Mayor Yen, the place is run by an Asian couple who charge a seven dollar try-on fee that includes a sanitary skull cap and stern advice.

After many try-outs I settled on a tousled dirty blond surfer number with thick strands. To complete the ensemble I chose a matching set of eyebrows and a discreet moustache.

To keep everyone guessing I purchased another set in gray-streaked brunette. Guided by the proprietor who hovered over us—especially Jimmy—I went for a Van Dyke beard with strands of gray, and salt-and-pepper eyebrows.

While I was admiring the transformation Jimmy was being fitted for a slicked back at the sides, Vegas-type wig reminiscent of Jerry Lewis. The proprietor suggested a moustache and Jimmy agreed transforming him into Wayne Newton. For a change of pace he chose a blond look with blond brows.

We walked out with two shopping bags packed with disguises and walked over to a Taqueria for lunch.

"I've got Sutter pinned," I explained over a delicious burrito and cold beer, "I know he's meeting Lady Sin for lunch tomorrow. I just don't know where."

Jimmy had to switch hands to lift his beer. "How do we find out?"

"The old fashioned way. Tomorrow morning when Sutter leaves his house I'll be on his tail and I'll stay on it until he meets Ky Sin."

"What then?"

"I'll eavesdrop on them chatting over lunch."

"Won't they notice your equipment?"

"All I need is a laptop and earphones. In this town I'll fit right in."

Back in our lush digs I started digging into Ky Sin's closet in earnest. Until then I'd been merely checking her in the context of Green Star Escorts. But as I began to peel back the layers a profile of a very serious business woman emerged.

My search showed she had arrived in San Francisco at sixteen and graduated from Mills College. From there her path becomes hazy, falling off the grid before resurfacing with Green Star. From there her rise was rapid. Within two years she became a partner.

Not only was she part owner of Original Sin and Green Star, her corporation Diamond Investments had acquired various properties in Chinatown. She also had an offshore account in the Caymans and a condo in Hong Kong. Among the companies owned by Diamond Investments were Eurasian Exports and Pacific Security Services both headquartered in Oakland.

Nice work by the lady from Shanghai.

***

Ky Sin blamed herself.

She had been too greedy and now she was saddled with a psychopath for a partner. When they entered their agreement some five years previously Doctor Sutter had contented himself with the occasional mock strangulations of the ladies she supplied. Ky Sin knew his special kinks and how to service them. And their financial arrangements had been extremely beneficial. Through Sutter and his clinic she was able to launder nearly twenty million dollars over three years. In return he received his pick of the girls in her stable and a sizeable profit on his investment in her various companies. All nice and tidy.

Until Sutter began killing the geese producing the golden eggs.

First she had to dispose of Susan who thought she could blackmail Sutter.

And then there was Mai Sun.

She had defied orders, refusing to return to escort work. In fact Mai had boldly declared she was leaving. Her rich American boyfriend would buy her freedom so she could marry him.

However it wasn't that easy.

It was a matter of face. Especially for her protector.

True Mai was an excellent earner but money didn't matter to her. Suppose all their assets decided they could leave any time they chose? Only fear and ignorance kept their girls in line. Her fault was letting Mai become educated.

Then there was her own skin to worry about. Her protector would blame her for Mai's defection.

Oh no, that wouldn't do, Ky Sin mused, examining her reflection in the mirror. Her plan would eliminate all problems in one stroke.

She was still a striking beauty. Admittedly her bee hive hair and cool grace made her seem severe but that was her intention. After all she was the CEO of a multi-million dollar enterprise.

And Ky's favorite perk was her private security service. Fredo had taken care of the Susan Wagner problem nicely.

The buzzer sounded. Ky knew who it was and let her in.

Mai entered hesitantly.

"Madam Sin."

"Well, Mai, here you are right on time. Please sit down and make yourself comfortable."

Mai sat but was clearly not comfortable.

"I hope you're not going to try to convince me to reconsider," she said, a defiant edge in her tone.

We'll soon see about that, Ky thought. "Of course not, dear. Did you bring the final payment?"

Silently Mai took a thick manila envelope from her Coach bag and handed it to Ky who took out the stacks of cash and began to count.

"It's all there. Seventy-two thousand."

Ky gave her a condescending smile. "Trust is an expensive luxury."

When she had finished she put the cash in her office safe and returned to the living room. Mai was still sitting where she had left her. After having lived in America for twenty-five years Ky's taste in décor was still heavily Asian running to plush couches, carved chairs, shaded lamps, long stemmed gladiolas curving over ornamental vases, and jade sculpture.

In the midst of this traditional splendor Mai looked every inch a modern CEO's lovely concubine in her classic camel hair coat and understated alligator pumps. *Probably bought by her wealthy white fiancé,* Ky noted. *Unfortunately his money cannot protect her from her obligations.*

"Very good, dear," Ky said. "There's just the one last thing. I'm sure you understand."

"Yes," Mai said tonelessly.

"Tomorrow at three o'clock you will have a visitor. You will see to his needs. And then you will be free."

Mai forced a smile. "You have taught me a great deal, Madame Sin."

"I'm happy for you, dear. When are you planning to marry?"

"We haven't set a date yet."

Just as well, Ky mused escorting Mai to the door. She knew Mai had to agree to meet a last client. If she declined, her family in China would suffer. Ky returned to the bedroom to prepare for her final meeting with Doctor Sutter.

Her silent partner had become too loud. Time to muzzle him.

Chapter 25

"You can go broke having lunch with rich people."
— David Prentice, Artist

At eight a.m. traffic heading east is light.

Armed with coffee and pastry we drove across the Bay Bridge both of us properly disguised. Jimmy had his Vegas sleaze wig and moustache while I sported the tousled number with matching stash.

With detached interest I observed the steady stream of cars headed for the city. Civilians with houses, kids, mortgages, driving early to their jobs, the good people who keep society's engine tuned.

Here we were two grown men in ridiculous disguise driving out to track a vicious killer. It made me wonder how many other dark secrets were concealed inside those staid commuter vehicles.

The Caldecott Tunnel cuts through the Berkeley hills, connecting Oakland to Contra Costa County which includes upscale hamlets like Danville, Walnut Creek, and Lafayette. The tunnel has a striking Art Deco façade built at a time when beauty was held in as high regard as function.

On the other side of the tunnel the landscape changes slightly. The wooded areas above the entrance on the Berkeley side give way to unbridled development in Contra Costa County. The hills overlooking the freeway are scarred brown, the trees uprooted by enormous houses of at least twenty plus rooms worth.

"How can you live in a place that big?" Jimmy said as a dwelling large enough for a tribe of dinosaurs came into view.

"Bill Gates' home is over sixty-six thousand square feet. It's called Xanadu. After the movie Citizen Kane, not the musical with Olivia Newton John."

I'm full of random bits of information.

"I'd be lonely in a place that size."

"Right. And your humble little pad in Pacific Heights is cozy."

We both started laughing at that.

Like the other homes in Lafayette, the Sutter estate was set back from the road, scarcely visible behind twenty yards of trees and bushes. I had Google-mapped the place and had a good aerial view on the twin computers Len Zane had folded into the dashboard. When they unfolded the Green Ghost became a command center.

Jimmy was as impressed with the custom touch as he had been with the late, lamented Mercedes 550.

"This car of yours has some nice details; radar detector, slide-out computers, racing suspension, five hundred horsepower...."

I hadn't told him about the two weapons compartments nor mentioned the police scanner built into my sound system. It might give him the wrong impression.

It was still early but I didn't want Doctor Sutter to slip away unnoticed.

Despite my access to his calls he never named his afternoon meeting place. So it was back to the old fashioned way.

Sutter's home had ten rooms and four bathrooms. From the floor plan the bathrooms qualified as full rooms. Three-car garage, pool, tennis court. Your basic California dream house.

Except like Marin County, the wooded estates of Lafayette had undesirable neighbors—the big oil refineries operating on the other side of the tunnel.

While petroleum seepage and outright leaks from oil tankers poison the waters surrounding Marin, the East Bay suffers another kind of pollution.

Toxic gas.

Less than thirty miles west, the burn-off from the oil refineries' flare stacks—those constantly burning towers that resemble huge pilot lights—pumps toxic waste into the air where it's sucked into the natural wind stream flowing between the valley that connects Berkeley to Contra Costa County. No coincidence that Lafayette has a sixty percent asthma rate.

However at the moment, on a lovely morning with birds chirping and sunlight raining on the trees and flowers everywhere, it was a nature lovers' paradise.

"Must be nice to live out here," Jimmy said.

I spared him the disclaimer. After all, where's perfect? And for how long?

I just nodded.

"Yeah," I said, "lots of fresh air."

"That could be him."

Jimmy was referring to a silver Lexus easing past the quaint letter box at the mouth of the driveway.

"I think that's his wife taking the kids to school."

As I said it I felt an unexpected sense of loss. The wife, the kids… Then I remembered the eleven odd strangling victims that filled out the portrait of Sutter's placid family life.

About fifteen minutes later a sleek black Mercedes nosed out of the driveway like a probing shark.

"Shit it's a CLS 63S," Jimmy said under his breath.

"That's code for what?"

I had parked a short distance uphill from Sutter's house and waited two minutes before pulling out. He was out of sight but I was confident I knew where he was going. And should I lose him somehow my trusty Stingray would give me the GPS location of his phone.

As I slowly passed Sutter's house I glimpsed another car zipping out of the driveway. A red BMW convertible with the top down, driven by a blonde woman. In my rear view I saw her turn and zoom off in the opposite direction.

Obviously the nanny had driven the kids to school and mommy was off to the races. And Nina wonders why I'm so cynical.

"You don't know much about cars," Jimmy was saying.

"I don't keep up. So long as this car can hold tight to the road at one-eighty I'm happy. All the rest is marketing and taxes."

Jimmy looked out the side window. "That model 63 S has a five hundred fifty horsepower engine. Handcrafted."

"Then it has lots in common with my Mercury. Do you see him up ahead?"

"Yeah, he's going in the right direction."

Minutes later we emerged from the curving suburban road onto a boulevard that connected to the freeway and whatever shopping malls and gas stations were nearby.

"There," Jimmy said, "see him?"

I saw him slowly turning onto the freeway entrance and sped up a bit to close the gap between us. We were two cars behind him as we joined the slow moving conveyer belt of commuters on their way to work. The coffee and pastries we had brought along weren't for the stake out but for the dreary crawl back through the tunnel.

Sutter kept banker's hours theoretically avoiding the rush but all it took was one overheated engine or a fender bender to bring progress to its knees. Some years back a truck actually caught fire inside the Caldecott Tunnel during rush hour wreaking all sorts of havoc.

This day we passed safely if slowly into the Berkeley hills.

Surveillance seems to bring on a sour stomach. One tends to eat fast food and drink too much coffee for an otherwise sedentary endeavor. We took turns keeping tabs on Sutter's clinic but our walks around the hood had to be limited lest someone tagged us as suspicious. As it was Jimmy's Vegas disguise made him look like a pimp compared to the academics from the nearby campus.

Me? I resembled an off-duty bartender.

Sutter finally left the clinic at one. As expected he headed for the city. We followed at a leisurely pace until he crossed the Bay Bridge. Unexpectedly he stayed in the financial district.

"This may get tricky," I said, referring to the heavy traffic and lack of parking, "get ready to take over."

Sutter's Mercedes turned onto Stevenson, a narrow street off Market, and pulled into a parking lot.

"Okay I'll take him on foot from here."

I stopped, stepped out, and took an attaché case from the back as Jimmy slid behind the wheel.

"Just stay nearby," I said, "I'll call when I'm ready."

"No problem."

I paused. "One more thing."

"What?"

"Bang up my car and I'll shoot you."

***

I lingered until Sutter left the parking lot then followed him into the restaurant across the street. The place was Yank Sing, an upscale Chinese bistro that specializes in Dim Sum which are dumplings stuffed with exotic combinations of pork, chicken, or vegetables. Pig in a blanket Asian style.

Fortunately there were tables available, however the table the hostess chose for me was off the beaten track, probably due to the way I looked in my unruly wig and thick moustache.

Sutter had taken a table across the room which defeated my purpose. So I pointed to an empty table a few feet from my quarry. "Excuse me, miss, would you mind if I sat over there? This table is a bit cramped."

"That table is…"

As she started to explain it was a table for four, I put three twenties on the table. "I understand, this should cover the inconvenience."

The hostess hesitated, smiled, and scooped up the bills.

"This way, sir."

I sat with my back to Doctor Wayne. Eye contact was unnecessary for what I needed to do. I took a small Mac laptop and what appeared to be a mobile phone from my attaché case and set them neatly on the table. I also removed a set of earphones from the case. Lady Sin had yet to arrive so I took the opportunity to order a tall beer.

The way it works at Yank Sing is the waiters roll carts bearing various types of Dim Sum dumplings between tables and diners choose the ones they wish to sample. I loaded up my plate from the first cart that came my way then quickly organized my surveillance kit.

It was simple really. The laptop acted as tuner and recorder while the innocent-looking 'mobile phone' was actually a powerful amplifier and transmitter.

Glancing around I saw one other patron on laptop over lunch and lots of others hooked into their mobiles in one form or another. In San Francisco a tech geek like me fit right in.

You couldn't miss Ky Sin's entrance.

Tall, regal, her athletic body moved gracefully between the tables and waiters rolling carts of dim sum. After a first glance I turned away but noticed many of the male diners were staring.

In less than a minute I had a fix on their table and when I slipped on the earphones could hear their conversation.

"I'm happy you were able to arrange things," Sutter said as soon as Ky sat.

"It hasn't been easy believe me."

"And the money?"

"Ah look. The food is here. What are you having?"

"My usual, the Shanghai dumplings and the duck."

"I believe I'll have the snow pea dumpling and the vegetable savory."

As I listened I nibbled on one of the dumplings I had selected at random and discovered it was indeed delicious.

"I have you scheduled for tomorrow at three, does that suit you?"

"That will suit me very well, Ky, my dear," Sutter said with unusual emphasis. Until now his voice had been a low drone.

"You know things…extremely difficult lately. We…to scale… operation." Intermittent gusts of static obscured her reply.

"And the money?"

"Of course. You'll receive your dividend at the end of the month."

"Why so late?"

"Mainly because of the difficulties caused by your own actions, Doctor. They have begun to call attention to us."

"After tomorrow the problem will be resolved."

"Really? How can we be so sure, Doctor?"

"I'll be taking an extended holiday. Six months, perhaps more."

"How nice. Where are you going?"

"Thailand, Cam…" Static cut off his reply but I got the bastard's drift. So did Ky.

"I see. Nothing's really changed except the location."

"Change isn't an option."

"Of course."

"Now then who is this girl and where do I meet her?"

"Her name is Mai…she…"

The waiter interrupted. "Today's special duck dumplings…" Abruptly his voice disintegrated into a burst of static.

"You're cert…" I heard Sutter saying, "…time?"

Ky's reply was lost in the clatter of dishes being exchanged. I tried to get better reception by moving the transmitter but it didn't help. The after lunch traffic of departing patrons, carts, waiters, and bus boys clearing tables fragmented what little conversation that followed.

I saw the heads turning when Ky Sin made her exit with Doctor Wayne in tow but averted my gaze. I paid the bill, gathered my equipment, and called Jimmy. My mission had paid very little dividends. I knew my lovely friend Mai was slated to be Sutter's next love slave and the time.

But not exactly where.

Very little for six hours of surveillance and an expensive lunch.

However one thing was terribly certain. Lovely Mai Sun was sitting on Death Row.

***

Back at our Pacific Heights mansion I hit the computer while Jimmy retired to his room. He was still nursing his wounded arm and fell asleep almost immediately.

I searched for Mai Sun's home but all I found was a Facebook page and a few transcripts from the University of San Francisco night school with a defunct address.

Finally I hacked into the DMV and found her legal residence.

But I was assuming that was where Mai would meet Doctor Sutter. It could very well be a neutral site. In which case we were both fucked.

It was still early so I went down to the den and poured a healthy scotch. Although I knew I had no part in Mai's fate I somehow felt responsible. If only because I knew what was coming—and no one should have to die like that at the whim of an upscale strangler.

I felt The Preacher stirring in the primal Chakra that fires my rage.

Won't do, I told myself. Emotion clouds judgement and any error could be fatal. I rolled a J, switched on the TV, and surfed for something to cool me down.

I skipped past the news and settled on a Giants baseball game. They were playing the Dodgers, always an intense rivalry. A few puffs into the game I was marveling at the skill of our new pitcher Johnny Cueto.

Some say it's The Great American Past-Its-Time.

Maybe…but so am I.

With my anxiety and anger lulled by a well-played ballgame my brain snuck out of its room and reminded me I could track Sutter's location via his mobile phone, compliments of the Stingray.

Thus reassured I watched the game to the end then tuned in an antique Fred Astaire, Ginger Rogers movie called *Swing Time*. Boy finds girl boy loses girl boy finds girl—in between they dance.

For some reason it made me think of Nina. At the moment we were in the boy loses girl stage.

And I'm a lousy dancer.

Chapter 26

"Live each day as if it's your last, someday you'll be right."
— Woody Allen, *Café Society*

Nina hadn't been able to reach Max all day.

Service in Zejuataneo wasn't always reliable but once she got to the airport she had hoped to connect. She wanted to alert Max that she was coming home. She couldn't sit on the sidelines any longer. If Max was in trouble she needed to be there for him. It was a no brainer.

Perhaps she could call him from the air, Nina thought, pacing as she waited for the plane. Of course it was late. As time passed her doubts increased. True, Max had told her to wait for him. But he hadn't called in two days, Nina reminded herself. Phone service in San Francisco was the best so he had no excuse.

Suppose he was in a hospital somewhere, or worse. It was maddening to not know. Nina understood all the reasons to stay put but she loved the crazy bastard. Even more she owed him a lot. If it weren't for Max her family would have been decimated. She and her cousin would be slaves in some grimy brothel, sold to the highest bidder.

Max saved them both and broke up the Vandals' human trafficking operation. Afterwards he helped her cousin Jordan get his college degree. In her mind Max would always be a superhero.

However in reality he was human. And vulnerable, especially when he drank.

Still doubting the wisdom of her impetuous return Nina shuffled onto the plane, hoping they would serve something to eat.

Once in the air Nina tried to call Max again but found her phone needed recharging. On the bright side Aero Mexico served a tasty lunch.

They landed in Los Angeles two hours late. After the plane landed it was further delayed on the runway for some inexplicable reason.

Bedraggled and pissed off, Nina grabbed a cab when she landed and went straight to her apartment. There she charged her phone, took a shower, and changed clothes. In turn, angered and worried about Max's silence, she went for a walk.

Before leaving, Nina took care to take the switchblade knife she'd left behind when she went to Mexico. She couldn't bring it on the plane and had bought a replacement as soon as she landed. Ever since she had been kidnapped by the Vandals, Nina kept a knife tucked into the small of her back as an essential fashion accessory.

It was a warm night and Sixteenth Street was teeming with movement: young techies on their phones, more young techies waiting to get into restaurants, local Latinos hanging out eying them suspiciously.

With good reason, Nina thought, rummaging through her bag for cigarettes. She had stopped smoking in Mexico but she was too stressed to feel guilty. She found a pack with three left and lit one.

A couple of long drags calmed her long enough to figure out what she was doing. The odds were better than even that she was just being hysterical. On the other hand she had a gut feeling that something had gone terribly wrong.

Call it female intuition or her Latina bruja insight or whatever, it was there warning her.

Maybe it's warning you to back off, Nina reminded herself.

She walked aimlessly for a few blocks then realized she knew exactly where she wanted to go and hailed a cab.

***

Nina was aware she was breaking a cardinal rule of their relationship by visiting Max's apartment unannounced. Especially in light of the fact that after knowing each other for two years Max revealed its location only two weeks ago.

It's his own fault, Nina fumed, *he's so fucking…distant. It forces me to break down the barriers he sets up.* Even though Max confided in her about his past and explained why he's been unwilling to take their relationship further Nina knew he'd left out a shitload of details.

North Beach was bustling when she arrived. The cab deposited her at Washington Square Park and she walked the few block to Max's flat.

When she pushed the outside buzzer it actually responded.

Elated, Nina hurried up three flights to the apartment but when she got there she stopped short.

An older man with long white hair and a neat white beard squinted at her curiously through the half open door.

"Uh, yes?"

For a moment Nina thought she'd gone to the wrong floor.

"I thought Max lived here."

"He does…Max is away now. Um, are you a friend of his?"

"Yes but I haven't heard from him in a few days."

"Me too and believe me I could use his help. Would you like to come inside and wait?"

He ushered her into the now familiar disarray of Max's flat. The front room had been converted into an office dominated by three Macs with oversized screens. An open laptop and untidy piles of papers and books occupied whatever space was left on the desk.

"Let's go into the kitchen. Would you like some tea?"

He led her down the long corridor. Max's room she knew was the last door on the right before they reached the kitchen. His door was closed.

A fitting metaphor for their relationship, Nina noted.

"I was just making tea when you buzzed. If I can figure out where to find some honey everything with be fine. This tea is very strong."

"I think there's a jar of honey in that small cabinet to your left."

The man cocked his head and regarded her with an owlish expression.

"So you've been here before?"

"Only once. You were in England."

"That right. I just got back. I stayed at the Saville Club."

"I hear very nice there."

"So how long have you known Max?"

"Two years. How about you?"

He seemed confused by the question. "Me?"

"How long have you known Max?"

"Oh—almost four years now."

He put two steaming cups on the table and sat down.

"Uh, what's your name?"

"Nina Fuente, what's yours?"

"Eli Sarfelli." He paused as if she should have recognized the name. "I'm a physicist," he added proudly.

"Oh." Nina tried to sound impressed.

"I hope he calls in soon, my laptop is frozen. All my notes on Gravity Waves…"

Nina nodded and sipped her tea. It was good actually, just what she needed to calm her. She tried to make conversation.

"Is Max a good housemate?"

Eli's face brightened and he looked like a six year old.

"The best. Pays on time, clean, courteous, and keeps all our computers in top shape."

"Sounds perfect," Nina said wistfully. She knew Max could be nice to live with…if he ever decided to live with her.

Eli peered at her through rimless glasses. "So uh, are you guys dating?"

"It's a little beyond that…I think."

Nina tried to smile and sipped her tea. *This was a really bad idea*, she suddenly realized. *When Max gets back Eli will tell him I tried to crash his privacy. Which should convince a guy like Max to change his zip code.*

Deflated, Nina finished her tea. She intended to go home and compose a formal apology.

"Thanks so much for your hospitality, Eli. I should be going."

"Do you want to leave a message?"

"Just say I'm back in San Francisco."

"Sure. Where were you by the way?"

"Mexico," Nina said, unwilling to name the place. Just in case Max should someday decide to run away with her.

"Did I say I was in London?" Eli said.

"Yes, the Saville Club wasn't it?"

"It's great there," he said opening the door. "If you see Max before I do tell him to call me."

From your mouth to God's ear, Nina thought as she descended the stairs.

***

It was cool outside but the sky was clear. *The Mission is always warmer than North Beach,* Nina mused, zipping her leather jacket.

She decided to walk over to Tony Nix and have a drink before going home.

As she neared the corner she noticed a large black car with two men inside. The man behind the wheel watched her intently as she approached. The other man in the passenger seat was on his phone.

For a moment Nina had a bad feeling but told herself to stay cool which she did—until the car door opened and an Asian man stepped out.

"Excuse me, are you a friend of Max?"

Max had told her about his friend Jimmy Shu. Maybe he was looking for him too.

"Are you Jimmy?" Nina blurted, instantly regretting it.

The man smiled. He had perfect white teeth.

"Yes," he said, "I'm Jimmy."

It didn't sound right.

Her fight or flight reflex kicked in and she turned to run.

She stopped and shrank back when she saw the large man looming behind her. He had a gun.

Nina tried to scream but a wave of nausea rolled over the sound.

Chapter 27

"No heart is so hard as the timid heart."
— Norman Mailer

Wayne couldn't sleep that night.

He was too amped thinking about his appointment the next day. It would be his last for a while. The last that is, until he got settled in Asia.

His plan was to set up headquarters in Thailand and take forays into Vietnam and Cambodia for his…special needs. No one would ever take notice of a dead prostitute in those countries and even if they did he'd be long gone.

They hardly took notice here in the States, he noted. If it wasn't for that meddler, things could have gone smoothly for a few more years. But it was just as well. For one thing he couldn't tolerate his wife for too much longer. Candi and her lover were an embarrassment. He had considered disposing of her the way he had his first wife. But it might arouse suspicion. And there were the children to consider.

A tight smile crossed his pudgy face as he thought of Candi's surprise when she discovered he'd left. She could keep the house, the cars, what little he had in their bank account. Candi would need it to raise the kids. He had also put some money in trust for his children's future.

As for him, he would retire with the twenty million he had in his offshore accounts. He wasn't greedy. Money was less important to him than his overwhelming obsession.

Of course his business partners at the clinic already knew. In fact his replacement was due next week. He had grown tired of catering to self-entitled bitches with leathery skin from too much sun at the country club, and egos as big as Brazil. Tired of catering to their constant complaints and whining that they had to look young again.

He switched on the CD player and tried to relax as the funereal chords of Beethoven's Fifth marched through the interior of his Mercedes.

Moving slowly across the Bay Bridge his anticipation of the afternoon's erotic entertainment grew. Sutter went over every minute phase, the wintery music serving as soundtrack to his festering fantasy.

First the small talk, putting her at ease.

Then something to drink or some cocaine. They usually liked that. Sutter didn't use the drug himself but as a dental surgeon he had access to pharmaceutical cocaine. Pure and effective.

After the opening ceremonies (as he liked to think of them) he would give her detailed instructions on what he wanted. Having already paid three times the going rate there was never an objection.

Especially since much of their participation consisted of posing in lingerie and high heels. Erotic posing. That was one of the best parts of his scenario. He felt like a film director, a great artist…he felt powerful.

Sutter was getting an erection thinking about it.

He was also sweating profusely even though the AC was on high. He took an oversized blue handkerchief from his suit pocket and mopped his face. His mother had given it to him decades ago. It was stained from use and had the sour stink of a farm towel unwashed for years.

After the show came the grand finale.

He turned the volume higher and let Beethoven's stormy passion sweep across his thoughts.

He would tell her to kneel with her back to him. She would assume it was just another pose. Instead he would rise and step behind her.

Sutter's fingers gripped the leather steering wheel tightly. He had strong hands, made stronger by the metal grips he squeezed nightly while watching TV.

And then he would start to strangle them. When they were close to death he would stop until she recovered.

Then he would strangle her again, and again until…

He could hardly contain himself.

…Blue Vengeance crushed her filthy throat.

Sutter relaxed his grip on the wheel as he nosed the car through downtown traffic.

He had been extremely careful. No videos, pictures, trophies—no trace.

Which paradoxically created a problem.

If he had saved trophies, an item of lingerie say, he wouldn't have to indulge his obsession so often. Fortunately after meeting Ky Sin it became easy.

Sutter's first encounter with Madam Sin was as a client, she being his escort. However she always seemed to be in charge so he restrained his urges to dark fantasy.

What Madam Sin did was allow him to indulge these fantasies, share them with her. She never condemned them, even appeared to be stimulated by them. For two years they were locked together in their unutterable lusts.

About that time she told him about her business plan. She was about to branch out on her own and he could get in on the ground floor for a sizeable investment. He readily agreed, especially when she explained he would have access to her stable of escorts.

In the intervening years his investment had garnered him a fortune and given him the opportunity to explore the exquisite art of killing. And today Blue Vengeance would take a final bow in the merciless drama of his mad soul.

Chapter 28

*"Do not wait till the iron is hot; but make
it hot by striking."* — W.B. Yeats

In the morning I drove to the address on Mai Sun's driver's license and parked a few doors away. In my business getting there early is half the game.

Like an athlete's first step against an opponent.

To while away the time I had both screens in my car's computer system focused on Doctor Wayne Sutter. Having jacked his mobile phone via the Stingray I had total access to his life. One screen tracked his location. The other was sifting through his private email accounts. And Wayne had more than his share.

Digging deeper I uncovered three separate offshore numbered bank accounts totaling twenty odd million. There were also visa applications to Cambodia, Vietnam, and Thailand. The Thai visa was for one year. The others for dates the following month. Apparently Wayne intended to take an extended vacation to deviate friendly pastures.

All the more reason to take him down now.

The other screen showed his normal schedule. I had brought along coffee, water, a sandwich, and pastry for the duration. Of course the coffee and pastry went first.

My first surprise came shortly after one. A silver Audi pulled up and Mai Sun exited. The driver got out of the car and said something to her across the open sun roof. She smiled and blew him a kiss. From her glowing expression she meant it.

On impulse I took a few quick shots with my phone. Having nothing better to do as I waited for Doctor Sutter to cross the bridge I ran the man's picture and license plate.

Turned out Mai's beau was a young entrepreneur named Mark Green. He was a principal in various online delivery services that included meals, medicine, and laundry delivered to your door. Photos of him embracing Mai or feeding her at dinner or out hiking together peppered his Facebook page. For her part Mai looked happier than the last time I saw her.

Digging deeper I found that Mark had graduated from MIT Summa and was a member of the St. Francis Yacht Club. No priors, no traffic tickets. I wondered if he knew what Mai did for a living. Considering Mai's spectacular beauty I would lay odds Mark didn't care.

His yacht was being steered by Captain Johnson.

Believe me I know how that goes. Come to think of it Mai's stunning good looks almost got me killed. Which made me wonder why I was trying to save her treacherous ass.

Speaking of treachery Ky Sin was deliberately serving up Mai to satisfy Doctor Sutter's lethal appetites. What was that about?

So I was somewhat astonished to see Ky Sin herself step out of a cab in front of Mai's apartment. Even more astonishing was Ky Sin's outfit, which consisted of a black Adidas track suit with red stripes and a pair of black Nikes. A large silver barrette held her signature bee hive hair in place. Without her high heels and usual Dragon Lady sheath she looked lean and compact, hips swaying and long arms dangling lazily like a basketball player.

I watched in amazement as she entered the building. Moments later my amazement morphed to confusion spiked with self-doubt. What the fuck was she doing there?

My heretofore carefully constructed plan to trap Doctor Sutter in the act was crumbling before my eyes. Unless Ky Sin was involved in the killings she was there for some other reason. Perhaps a business meeting, maybe a three way.

And there I sat with my head up my ass.

I called Jimmy who was positioned a block away in his rental and told him what was up.

"Why do you think she's here?"

"No idea."

"Maybe we should back off until we know?"

"Give me a minute."

I hung up and sorted through my options. There were two. Crash the scene or go home.

I still had my disguises in the trunk and was already wearing my Kevlar vest. I checked Sutter's progress on the computer. He was at least twenty minutes away.

I popped the trunk and quickly retrieved my gear. Back inside the car I donned the gray black wig and matching Van Dyke beard. Practically as good as a mask.

My plan (such as it was) involved picking the outside lock, sneaking up to Mai's apartment, and breaking in if I heard anything like a struggle.

Primitive and possibly disastrous. Still it seemed like my best chance to get Doctor Sutter and Ky Sin in the same room before Sutter split the country.

Worst case scenario I could always leave the country myself.

I called Jimmy. "Can you see the house?"

"Yeah. I saw you leave the car too."

"Good. Fifteen minutes after Sutter gets here I'm going in. When you see me enter the building, walk to my car, get in, and start it up. Keys are under the mat. Most likely I'll be coming out fast."

"Got it."

"The bastard's halfway across the bridge, stay frosty."

When Sutter arrived he circled the block looking for parking. I saw the dot on my screen stop and a few minutes later a paunchy, pasty white man who resembled a steamed bun stuffed into an expensive suit was let into Mai's building.

I waited fifteen minutes then took a quick check before getting out. My Kevlar vest was snug under a loose-fitting blue oxford shirt, my Taurus was tucked in the small of my back, and my set of lock picks was in my pocket. I glanced in the rear view to make sure my wig was straight.

Good to go.

There was no problem picking the outside lock.

Mai lived in a well-kept Edwardian on Russian Hill. Thankfully the stairs were carpeted but I hadn't counted on them leading directly to her flat.

I should have noticed that unlike my North Beach pad where the apartments were connected by a common stairway, all three flats in Mai's building had separate entrances.

Sherlock had blundered inside like Inspector Clouseau.

One hand gripping the door knob, I stood stock still, staring up at the hall landing.

There was no barrier between the people upstairs and me. If anyone should glance over the bannister it was over. I heard a voice and crept up the first few steps, eyes on the railing above me. I tried to remember what I knew about Edwardians.

Basic floor plan for that style had a long hall that connected a kitchen and dining room in back to two front rooms, with bedrooms and bathrooms between. High ceilings were also a feature of that style and they amplified the male voice that drifted from somewhere upstairs.

I paused and carefully took the Taurus from its resting place at the small of my back.

I heard the male voice again. I couldn't make out the words but the tone was soothing, like someone calming a pet. Slowly I cocked the hammer of my .45. The metallic *snap* sounded like a gunshot. I froze expecting someone to appear on the landing. But it remained quiet.

Too quiet.

It was a dense silence, like swimming underwater. I remained as still as a crocodile. Until I heard a high feminine shriek and mounted the stairs two at a time.

The hallway was deserted. There was a room behind me. I stepped back and swept the area with the muzzle of the .45. Empty.

Taurus extended, I moved along the hall taking quick, quiet steps the way I learned at Marine combat school.

I saw a doorway just ahead but as I went to check it…a gargled shriek pulled me to another door—too late.

Mai was sprawled on the floor face up, her eyes shut and mouth contorted. A blue handkerchief was twisted around her bruised throat.

A naked man lay a few feet away, a knife protruding from the base of his skull.

I stepped inside.

Wrong move, jarhead.

A ferocious thunderclap blew me off me off my feet.

Chapter 29

*"I long ago came to the conclusion that all of life
is six to five against."* – Damon Runyon

I kissed the floor hard enough to leave an imprint of my lips.
Stunned, my instincts kicked in.

I rolled and lifted the Taurus.

Except it wasn't there.

Still disoriented I rolled again in time to deflect the full force of a hard swung sneaker. I grabbed an ankle and yanked.

It threw the other leg off balance long enough for me to recover mine. Still clutching the ankle I pulled myself up and turned a half step. The momentum pulled the leg from my grasp and flung my attacker out of reach.

I stumbled back not really surprised to see Ky Sin stop and spin.

She lowered her lean body in a cat crouch as I circled away. I considered myself above average in close combat but Ky Sin was flash fast—and speed kills.

One balletic step and she was airborne, her whip-like foot snapping off my skull.

I scrambled away, frantically looking for my lost Taurus while trying to keep Ky Sin in view. Her quickness closed the gap in a blur. I blocked one kick to my groin, a fist to my neck, and began to bob and weave like Ali except I was bobbing backwards.

A wave of adrenaline washed over my limbs and The Preacher surfed right in with it. She came at me again but I wasn't playing defense anymore. I slipped a sharp kick, stepped inside, and drilled my knuckles into her belly.

She gave a short *huff* and retreated a step.

It didn't seem to faze her.

As we circled she reached up and took the barrette from her bee hive. Except her barrette was a silver stiletto with a seven-inch blade.

Her sleek black hair uncoiled like snakes on Medusa, her eyes burning coals of hate. When she saw me shrink away from the dagger her lips contorted in a ghastly smile.

She darted in like an angry bee slashing the air.

My back slammed against a wall and she lunged. The stiletto dug into my chest just below my rib cage.

It tore my shirt but failed to penetrate flesh.

The Kevlar saved my ass.

A backfist swat across her face drove her away. I spotted my gun near the door and dove for it. As my fingers closed on the Taurus the bitch stamped on my hand with one foot and booted me across the skull with the other.

The Preacher would have none of it.

Ignoring the pain I twisted and somehow heaved myself erect. My numbed fingers were still wrapped around the gun but it was pointed the wrong way. Vision in one eye was blurred from the kick and I knew the second it would take to right my weapon would be fatal.

Ky Sin was too swift. She'd figured out I had body armor and zeroed in on unprotected flesh.

Searing pain burned my arm as her dagger slashed my exposed forearm. I dodged and scurried back.

It's tough to fight when you're trying to avoid two dead bodies and Ky Sin was expertly cutting off my wiggle room.

She worked me into a tight corner with corpses on my right and a wall on my left. My arm was bleeding and one eye blinked in and out of focus.

Out of nowhere her foot whacked my crotch and I dropped to one knee. With a triumphant howl she grabbed my hair intending to jerk my head up and slit my throat.

Except it wasn't my hair.

For a confused moment she stood holding my wig aloft, which gave me the space to come out of my crouch and head-butt her in the belly. This time her *huff* was loud and hoarse and she staggered back a few feet.

All The Preacher wanted now was to blow her face off.

I curled my swollen finger around the trigger but again she was too fast. She sprang high and lashed out with her foot, catching my gun. My hand was still numb from being stomped and the Taurus slipped slightly. I barely managed to hold on but I was off balance and she was bobbing closer, the dagger a blur. At best she'd slice my arm into cold cuts before I could switch hands.

She came at me from my near blind side and punctured my forearm. I roared and swung the gun with two hands, smacking her cheek.

The blow stunned her.

She stepped back.

I went into a shooter's crouch, aiming at her torso.

She crouched to spring…

She stopped short, eyes wide with surprise.

But it wasn't my .45 that surprised her.

She turned stiffly, limbs twitching, and I saw the knife protruding from her neck like the key in a wind-up toy.

As she collapsed I saw Mai Sun standing there.

She was naked except for a garter belt and sagging stockings. She held up her arms.

"Don't shoot, please…" Her hoarse voice trailed off to a low moan. Her eyes were glazed bright and she was trembling from shock.

I lowered the gun.

"I think you killed her."

She spoke with some difficulty, voice a low monotone. "It was self-defense. You saw, she tried to kill you."

"What happened?"

"He…choked me. She was there. I passed out. When I woke up he choked me again…and again… It was horrible. And she…"

"What did she do?"

"Pushed him on…she was getting off on it."

Mai began to shiver.

"You better put on some warm clothes," I said.

She nodded and went to a closet. Absently she put on a flannel shirt and sweatpants.

I waved my gun at Sutter's body. "Who killed him?"

"I don't know. When I woke up he was beside me. Madam Sin must have…I need to sit down."

She walked unsteadily to a connecting bedroom and sat on the bed.

There was a blanket at the foot of the bed. I put it around her shoulders.

"Where did you get the knife?"

"What?"

"The knife you used to kill her. Where did you get it?"

"I woke up and you were fighting her. I was afraid she'd kill me if you lost. So I pulled the knife out of…him…" Mai pointed at the other room.

"She didn't see me get up. Then you knocked her back and I…stabbed her." Mai looked up at me. "Who are you?"

It was then I realized I was still wearing my salt and pepper beard. Which reminded me. The wig was still in the other room somewhere.

Evidence easily traced.

"Who are you?" she repeated.

"A friend."

I went into the other room and retrieved my hair piece, grateful she hadn't recognized me. To make sure I put the wig back on my head. As I started to leave she called out.

"Wait…please."

I came back for a moment.

Her glazed eyes pleaded with me.

"What should I do?"

"Call your boyfriend to pick you up. Tell him to get a lawyer. Then call the police."

Which should give everybody time to work out a solid self-defense alibi, I thought, hurrying down the stairs.

The moment I hit the street, Jimmy pulled up in the Green Ghost.

"What happened?" Jimmy said as he turned the corner and sped away.

I removed the wig and took a deep breath.

"You won't believe it."

***

By the time we got back home my body was feeling the effects of my death battle with Bruce Lee's feminine side. My eye was throbbing. I was bleeding from at least three cuts and my hand was swollen. Not to mention stiff joints and strange bruises. Fortunately I had an in-house physician.

Despite his own injury Jimmy cleaned and bandaged the cuts on my forearm then went to work on my body. He brewed a hot herbal bath for my hand that reduced the swelling and gave my back and shoulders a deep massage that had me moving around without pain. Then he brewed up an herbal compress for my eye that brought my vision into focus.

Three hours and a fat J later I was near normal, which wasn't saying much.

Jimmy was full of questions and I tried my best to answer them all.

"So you think Ky Sin killed Susan Wagner?"

"Or had her killed. High Class Sluts was one of Ky Sin's satellite operations along with Oracle Escorts."

"But she definitely killed Doctor Sutter."

"Oh yeah. Sutter liked to play with his victims. Let them breathe then strangle them again. And Ky Sin was his enabler. Until she shoved a knife into the base of his skull."

"And Mai Sun used that knife to kill Ky Sin?"

"Yeah. Homicide forensics will have a great time figuring out who did who."

"So it's over?"

"Not until we get paid."

I picked up my phone and called Albert Chan.

He answered on the first ring.

"Yes?"

"I have good news."

There was a long pause.

"You need to check your messages. Call me."

Check my messages? I was using an untraceable pre-paid phone. Only two people had the number to my other phone. And one of them was with me.

My belly went into free fall.

Nina.

Frantic I went to the bedroom where I had left my personal phone.

There it was. A call from Nina.

I took a deep breath and tried to think. This was no time for The Preacher to get hysterical. Another breath and my animal rage turned cold assassin. I realized I needed an edge. Then it came to me.

I ran past a confused Jimmy to the garage. I retrieved the Stingray from my car and ran back to the bedroom. I hooked my Stingray to my laptop and started making calls. The first to Nina.

"Max, I'm so sorry," she blurted, "I should have listened."

"Are you alright?"

"Yes, unless you count being locked in a closet."

"Do you know where you are?"

"Somewhere near North Beach. Maybe Chinatown."

"Hang on. I'll be right over. Now listen…"

"Somebody's coming.…"

"Hide your phone…somewhere on you. Understand?"

The call ended. I immediately called Shark Boy.

"I see you got the message," he said.

I could see his broad smirk but I stayed calm.

"We had a deal."

"And I intend to honor it."

"What does Nina have to do with this?"

"I'm going to negotiate a better deal. Just like Trump."

"What do you want me to do?"

"I'll call you back."

Now I had access to Shark Boy's life: phone, text, emails, location. A slight edge. If I lived long enough.

No doubt he would want me to meet him somewhere. And no doubt his boys would frisk me. Something else occurred to me. Who else was involved in Shark Boy's renegotiation? Could be he'd decided to collect the Vandal's bounty on me. Which would leave Nina at their mercy. Most likely they'd sell her—if they let her live.

I had no illusions about what they would do to me.

My mind rummaged through my options. Cyber skills are no match for bullets. I would have to go in there unarmed and alone. Jimmy was no match for professionals no matter how big his heart.

I made a quick call to the cavalry.

Captain Robert Lowell of the Petaluma PD responded after a grueling three rings.

"It's me," I said, "I need a favor."

"What's the problem?"

"The bastards abducted Nina. They're about to call back, probably deciding where to smoke me. I need back up."

"Who took her, the Vandals?" Referring to our vigilante raid on the motorcycle gang a few years back.

"Right now it's Albert Chan AKA Shark Boy."

"We've heard of him up here. I'm in. Where are you?"

"I'll probably be where they want me. My friend Jimmy Chu will trail me. He's a civilian. He'll call you from his phone now. That way you can stay connected."

Jimmy called Lowell immediately,

"He says he's already on his way," Jimmy said.

I felt slightly relieved. Petaluma is a thirty minute drive—if you're a cop. Bad traffic could slow him down another thirty. Either way I would have to go in alone to make sure Nina was safe.

"You'll have to follow me," I told Jimmy, "but only if you're up to it. They want me, not you."

"If they get you they'll come for me next. Anyway I owe you—end of discussion. I'll get the Mercedes."

"Too visible." I handed him the keys to the Green Ghost. "People don't notice an old Mercury."

***

As we waited for the call I paced up and down. Trying to come up with some kind of Sun Tzu strategy. I took stock of the weapons at my disposal.

My arsenal consisted of a flat throwing knife, a combat knife, a Cobra spring-loaded blackjack, a short barreled .38, a Sig Sauer nine, a Taurus .45…and not much chance of using them.

Shark Boy probably thought he was wearing me down by making me wait but I knew he wanted *me*—personally. That was my edge and the only thing keeping Nina alive.

The Preacher was in a frenzy and had to be restrained like a wild horse at the starter's gate. We went to the garage and Jimmy helped tape some weapons to various parts of my body: the flat throwing knife inside the bandage on my wounded forearm, the Colt .38 taped sideways to the middle of my back within reach of my fingers, and the Cobra taped between my shoulder blades just under my neck.

Find one you find them all.

We were nearly finished when Shark Boy called.

"Forty-five minutes be at the corner of Jackson and Grant. If I think you're followed the girl dies," he said and clicked off.

He couldn't have chosen a more public place, usually teeming with tourists. His crew would walk me somewhere to make sure we weren't tailed.

"You go there now and park the car." I took my bike out of the trunk and slid it onto the back seat. "They're picking me up on Grant and taking me somewhere else. The bike is the best way to follow."

"Will do," Jimmy said.

I put the Stingray in the trunk.

"They know you in that neighborhood. You better wear this." I handed him the salt and pepper wig that saved my life. "It's my lucky piece."

Chapter 30

"Tom, you have plenty of enemies and they're all doing well."
— Kathleen Brennan Waits

My appointment with disaster was about forty minutes away so rather than waste time fretting I went on foot. The walk helped me harness the excess energy racing through my body. It also helped loosen my battle-scarred limbs. Jimmy's healing skills had eased but not erased the stiff aches and pains.

Along with my hidden weapons the Sig .9mm was stuffed in my waistband under my leather windbreaker.

It was little comfort.

I hadn't bothered with the Kevlar vest. The other kids would laugh.

They would be waiting when I got there, at least three maybe four. Two stationed as lookouts, two to intimidate me. Maybe they'd frisk me right there, maybe not. Then they'd take me to wherever Shark Boy planned to kill me.

On my end I had Jimmy already there. He'd follow on foot or bike and direct Lowell, who was on his way. That was the extent of my brilliant strategy.

That and The Preacher.

His sheer ferocity was a point in my favor.

All I needed was a thousand more points.

I thought about Nina. What the hell was she doing here anyway? Not important. My only goal was to get her out safely. Nothing else mattered.

***

They were there as expected.

Two on the corner, another across the street. The sentries could be anywhere.

I actually spotted one as I came through Kerouac Alley onto Grant Street. He was on the roof of a low building. I wondered how many more were stationed around me. They would stay in place long after my handlers took me away to make sure I wasn't followed.

The two standing the corner of Jackson were textbook.

In the flow of tourists and locals jostling each other they stood out.

The big one wore a permanent scowl over a red and black check shirt and new designer jeans. He had a broad face reminiscent of a Chinese Edward G. Robinson with heartburn. He was pretending to browse a souvenir bin but he kept looking around to scan the street. Considering the merchandise on display he didn't look like the type to buy a plastic happy cat with one constantly waving paw.

His black Nikes were at least size seventeen and his shoulders stretched the seams of his shirt which was untucked either to conceal his belly or a weapon. Probably both.

The other one was leaning against a parking sign reading a Chinese newspaper. He was smaller and wearing a hooded sweatshirt and jeans. Every ten seconds he would drop his newspaper and check the street like a nervous tick. He seemed vaguely familiar.

I glanced up to see if there were any other spotters on the rooftops. Nothing. Walking slowly I tried to pick out Jimmy on the crowded street. Nothing.

That's a good thing, I told myself, not convinced.

To disarm them, so to speak, I smiled as I neared and opened my hands in a Guido style greeting. The smaller guy smiled back uncertainly and I recognized him. I also knew why he was nervous. The last time we met I had left him taped up at the Wu Sing Ki Tong. The scumbag with the perfect teeth who had helped grab Jimmy's little girl.

Smiling I approached him arms open.

"Still in the kidnapping business," I said, "you want to frisk me here?"

Before he could answer a large, heavy hand fell on my shoulder.

"You come with me."

I didn't have to turn around to see who it was. I began walking in the direction the hand pushed. The scumbag with the teeth trailed behind. I noted the big guy said *me* not us. I also noted he hadn't checked for weapons.

Not that it made any difference. If I went in blasting, Nina would be dead. I didn't know where she was or how many guns I'd be up against.

Shark Boy was in the catbird seat and I was the pigeon.

The hand guided me down Jackson and through Ross Alley, a narrow lane housing some rickety Chinese businesses including the Golden Gate Fortune Cookie Factory. As I turned the corner I saw that a third hood had fallen into step behind us.

As we emerged from Ross Alley the hand pushed me towards another alley called Spofford Street. If Ross was colorful, Spofford was grim. Not even the row of skinny plants standing in concrete pots at the edge of the sidewalk, gaunt sentries against car traffic, relieved the sense of isolation.

The alley was quiet except for the atonal Chinese music drifting from the ubiquitous basement social clubs.

The hand pulled me to a firm stop in front of a nondescript brick building. I waited patiently for the customary pat down. Surprisingly it never came. Instead perfect teeth went to his phone. After a brief conversation he said something in Chinese. The third guy nodded and went back in the direction we came.

Perfect teeth went to the door and unlocked it from a ring of keys. The hand pushed me inside. I was looking at a long hall at the end of which was a door facing me and another door to my left. Both had intercoms and cameras. From habit I kept my head down as I was prodded to the door on my left.

So they couldn't identify my corpse.

The door opened onto a well-lit stairway. Having the Sig still in my waistband gave me a false sense of confidence as I descended Perfect Teeth leading the way. So far I had only two to deal with.

Teeth produced his keys when we reached the base of the stairs and unlocked a steel door. I entered a large, damp room illuminated by stark fluorescent light.

Shark Boy occupied a good part of the room. If possible he was bigger than the hood who still had his heavy hand in my shoulder. He sat behind a black desk in an oversized carved wood armchair reminiscent of a throne. The only thing on the desk was a mobile phone. There were three other people behind the desk, two on one side of the throne and one on the other. I recognized the other.

Taylor Kingston's personal assistant Mark. His face sported a large bandage below his blackened right eye, a souvenir of our previous encounter. Now both eyes blazed with a mixture of hatred and triumph.

The other two were born angry. One tall and beefy, looked like a blond Neanderthal with a full beard and ponytail. The other was short and broad with a hawk-like face and a black Van Dyke beard which gave him a Satanic air.

Both wore armless jean jackets to better display their tats. I didn't need to see the colors on their backs to know they were Vandals. Members of the motorcycle gang offering a cash reward for my ass.

The only one in the room who was smiling was Shark Boy.

The smile pissed me off.

"We had a deal," I said.

Shark boy kept smiling. "And I intend to honor it, Max. When you give me your report."

I looked around at our disgruntled audience and when Shark Boy didn't comment I thought what the hell and told him the news.

"The freak who strangled your hookers was Doctor Wayne Sutter. He's dead."

"Did you kill him?"

"No. He was killed by his partner. A woman called Ky Sin."

The fixed smile faded. "His partner you say?"

"Yes, the two of them were in the sex trade. I've got evidence from his phone and computer."

Without warning he slammed his huge fist on the table. The phone jumped and so did half the guys in the room. Anger twisted his expression from benevolent to brutal.

"Son of a fucking bitch! Who the fuck can I trust?"

Nobody answered.

"Where the fuck is Ky Sin now?"

"Dead."

He relaxed a notch.

"You killed her?"

"No. The girl Sutter tried to strangle. She killed Ky Sin while I was fighting her off."

Shark Boy chuckled. "The bitch was good right? Black belt. Worked out. Lucky you didn't get hurt."

"Oh I got hurt alright." I didn't mention I was about to blow her away when Mai Sun intervened.

"How did you find out about her and this psycho?"

"That's what I do." I tilted my head at Mark. "Ask him."

Shark Boy laughed. "You're a real piece of work, Max. But a pain in the ass."

"So we're square?"

He stopped laughing and nodded solemnly. "We're square, Max."

When he reached into his jacket I half expected a gun to come out. Instead it was a thick envelope. He tossed the envelope onto the table. "Thirty thousand, Max. The twenty I owe you plus a ten grand bonus. You did me a favor sniffing out that treacherous bitch. She was using me to protect her, can you believe it?"

"Then maybe you'll return the favor." I stepped forward and took the envelope.

He regarded me through heavy lidded eyes. "If I can I will."

"Let Nina go. You can turn me over to these gorillas and collect the bounty, I won't argue."

"*Argue?*" He grinned and looked around. "You're in no position to argue, Max. I'm afraid I can't grant you that favor. We need her. We need her to convince *you* to give up that video you took."

"In that case…"

I unzipped my jacket, put the envelope away—and pulled the Sig out of my waistband.

"Whoa," someone yelled. The two bikers hit the floor, obviously well-trained. Mark stood frozen, a stricken look on his face. In my peripheral vision Perfect Teeth had backed against the wall. I took a quick glance behind me and saw the big guy stepping away, hands half raised.

Only Shark Boy remained calm.

"Don't be stupid, Max. Anything happens to me and the girl's dead."

"For all I know she's dead already."

"I told you, we need her."

"And I need to be sure she's okay."

Shark Boy picked up his phone. "Put the girl on."

He had it on speaker and I heard her voice. It sounded strained and weary. "Max, is that you?"

"Hang in, baby," was all I could manage through a wave of emotion.

"If I don't call back in ten minutes, snuff her," Shark Boy said. He sat back on his throne.

"Satisfied?"

"Bullshit. Bring her here or I'll smoke you now."

He looked at me hard, trying to determine how far I was willing to go.

The Preacher was ready to kill everyone in the room.

Shark Boy was a good judge of character. He picked up the phone.

"Bring the girl downstairs."

He said something else in Chinese. I don't speak the language but I had a good idea of what he said. By now the bikers had regained their feet and stood watching me, like lions stalking a stray calf.

For that matter so was everybody else in the room.

I waved the gun at the big guy and directed him to stand in my line of sight next to Perfect Teeth.

All nice and tidy until the two goons showed up with Nina.

As I expected both came packing. One UZI, one Glock.

"Max…"

Nina had seen better days. But even with tangled hair, sunken eyes, and rumpled clothes she was still the best looking thing in the room. She didn't say anything but it was all in her face.

The boys with the guns were more professional than my escorts. They swung their guns at me and separated. One nod from Shark Boy and I'd be ground meat.

After a tense moment I slowly put the Sig on the desk.

Shark boy snatched it up immediately and glared at Perfect Teeth. "You didn't frisk him? You stupid piece of shit."

"You said bring him here when he shows up," Teeth said, hugging the wall. "Anyway Bobo brought him in."

"Who was in charge of the crew?"

Perfect teeth hung his head. "Me."

"Come here and take his gun."

Cautiously Perfect Teeth approached the table and reached for the Sig. With snake speed Shark Boy grabbed his wrist and slammed his hand on the desk. An instant later he whacked Perfect Teeth's knuckles with the gun.

"You bring anybody here, you frisk then first. Understand?"

Perfect Teeth was too busy howling to hear.

Shark Boy raised his voice. "You understand, Fredo?"

"Yes, understand," Fredo said, his white teeth set in a grimace.

"You see what I have to deal with?" Shark Boy said.

"You don't know the half of it."

"Educate me."

"The last time I saw your boy Fredo he was working with Victor Kang at the Wu Sing Ki Tong. They kidnapped a little girl." I tilted my head in Mark's direction. "Probably working for this asshole."

To my surprise Shark Boy began to laugh.

"Don't you get it, Max? This is Chinatown—by way of the Hong Kong Triads. We have interests from San Diego to Seattle…including New World Developers. Victor Kang was a fool but he was working for me. I sent Fredo to protect my end but I see now I made a mistake."

He glared at the big guy in the checked shirt who had taken me there. "And you. What kind of security man lets somebody in the door without checking him out for weapons? Tell me, Bobo."

Bobo hung his head. "Very bad."

"Mr. Chan?"

Everyone looked at the man who spoke. The biker with the Van Dyke.

"Yes," Shark Boy snapped.

"Now that everybody's said their piece maybe we can just pay you," Van Dyke lifted a leather briefcase, "and be on our way."

Shark Boy put a thoughtful finger to his lips.

"That might be a problem."

The bikers looked at each other.

"What the fuck does that mean?" Van Dyke said.

"It means the circumstances have changed." He waved a hand at Mark. "This is now an auction."

"Yeah? Well this here's what we agreed on. Four hundred grand for both. Just remember we've had a bounty on this asshole for over three years. Ain't *nobody* changin' that. We got a code, man."

The Neanderthal next to him nodded and crossed his arms.

The two guys with guns were now watching the Vandals as was Fredo who held the Sig loosely in both hands, one of which was badly swollen.

The electricity in the room was creeping to overload.

Nina looked at me and we locked eyes. Something passed between us and she straightened up as if energized.

She got a whiff of The Preacher.

I took a step closer to Fredo.

"We have a code too," Shark Boy said, "it's two thousand years old. It's very simple, Duke. We found this man and this woman. *We*—not you. They are *our* property."

He lifted his hands in a gesture of compromise. "So in all fairness I'm holding an auction and you are free to bid."

"Bullshit."

"You already said that, Duke."

The Neanderthal's neck reddened. Duke tossed the leather bag on the table.

"Four hundred grand for the asshole. You keep the girl."

"Negotiation…good. Very fair offer." Shark Boy lifted his hand. "Mark, do you have a bid?"

With one foot Mark shoved a metallic Haliburton suitcase over to Shark Boy's chair.

"A million dollars cash for both."

I took a step closer to Fredo. One of the gunmen with Nina saw me and jabbed his Uzi in my direction.

I lifted my hands and stepped back.

"Well, gentleman," Shark Boy was saying, "the ball is in your court."

Ostensibly holding my hands up in surrender, my fingers started a spider search for the Cobra taped to my back.

Duke glanced at his friend, then at Shark Boy. "Hey we always done straight business with you people. This ain't right."

"You people," Shark Boy repeated slowly, "that's almost disrespectful."

"You people can have what's left of them when we're done," Mark said. "For free."

Big mistake.

The Neanderthal's neck flushed and he advanced on Mark fists clenched. "And you can shut your punk ass up. This ain't about fuckin' money! I was there when we made this deal."

Nina's guard moved behind him and prodded him with the Uzi.

Big mistake two.

Without bothering to look, the Neanderthal reached back and yanked the Uzi out of the goon's startled hands.

I was already moving towards Fredo, my hand gripping the Cobra.

The other goon with Nina fired his Glock at the Neanderthal.

Big mistake three.

First of all he missed—and hit Mark.

The loud blast ignited frantic movement and panic.

Mark shrieked.

Nina screamed.

In the echoing confusion I whipped the spring-loaded blackjack across Fredo's injured hand. He yowled and dropped the Sig. I hit the floor and scooped it up before anyone noticed—their attention riveted on the biker with the Uzi.

"Everybody cool it!" Shark Boy yelled.

Bobo spotted me and shouted. "Hey he got a gun."

Fortunately he didn't.

I knew the Neanderthal would be looking to shred me with the Uzi the moment he got his bearings. I rolled and lifted the Sig.

"Over there," Duke said, "kill the asshole."

The goon had his Glock on me but I wasn't worried about him.

I worried about the fifty rounds the Uzi could spit out in three seconds. Nothing in my immediate area would survive. Especially me.

So as the Uzi swung my way I fired.

A bullet *cracked* past my ear. I twisted and dropped the goon with the bad aim. The Neanderthal was hit but still on his feet, weaving drunkenly as he brought the Uzi up and around.

The other goon tried to snatch his weapon back.

Another big mistake.

A short burst from the Uzi threw him against the wall like a broken doll.

Enraged, Bobo charged. Still unsteady and chest spitting blood, the Neanderthal fired.

Shark Boy was on his feet before Bobo fell.

In one blurred move he pinned the Uzi to the blond man's side, then slung his other arm around the man's neck.

The Neanderthal was no slouch. Despite his wound he rammed an elbow into Shark Boy's belly.

The jackhammer blow bounced off.

An instant later Shark Boy twisted, hoisting the man off his feet. He dropped down on Shark Boy's waiting hip, snapping his spine.

I heard another sharp crack. Shark Boy wrenched the Neanderthal's neck before tossing him aside.

"FUUUCK!"

I looked back and froze.

Duke had one arm around Nina, using her as a shield. He had picked up the Glock and swept the room with it. Along with Nina he had retrieved his briefcase. When he spotted me he fired.

Nina screamed and struggled, throwing off his aim. Unable to shoot back I stayed on the ground.

Shark Boy was clawing for the Uzi pinned beneath the Neanderthal's lifeless body. At the same time Fredo was creeping behind Duke.

"Now, Fredo!" Shark Boy roared, wrenching the Uzi free.

Duke half turned and put two bullets in Fredo's lungs. As he retreated through the door with Nina, he fired another pair at Shark Boy. At least one shot connected. A bright spot blossomed like a red carnation on his expensive lapel.

Fredo slowly crumpled, leaving a blood trail on the wall. Shark Boy slumped back on his throne, the Uzi on his lap.

By then I was crouched behind the Neanderthal's body. Duke fired in my direction and disappeared.

I got to my feet and ran after him. The moment I peeked out the door, a burst of flying splinters drove me back.

I could hear Duke shouting, "Mayday, mayday!" above me. Probably on his phone. A quick look around the corner drew another eruption of shrapnel.

I was pinned down in a room full of dead bodies and a million dollar suitcase.

Unable to stand helpless any longer, I darted out hoping to get a leg shot but there was nothing on the stairs except gun smoke. The smell of cordite hung heavy in the cramped hallway and my ears were clanging as I rushed up the stairs and out the door oblivious to the risk, thinking I'd have more room to maneuver in the open alley.

I reached the street in time to see Duke hauling Nina into a black van, still using her as a shield. The pavement exploded at my feet and I jumped back inside.

I crouched down and inched around the doorway hoping to blow a tire. At the same time I pulled out my phone and speed-dialed Jimmy.

"Black van coming out of the alley. They've got Nina. Where's the car?"

"Three blocks. Wait I see it!"

I fired at the rear left tire just as the van pulled away hitting nothing but cement. The van paused at the end of the alley, then screeched around the corner.

For a desolate moment alone in the empty alley, Nina gone, I was the last man on Earth.

Then Jimmy shot across the street in pursuit of the van. I called for him to stop but he went out of sight too. By the time I reached the end of the alley he was back, perspiring and breathless just like me.

"I got a partial plate."

"Give me the bike," I said, "where'd you park?"

"Jackson, a few doors from my clinic."

"Call Lowell and give him the plate. Tell him I'm going after them."

"Where do you think they're headed?"He had me. The Vandals were headquartered north near Petaluma but they just as well could be going south.

Or any fucking where.

I had one slim chance.

"Call Lowell," I repeated as I pedaled into the street.

Dodging shoppers, hand trucks, cars, and buses I weaved through Chinatown traffic averting disaster at every turn. When I reached the Mercury I popped the trunk, took out the Stingray, and dumped the bike inside.

Working feverishly I started the engine and jacked the Stingray into the car's computer. My one hope was that Nina's phone was still with her or Duke. What if it was back with the Neanderthal's corpse? I punched in Nina's number and waited a few tortured seconds.

Bingo. I had her on the GPS moving south towards the freeway.

I started a hot chase until traffic and the realization that I didn't have to break any speed laws to track the van slowed me down and gave me a chance to get organized. I phoned Lowell and put him on speaker.

"Where are you?"

"Here in Chinatown. Where are you?"

"Driving south on Sixth heading to 280. I've got them locked on my GPS."

"I'm on my way."

"Jimmy call you with the plates?"

"Sitting next to me."

"Hello, Max."

"You agreed surveillance only remember?"

"All I remember is what you've done for me."

Too late for sermons and truth be told it felt damned good to have back up.

It was difficult to keep The Preacher from stomping on the pedal. No electronic tracker can ease the fear, anger, and raw panic when separated from a loved one in danger. But I wasn't about to engage in a shoot-out on the freeway. I hoped to free Nina first and shoot later.

Every few minutes I would check in with Lowell and Jimmy.

"Don't use your siren," I reminded.

"I'm in my own car. Black Mustang. I have a police radio and if I have to I can put a blue light on top."

"Don't. They'll kill Nina if they feel any heat."

"How do…?"

"Hold on," I said, my attention diverted by the computer screen.

"They're turning off towards Pacifica."

For a mile or so I remained intent on the GPS. The freeway widened at that juncture and I revved it up a bit.

"Are you there?" Lowell said.

"I'm tracking them. They're headed for Route 1."

"We're about five miles behind you."

The freeway narrowed when it merged to 1 and the speed limit did the same. Local cops lie in wait for unsuspecting motorists. I knew it and apparently so did the driver of the van ahead who had slowed.

I watched the van continue past the foam misted surf coves in Pacifica into the wooded slope that preceded Devil's Slide.

Driving towards the sea cliffs brought up memories of the night Jimmy and I disposed of Peter Ng's corpse. Only a few weeks ago but it seemed like a year. A very bad year.

The thought made The Preacher twitchy. I sped up passing through the wooded area and to calm myself a bit I took inventory of my arsenal.

The Sig had seven rounds in the clip and there was another clip in the overhead panel. The Taurus was in the dashboard panel fully loaded. I still had the .38 taped to my back and the throwing knife bandaged to my wounded forearm. There was also the Kevlar vest in the trunk.

The inventory failed to calm me down. In fact it only served to stoke me up. The Preacher was straining at the leash.

"You still there?" Lowell said.

"Locked and loaded."

"Don't start shooting without us."

"With Nina there I won't be shooting at all."

"Any plan?"

"Track them to where they take her. Get her out somehow."

"Somehow…"

"We'll do it, Max," Jimmy said.

I wished I had his optimism.

As I emerged from the woods and started driving over the sharp cliffs high above the wide expanse of hard green water, I tried to spot the van ahead of me. When I did I had to keep from turning on the Green Ghost and cutting them off at the pass.

All I could do was follow the small black vehicle below me.

"I've got eyeballs," I told Lowell.

"We're almost at Devil's Slide. Made up time coming through the woods."

"Mustang is pretty fast," Jimmy said, "Not as fast as yours though."

"He's been telling me about your ride."

"So far these guys have been straight south," I said, to change the subject, "but you know what worries me?"

"What's that?"

"There's an airport up ahead."

This observation was met by silence

"Cross that bridge, Max…" Lowell said finally.

I was on the downhill side, having passed the crest where we flung Peter Ng's body onto the wave-battered rocks below. Once I hit level road going past Moss Beach, the van was out of sight. I kept the speed down mindful of small town cops. This whole stretch was coastal with small weathered houses and the occasional café.

I breathed a bit easier when the van went past the small Half Moon Bay Airport having had visions of ramming their plane before they could lift off.

Cinematic but it wouldn't do Nina much good.

My pulse rate surged when the van made a right turn to Pillar Point.

Set on the other side of the famed Maverick's big wave surf beach, Pillar Point is a natural harbor. The bluffs around it are part of a state park known for its scenic hiking trails.

As I followed I drove past a bar with several motorcycles parked outside. However the van was at the harbor a half mile away.

"You with me?" I said to the speaker.

"We're here."

"Make a right onto Princeton. They're at Pillar Point Harbor."

"Harbor?"

"Go figure. You'll pass a biker's bar called the Silver Dollar. Maybe there's a connection."

"If they're at the harbor there's only one way out."

That's what I was afraid of.

For Nina's sake I wanted to avoid a confrontation if possible. But The Preacher knew better.

It would get bloody.

I drove the Green Ghost past a wooded area and nosed out onto the harbor. There was a parking lot nearby but I could see the van wasn't stopping. It was moving slowly toward the marina crowded with pleasure boats, yachts, and fishing vessels of all sizes.

Following the van on the open pier would alert them. So I decided to infiltrate.

I parked the car, opened the trunk, and took out my trusty bike. I stripped off my jacket and donned my Kevlar vest.

To the casual observer it could have been part of a surfer's wet suit. To complete the illusion I put on the wig with the tousled hair.

I phoned Lowell as I rolled. "I'm tailing them on my bike. Block the pier with your car and wait for my call. And Bob…"

"Yeah I hear you."

"This might be a good time to put that blue light on top of your Mustang."

I put the phone away and pedaled slowly along the pier as the van stopped near the fishing boats docked at the end of the harbor.

Chapter 28

George "Duke" Disgrazio was seething with fury.

"You cost me my best bro," he said to Nina who was huddled in a fetal position on the floor of the van, "and you *are* gonna pay."

"What the fuck happened back there?" the driver said carefully. Duke had a vicious temper.

"Motherfuckers double-crossed us. Bait and switch. Slant bastards treat us like shit after all the business we done with them. You know how Thor is. He got offended and things got out of hand."

Duke shook his head.

"Shit turned into a gun show. Thor got taken down but I smoked the head slant and got out with the bitch and our cash."

"What do we do with her now?"

Duke smiled. "Anything we want. Maybe we'll sell her back to her boyfriend after we're done. You hear me, bitch? Your gonna pull that train."

Under his bravado Duke was feeling the loss of his second in command. As president of the Vandals MC he controlled a criminal network that dealt in drugs, guns, and prostitution. Not returning with LeBlue's head weakened his credibility. His authority was further eroded by losing Thor, his main enforcer.

Duke had been entrusted with his command by the legendary Shane Hazer who was currently running things from their Montreal chapter.

It was Shane who had put out the bounty on LeBlue after the asshole blew up his operation in Petaluma. But the guy was a ghost. No trace of him anywhere. They even had the cops on their payroll check him out, and they came up with nothing. For over three years no sign. Everybody figured he was in the wind.

Until Shark Boy flushed him out.

Smoking that fat Chinese bastard might have been a mistake. Or not.

Either way it would have been war with the Tongs and there was nothing else his crew liked better.

His Vandals controlled the distribution routes and could squeeze their territory down to ten square blocks in Chinatown. Fuck those Hong Kong Dons.

Duke hoped Shane Hazer would approve when he got the news in Montreal.

The driver, whose name was Wallace Fenton AKA 'Guns' (the gang name referring to his melon-sized biceps) was coming down from his daily cocktail of meth, HGH, and Red Bull.

He turned to the man riding shotgun beside him. "Hey, Half Pint, you holdin' some pills? I got me a mean headache."

His companion, who indeed was short, gave Guns a hard stare.

"I told you not to call me that. My name is Pinto, you fucking 'roid runner."

"Chill, dude, no disrespect."

"Then call me Pinto alright? And I ain't got no fuckin' pills."

"Both of you chill. When we get her aboard I'll break out the skag." He leaned closer to Nina who lay beside his motorcycle. "And baby here gets the first shot. So she'll be nice and quiet."

"Where we goin' this time?" Guns asked.

"El Salvador."

"That's a long fuckin' trip, man."

"You got somewhere else to go?"

Duke's tone warned Guns to can his complaints. Duke was known to have damaged guys for less.

Duke had decided to multitask. The fishing trawler would take them down to El Salvador where the weapons stored in the hold would be exchanged for heroin and prostitutes, both imported from China. The girls were all under sixteen. During the five day round trip Duke intended to train his new mama. By the time they returned she would be addicted and submissive. And he would dangle her as bait for this asshole LeBlue.

He did have balls walking right in there with a Sig Nine in his pants, Duke brooded. The same gun that smoked Thor. He was going to make the bitch pay extra for that. The asshole too.

"Take your time drivin' up to the boat," Duke said, "don't attract attention. We're just making a normal run. We wrap the bitch up and take her up the gangway like a sack of flour."

"You takin' your bike too?"

"This bike goes where I go."

Pinto nodded solemnly. "Word."

Duke's bike was basically a Dark Custom forty-eight Harley with a Screaming Eagle twin Cam 110. But there was nothing basic about it. He had tricked it out with extended handlebars that made it seem like a chopper but was actually one of the most powerful racers on the street. The engine had been supercharged and the Hollywood high bars could be hinged down low so Duke could lie across his bike and air the beast out.

A mechanic by trade Pinto was impressed by the bike's performance.

"Where do you want me to stop?" Guns said, anxious for his heroin. He had a headache and his stomach was sour. Too much Red Bull.

"Stop at the gangway. Like we're making a delivery."

Guns parked then went around back to roll Duke's bike off the van and onto the gangway of a large fishing vessel. The girl was on the floor but the doors concealed her.

As soon as Guns reached the deck he was met by two Vietnamese crewmen who took the bike. Guns followed to make sure it was secure. All he needed was for one of these gooks to fuck up Duke's ride.

When he returned to the gangway he scanned the pier. Except for some people at the brewery across the harbor and a local on a bicycle it was quiet. He went back to the van for the girl.

"Bike good?" was the first thing Duke said.

"Yeah." He gestured at the girl balled up on the floor. "Let's wrap her up."

"There's a guy out there," Pinto said, "on a bicycle."

"I know," Guns said impatiently, "so fuckin' what?"

"We're comin' from a fuckin' war zone with a hot body that's what," Pinto said. "Murder, assault, kidnapping…we're looking at life in Pelican Bay."

"Yeah right," Gun's snorted, "and this guy followed us from 'Cisco on his fuckin' *bicycle?*"

"I'm just sayin' we gotta be careful," Pinto said, walking it back. He had just done a deuce in Quentin and had no eyes to go back inside.

"Pinto's right," Duke said. "You two take the girl to my cabin. I'll stay with the van and make sure. I'll follow in a few minutes. Don't unwrap the bitch till I get there."

He reached under the dashboard and removed a Mossberg shotgun with both barrel and stock sawed off. It was his favorite weapon. The three notches on the wood grip represented his progress. Plenty of room for more.

Duke sat behind the wheel with the shotgun on his lap while Guns and Pinto rolled a tarp over the girl. Then Guns hefted the tarp onto his shoulder and walked onto the gangplank with Pinto trailing behind.

As they boarded the ship with their human cargo, Duke watched the man on the bicycle roll past and continue to the end of the pier.

***

Nina couldn't breathe.

They had rolled her in a foul-smelling tarp and it was suffocating her. Seeing Max had given her hope but it had faded fast. For all she knew Max had been shot. And it was her headstrong stupidity that caused all this. Max had warned her more than once that he was playing with dangerous people but she never thought the Vandals were involved. She knew about the bounty on Max but…

Someone picked her up and started moving. She was suddenly nauseous and had to fight to keep it down lest she choke to death on her own vomit. Teeth clamped shut she struggled to breathe through her nose.

Nina felt light-headed and wondered if she was dying. She felt herself swinging back and forth. Her brain seemed to be melting inside the hot airless tarp. It was squeezing her like a python. She was spinning, drowning...

And then it was light. Nina took a gasping breath. Air. She blinked. Looked up.

Duke and his muscular sidekick were looking down at her.

"Oh yeah. We're gonna' have us a good time with you, babe." He turned his head. "Pinto—You want a piece of this?"

"Later," Pinto called. "After I check out what's happening on deck."

Nina carefully reached for the switchblade in her waistband at the small of her back. ---The metal weight in her palm was reassuring although she knew it was like fighting them off with a toothpick. But with luck she might get one of these animals before she was overcome.

Duke leered at her. He looked truly demonic with his sharp beard and cruel smirk. But it was his eyes that were truly frightening. Hard and pitiless, black suns in a dark sky.

"Hot in here ain't it? Why don't we just take this blouse of yours off…?"

As he reached down Nina snapped the blade free and lunged wildly, choking with fear.

Duke jumped back and looked at the blood oozing from the back of his hand. He grinned.

What do you know, Guns, bitch here has a concealed weapon. That carries a heavy sentence, don't it?"

He came closer, eyes bright, focused on the switchblade.

Nina moved back brandishing the knife. She tried to get to her feet but Duke lashed out with his foot and kicked the blade aside. A moment later a hot flash of pain shattered her skull. Stunned, she fell back.

"Let's see what else our bitch is hidin'," Duke said, roughly unzipping her jeans and putting his hand on her crotch.

"And what the fuck is this?"

Nina's heart stopped when he found the phone she had hidden. It was her last fragile link to hope.

"Gonna have to search her real fuckin' close to make sure there ain't nothin' else. Get them designer jeans off, bitch."

The biker with the bulging biceps laughed. "Make her dance naked for us, Duke."

"She'll do anything we want, won't you, babe? Now get them jeans off before I slap you into next week and Guns here'll take 'em off for you."

Belly churning with nausea, Nina started to comply.

Chapter 29

"Come out to the coast. We'll get together,
have a few laughs…"
— Bruce Willis, *Die Hard*

Pillar Point Harbor was a postcard of the California dream. Blue sky, green sea, majestic cliffs, rows of sail boats and yachts, surfers catching their last waves, and in the distance a red hang glider hovering over the restless Pacific.

The sun was setting, wrapping the landscape with a mantle of gold light as I pedaled closer to the van. The Sig was jammed in my waistband and the Taurus tucked into the small of my back. The knife taped to my forearm was visible but most surfers carried knives. Okay, not throwing knives, but I was reasonably sure I could get next to the van without attracting undue attention.

However as I rolled slowly past the van it was clear a lone cyclist on the empty pier was the center of attention. I could feel the stares and pumped faster to the end of the dock. Then I slowly got off the bike, sat down with one leg dangling over the water, and lit a cigarette.

Over my shoulder I saw a bodybuilder type with bulging arms haul a rolled carpet or tarp onto the boat.

Nina.

It was all I could do to keep The Preacher in check. My limbs were literally trembling. I willed myself to stay put and finish the damned cigarette.

If anything the nicotine jacked me up but at that point a shot of morphine would have done the same thing. Uncut adrenaline shot through my veins, and as soon as the bodybuilder and Duke boarded the boat The Preacher took charge.

I jumped on my bike and started pedaling madly like a sprint-er in the Tour de France. Leaning into the turn around the van, I coasted right up the gangway, tires bumping on the planks.

The moment I hit the deck I dismounted. I drew the Sig just as a short, broad-shouldered biker came through the doorway.

Without hesitation he charged.

Without hesitation I shot him twice.

He kept charging all the way to the deck, then lay there unmoving. A heavy stillness fell over the boat and I knew the shots had been heard and registered.

One thing about a big boat, there are lots of places to hide. At least two bikers were somewhere inside with Nina but I had no idea how many others could be aboard.

I stepped in the door the short guy had exited and ran into an Asian crewman. His eyes widened when he saw the still-smoking Sig and he threw his hands high.

I grabbed his shirt with one hand and slammed him against the wall.

"Where's the girl?"

He shook his head vigorously, averting my eyes as if he didn't understand.

I slammed him again, much harder, and shoved the Sig into his neck.

"Where's the girl?"

Something in The Preacher's eyes convinced him.

"There…" He pointed frantically to a stairway leading to the upper deck.

I spun him around and shoved him to the stairs.

"Show me."

Very reluctantly he began climbing the stairs, taking them one at a time, fearful of what was coming.

The second tier was deserted. It consisted of a long narrow hall with three rooms on each side. Probably the cabin deck for officers and select passengers like the Vandals.

I put a finger to my lips and gestured with the Sig.

The crewman took a tentative step and pointed to the middle door on the left. Uncertain of what to do with him I made him lie down on the floor. I momentarily took my eyes off the door—and that's all it took.

As I turned, a massive body collided with my spine. When I hit the floor the Sig popped out of my hand.

***

Like an NFL quarterback's protective vest, my Kevlar muffled the impact. But it woke up all the injuries I'd accumulated over the past month. Stunned I realized a crushing weight threatened to crack what was left of my ribcage.

The bodybuilder was sitting on top of me, his oversized arms doing pushups on my chest.

"I got him," he yelled over his shoulder.

"Any more?"

"Not yet."

"Find Pinto."

"Okay."

Again—that's all it took. An extra two seconds looking away. Enough time to tear the knife from my forearm bandage and jam it into his throat.

When I pulled it free, blood gushed out like red oil.

He let out a gurgling roar, grabbed at his neck with one hand—and lifted the other to smash my face. I twisted and punched his exposed torso with the knife once, twice…then the blood-slicked blade slipped from my grasp.

I waited for his huge fist to fracture my skull but both his hands were trying to cap the glistening red gusher spurting from the gash in his throat. I pushed and he toppled over… still gurgling.

The Sig was a few feet away.

I started crawling over to retrieve it when the middle door burst open and a thunder blast boomed through the narrow passage splashing me with hot stinging rain.

The door stayed half open with only the nasty muzzle of a fuming shotgun visible. I yanked the Taurus from my waistband and pulled the trigger.

It was the first shot I'd taken with my new weapon and I was impressed. The .45 slug ripped a hole in the metal door and the shotgun muzzle retreated out of sight.

Keeping my eye on the door I scrambled across the floor and grabbed the Sig. As my finger curled around the trigger another blast tore a trench in the section of the floor I had just occupied.

I fired back blindly with the Sig. The 9mm's penetrated the metal door but I wasn't sure they went through.

My answer came when Duke came howling out the door hopping on his one good leg, the sawed off shotgun cradled in his arms. He fired as he retreated but his off balance shot slashed the wall. When I lifted my head he was skipping awkwardly down the hall.

Wary of the shotgun, I came up into a combat crouch and fired after him as he turned a corner. I started to follow but as I passed the open door I glimpsed a body on the floor.

Nina.

I leaped inside ready to kill anyone in sight but the cabin was empty.

"Nina, it's me. Are you okay?"

Her head was down, eyes closed. Her jeans were at her ankles and her shirt was open.

"Max...?"

"It's me, I'm here, are you hurt?"

She lifted her head, eyes fluttering. "Max, you're here...?" Then her eyes opened wide and she shrank back "...*Oh my God!*"

"Baby, it's me, it's okay."

She extended a tentative hand to my face. "You're covered in blood...and your hair..."

I was still wearing my surfer dude wig. I tore it off and tossed it aside.

"Better…?"

She nodded uncertainly.

"Can you walk? We've got to get out now."

She pulled up her jeans and I carefully lifted her to her feet. But as I stepped out the door I heard a loud shot and a metal fist smacked me in the chest.

I fell back inside the cabin.

"Get down," I yelled.

I had managed to hold on to the Sig but the .45 fell from my blood-oiled hand. I couldn't seem to hold on to both weapons at once.

"Max, you've been shot."

I looked down at the bullet imbedded in my Kevlar vest.

"I'm cool. Stay back."

The bullet may not have hit flesh but the wallop bruised every bone and tendon in my damaged rib cage. With agonizing effort I crawled into position and poked my head around the door.

Three Asian crewmen were advancing reluctantly down the hall, including the bastard I'd turned loose. Had I listened to The Preacher he'd be safely dead.

The lead man was armed with what looked like a Glock 9. It was trailing smoke. The others held revolvers at their sides.

My first shot hit the shooter's thigh, my second his sternum. He was a corpse before he dropped. The remaining pair took stock of the two bloody bodies in the hall and ran for the stairs.

"Let's go," I said, pushing myself up and into the hall. I felt a flash of pain as I bent to retrieve my Taurus. Moving in a quick crablike shuffle I guided Nina to the stairs. Before going out on deck I checked both ways.

All clear.

It was dusk and I could see Lowell's blue police light glowing at the end of the pier. My head on a swivel, I had Nina lead the way down the gangway while I protected the rear.

Nina had reached the pier when I heard a thundering howl above me. Instinctively I lunged off the gangway and pushed

Nina to the ground. At the same time a lightning blast of searing heat slashed my arm.

Like a jet fighter with a shotgun in its nose, Duke's motorcycle zoomed high overhead. It seemed to hover in mid-air before it made a skidding landing six feet away.

I rolled under the van pulling Nina with me.

"Max…you're bleeding."

I glanced down and saw a red sleeve of blood where shotgun pellets had raked my arm. Afraid he'd try again I raised the Sig and fired.

But my angle was off and Duke wasn't looking at us anyway. His focus was on the rotating blue light on top of Lowell's Mustang. He had paused to adjust his bars and was now lying flat on his motorcycle, the hand grips low like the controls on an airplane. I heard the unmistakable *rack* of a shotgun reload and squeezed off two rounds.

The shots were lost in the thundering squeal of charging machinery and scorched rubber as Duke's motorcycle rocketed straight for Lowell who was standing beside the Mustang. Lowell ducked behind the front fender his weapon raised but Duke fired both barrels into the hood and the Mustang erupted into a volcano of orange flame and dirty black smoke.

Duke's bike swerved and disappeared in the boiling cloud. Then I saw Jimmy pulling Lowell's limp body away from the fiery Mustang.

The sight enraged The Preacher beyond control.

I crawled from beneath the van and opened the door. The keys were still in the ignition. I helped Nina to her feet and climbed behind the wheel.

"Get in!"

Nina said something as she got inside but I didn't hear. I started the motor and pulled away. When I passed the still-burning Mustang I stopped.

"Is he okay?" I yelled to Jimmy who was kneeling over Lowell's body.

"Don't know! What happened?"

Without answering I stamped on the gas and drove to where I had left my own car.

"Max, where are you going? You can't…"

With some difficulty I climbed down from the van and settled into the embrace of my Mercury. I opened the window.

Nina stared in disbelief, confusion and massive indignation.

"Stay here. Call 911," I said.

"I can't…"

But I was pulling away. People were running towards the flames. I nearly hit a few on my way out to Route 1.

When I reached the highway I stopped, turned off the engine, and listened for sound of the motorcycle. He was too far ahead. He might be heading north to Petaluma or south to LA for all I knew. Then I realized what Nina had been trying to say. They took her phone. Praying it was in Duke's pocket and not back on the boat, I started the engine and opened my computer.

It was still jacked to the Stingray and there, clear as Sunday morning, was Duke moving south. Very fast.

I knew it wasn't necessary to pursue him but The Preacher knew better. Back there with Shark Boy Duke had acted as spokesman for the Vandals. Probably their leader.

He was the bastard who was dangling a price on my head. The only Vandal alive who knew my name or had seen my face. With him on the loose Nina would always be in danger. And I'd be a walking retirement fund for some ambitious bounty hunter.

No. I had to put Duke down.

First I had to catch up to him.

Route 1 south shrinks from four to two lanes with many scenic curves, perfect for a speeding bike but challenging for a car. Even one like the Green Ghost.

Fortunately my man Len had reworked the suspension so it held the road at high speeds. But the best of race cars will fishtail at tight curves. And these curves were tight. More than once I was on the cusp, one hand too slick with blood to hold the wheel.

As I drove I made a mental inventory of my arsenal. There were three bullets left in the Taurus, maybe six in the Sig. No matter, I had another clip for the 9mm along with extra .45 rounds for Mr. T. The knife was gone but I still had the .38 taped to my back. However my ability to reach for it was severely compromised.

Hard to wipe your hands on leather seats, but overhead, the Mercury was upholstered with gray fabric which I used to smear the blood from my palm. Problem was I was still bleeding. That was the least of my problems. It was painful to take deep breaths, my spine was out of whack, and I was trembling with anger and shock.

With all this assessing, one might assume I was conscious. But my awareness had been reduced to the road ahead and the tiny red dot on my computer screen.

In the darkness I caught glimpses of the moon reflecting on the sea below. The road was deserted and I nudged the speedometer past eighty-five. Duke was still a few miles away but I was slowly reducing the distance between him and The Preacher.

Below Half Moon Bay Route I has long stretches of wilderness and cliffs. As time wore on, my adrenalin was draining and my arm oozing more blood. I half considered blasting music to keep me pumped, then forgot about it. The raging silence wrapped me like a blanket.

I perked up when I saw Duke was turning off in Pescadero. I knew the place from previous visits. It's an idyllic little farm and ranch community. The population is less than a thousand and it has a beautiful state beach and lighthouse. I would go there to unwind when things got too tense.

At the moment my nerves were sizzling way past tense.

I drove through Stage Road in the moonlight. Most of the buildings date back to the nineteenth century giving it the rickety feel of a frontier town.

Two blocks later I was in the country with occasional farmhouses on either side. Duke turned onto Creek Road. The terrain became even more rural and in a few minutes the red dot on my screen stopped. I switched off my lights and rolled slowly to my destination.

The GPS led me to a small driveway marked by a letter box. A few hundred feet up the driveway was a house. I could see its lights through the trees around the property.

Before I left the car I reloaded both of my weapons. I left the keys in the ignition anticipating a hasty departure. Then I opened the trunk, found a towel, and wrapped my arm. One hand was still a bit swollen but serviceable.

I gave the Sig to that hand and gripped the Taurus with the other. The Sig was an automatic which required minimal trigger pulls. The Preacher had thought of everything.

Except what to do when I got there.

Relying on my old combat training, I crept onto the property along the tree line. Perhaps crept is a generous term for the way I was moving. It hurt to breathe, my spine was locked, and my arm was throbbing like a martial drum.

I managed a sideways crab crawl towards the light actually having to stop twice to stretch a stiff knee.

As I neared I realized the light wasn't coming from the house but the garage. It was about a hundred feet from the house and had two small windows on the side. The door was partially open, illuminating the three motorcycles a short distance from the garage.

Leaving the protection of the trees I scuttled to the windows like an oversized lizard, pausing every few feet to sniff the air. Far from farm fresh, it smelled vaguely sulfurous. It was very dark and very quiet and I could hear voices inside.

When I peered through the window I saw Duke sitting on a table while a burly red-haired man examined his wounded leg. His shotgun was on the table beside him. His hair was in disarray and features contorted either in anger or pain. Probably both.

All around them were tables laden with heat-resistant flasks, large glass coffee pots with filters, a large gas oven, two industrial sinks, and a pair of large metal tanks in the rear. There were also banded stacks of glassine bags, gas masks, rubber aprons, and rubber gloves on the wall shelves.

Perfect. You find a quaint old farm in a small friendly community by the sea and install a fucking meth lab.

The new American business model.

The burly man started to cut Duke's jeans away from his wound but the Vandal leader lifted his arm and said something I couldn't quite hear. The third man who was tall and lanky had a gun holster around his hips which held a Smith and Wesson 9mm revolver. I knew because I carried one for six months while undercover for the DEA. Very dependable. I wondered how good he was.

I was about to find out.

The lanky man went to a cabinet and came back with a vial of powder which he gave to Duke. Using the tip of a knife Duke scoped out a tiny mound of powder and snorted it. He handed the vial back and a few seconds later the knife fell from his hand. He slumped to one side and beckoned to the burly man who resumed cutting around his wound. Apparently Duke had inhaled a bit of heroin for his medical procedure.

The Preacher had seen enough.

I moved back to the front and slipped inside the half open door, both weapons extended and yelling.

"Freeze Dammit!"

Nobody froze.

Duke grabbed the shotgun and rolled off the table, the red-haired man dove to the floor, while the lanky dude drew his Smith and Wesson.

He was slow. I hit him with two quick shots and he collapsed.

I looked to see what happened to the redhead and the door beside me blew off its hinges and knocked me to the floor.

I hadn't been hit but I was on exposed ground. I crawled awkwardly to a nearby lab table and crouched behind it. Across the floor and through a frame made by table legs, redhead was on his belly, holding an AK47 the way they teach you in the military.

He was looking in the wrong direction so I eased myself back further and found cover behind an industrial barrel. I fired twice at the framed figure and ducked back.

"Shit!"

His yowl told me something made contact but when I took a peek, my protective barrel shattered into a green cloud of chemical powder and cardboard shreds. I scrambled for sturdier cover, firing behind me as I went.

I bumped into a steel sink and made it my home.

Redhead sprayed the barrels where I'd been, sending up even more noxious powder and a rain of burning paper shreds. Huddled behind the sink, I was more worried about the bullets ricocheting off the concrete walls. Apparently so was Duke.

"Cole—hold your fire damnit! You'll blow the place."

Then he added, "Asshole can't get out anyway."

I heard that.

I also heard the double *rack* as he reloaded.

I tried to remember what I'd seen through the window. Three rows of lab tables on either side, a large oven, propane tanks. I stopped there.

Cooking meth is a volatile endeavor. One mistake and the kitchen explodes in your face.

At the moment I was cornered by two wounded but mobile killers with serious weapons. And The Preacher was certifiably insane.

If I took myself out with them at least I'd know Nina would be safe.

But Preacher aside, I didn't want to take myself out just yet.

I looked around for other options, or should I say distractions. Either way I would have to blast my way out. I saw an empty beer bottle against the wall and reached back to take it. It reminded me that my entire body was bone dry, a walking Death Valley.

I tried to make a mental evaluation of who was where. I was pretty sure Duke was close to where he had landed but Cole could be anywhere. My guess? He was crawling through the chemical fog like the trained combatant he was. Once he rounded the corner my steel sink sanctuary would be imbedded in my flesh.

I tossed the beer bottle into the mist and half stood.

Wrong on both counts. The two men had switched places.

Cole stood up and began cutting holes in the fog with his AK47. Braving the bouncing bullets I fired three rounds.

Twin jets of blood spurted from his chest. He fell face down, the weapon clattering on the concrete floor.

Which left me and Duke.

I heard a shuffle and peered through the mist. I expected he was covering the exit.

Actually, was making an exit, hauling his crippled ass out the ravaged door. I went after him disregarding the possibility that he could turn and burn me with the shotgun.

Unfortunately he did just that.

Duke twisted and fired wildly driving me to the floor. I popped up ready to shoot but he was limping into the night. I got up and half ran after him, my lungs screaming in agony.

I heard a grunt behind me and saw Cole had found the AK47 and was making an effort to cut me in half. Maddened with pain and primal fury I emptied my clip into the propane tanks next to the ovens.

A massive *whump* shook the earth throwing me to the floor. Suddenly everything erupted in flames. I got up and staggered outside. Duke was struggling to get to his feet. He saw me and lifted his shotgun.

Realizing I was a perfect target silhouetted against the blaze I dove for the shadows. His shot went high and when I lifted my head he was scuttling for his bike. I raised my Sig and pulled the trigger.

Nothing. The clip was empty.

As Duke neared his motorcycle I took a shot with the Taurus. The bullet plowed up a geyser of dirt in front of him and he veered a few steps before he stopped, teetered on his good leg, and fired point blank.

My tongue tasted dirt. I rolled and fired back as he tried again to reach his bike. Another near miss convinced him to take cover and he ducked into the tree line, out of sight.

Aware I was outlined against the bright orange flames behind me, I cautiously went in after him. I paused behind a tree and listened for, but didn't hear, that unmistakable sound of a shotgun reload.

So I moved a bit faster. Although Duke knew the area a lot better than I did, the burning garage afforded me enough light to avoid falling over tree roots and see a few yards ahead.

I heard rustling in the distance and realized Duke had built a considerable lead.

Then I heard a car door open and began to trot. The growl of an engine starting brought me up short.

I glimpsed red tail lights moving away.

There was only one car out there.

Mine.

Chapter 30

"If you're batting a thousand you're playing in the Little League."
— Warren Buffet

Fuck me.
For a petrified moment the massive import hung in my brain. Then it all came hurtling down and crashed in the pit of my belly.

Duke had taken my car.

Which left me alone with two dead bodies and a blazing meth lab.

Worse, he had the computers built into the Green Ghost. I—and everyone I knew—would be totally exposed. I felt impotent with loss, my lungs heaving air and knees wobbly.

Until The Preacher straightened me.

Raw fury fused my spine like a hot blue welder's flame and I trotted back to the burning garage. There were three motorcycles standing there. I had to get one of them to start.

Two were Harley choppers. I tried them both without success. I even considered braving the fire to frisk the bodies. Then I saw the key in Duke's bike and mounted.

At first it was difficult for me to lie across the tank and steer with the low-hinged handlebars. Especially with the Taurus in my hand. The bike started up like a reluctant horse and threatened to throw me until I got the feel of the reins.

It was a powerful mother.

The roads were empty and I let the steed loose. In a few minutes I spotted the red tail lights. He was headed for Route 1. I had the speedometer up to ninety roaring down Stage Road, hoping no cops were around.

I rode without lights so Duke wouldn't see me until I was within shooting range but as we neared Route 1 it was no longer an option. The moment I switched on the headlight the red tail lights surged faster.

No matter. Route 1 goes either north or south.

Duke went south. Very few exits.

It was time.

The road south is the scenic route you see in the pamphlets. Magnificent cliffs rising over the Pacific, secluded cove beaches, long wooded stretches without rest stops.

All I saw was the white line and the red lights ahead. Occasionally I'd glimpse the moon-flecked water far below. The road was separated from the steep drop by nothing but a low white rail.

The Preacher didn't care.

Nothing else existed but those red lights. Not the pain racking every part of my body, not any law, and not the possibility that I might go over the high side any second. Mad rage and fresh adrenaline rushed through my veins like a flash flood.

When the road straightened I pushed the speedometer past 100. The red lights grew larger. I visualized pulling alongside and blowing his brains out. A tight curve brought me out of my reverie. I pulled the beast back to eighty and watched the red lights recede.

But now my focus was on keeping the monster bike upright. The motorcycle was heavy in the center with a supercharged engine and big tires, not ideally suited to leaning into curves. Especially with a .45 in one hand and the other semi-functional.

The Green Ghost on the other hand was built to take tight curves at speed.

Which meant the next straight stretch was my best shot.

Literally.

Silently I thanked whoever invested the Taurus with a rubber grip. Through it all the.45 clung firmly to my busy hand.

I hugged the bike, trying to get the feel of the curves but the red lights remained out of range. Coming out of a series of S curves I saw it as my chance.

Outlined in the moonlight the white line dividing the highway went directly uphill for at least three hundred yards.

My eagerness nearly killed me. I tried to accelerate too soon and the bike began to drift toward the low white fence that separated me from the rocks far below. Like wrestling a steer I held the handles as steady as possible, slowed down until the tires grabbed, then twisted the throttle.

The bike leaped forward, accelerating rapidly up the steep incline.

For all its virtues the Mercury was heavy, which gave my lighter machine a distinct advantage. Halfway up the hill I found myself only fifty feet from the red tail lights.

The lights started edging away. Dumping the idea of coming alongside, I extended the Taurus and fired.

The high-velocity .45 slug must have punched through the trunk to the gas tank because smoky yellow flames jetted from beneath the car. Duke accelerated but I was locked in by then. The right rear tire was illuminated by the fire giving me a clear target.

My shot blasted rubber just as the blazing Mercury neared a curve at the top of the incline. The burning car went a slow skid. Suddenly the red tail lights went bright, like frightened eyes.

Not wise, Duke.

Braking hard while rounding a curve on three wheels sent the fiery car fishtailing dangerously near the edge. He gunned it but the Mercury kept skidding…then sliding…until it smashed through the guard rail and tumbled down the cliff like a sparkling pinwheel before it crashed below and expanded into a giant orange balloon of dirty flame.

I slowly got off the bike and limped to the gap in the twisted guard rail.

The car was impaled on the sharp rocks jutting from the dark, restless water. It was still burning, its fiery light skipping over the white foam.

For a long time I stood there watching my beloved Green Ghost—and the ashes of my life—disintegrate and wash away on the tide.

Chapter 31

"Yesterday doesn't exist and tomorrow
belongs to somebody else." — FL

Numbly I got back on that fucking trick bike and head-ed for the nearest shelter which happened to be Santa Cruz.

A beach town trending upscale it was still a haven for surfers, bikers, artists, and eccentrics. At one time the Santa Cruz Mountains boasted the largest population of witches in America. Not surprising when the town motto is *'Keep Santa Cruz Weird'*.

So I was confident when I pulled into a funky motel situated between a surf shop and a liquor store that the night man wouldn't freak when a bloody, wild-eyed maniac limped into the lobby.

To lessen the bad impression I took off my Kevlar vest. As I went to stuff it in the bike's saddle bag I noticed a familiar brown leather case inside and took it with me.

Looks better if you have luggage.

I had shoved Shark Boy's fee in my jeans and miraculously the envelope was still there. Rather than flash my cash I re-moved five Franklins before I went inside.

The night clerk was actually reading a book. He took one look and put the book aside.

"Are you okay?' he said, brow furrowed.

A big step up from the American battle cry, may I help you. He was somewhere between twenty-five and thirty, tall, with narrow features, short red hair.

"Ugly accident," I said, "had to lay down my bike." My voice coming through low and raspy, "I'd like a room please."

"Are you sure you don't want to go to the ER?"

"Nothing's broken but I can use a hot shower." As I spoke I lay three hundred dollar bills on the counter. "And some extra towels."

He regarded the money with a studious expression, picked up the bills and replaced them with a form. "Just fill this out please. I'll send someone with the towels."

As soon as I entered my room I drank six glasses of water. Then I called Nina.

"Max, you bastard! I'm worried crazy. Where are you?"

"I'm fine, baby, how are you?"

Her tone softened. "Sorry, Max. Do you need help?"

"I'll be okay tomorrow."

"Oh no you don't. Fuck tomorrow. Where the hell are you?"

"The New Moon Motel in Santa Cruz but…"

"No buts—we're coming to get you."

"Who's we?"

"I'm with Jimmy at his mansion." She paused. "Bob's in the hospital in Half Moon Bay."

My momentary elation evaporated. "How bad?"

"A piece of metal speared his leg when his car blew up. His doctors say he should recover. Now give me the address there."

I barely hung up when there was a knock at the door. Reflexively I reached for the Taurus. My fingers not far from the .45, I opened the door.

Standing there was a slender man with long blonde hair, a Zapata moustache, plaid shorts, and a T-shirt that read 'Life is a Beach'. He was holding a stack of towels.

He didn't seem surprised by my appearance. "Need anything else?"

"Possible to get a bottle of ninety proof bourbon and some aspirin?"

"Anything's possible, is that all?"

I caught his drift. "What's available?"

"Weed, Ex," he nodded at the bloody towel wrapped around my arm, "you might want some downs."

"No thanks I get down on life."

I handed him two hundred. "Is this enough for the booze and a couple of joints?"

He took the money and smiled. "Back in fifteen minutes. Take care of that arm."

It took me all that time to get my shoes off. My ribs were cramped with pain and the rest of my body was either bruised or swollen.

The Preacher was long gone, stiffing me with the tab.

The clerk returned with a large paper bag which he set down on the night table with some ceremony. He extracted a bottle of Jim Beam, a baggie with four fat Js, a book of matches, a bottle of aspirin, and a bottle of peroxide.

"Let me know if you need anything else. My name's Ray as in Sun Ray."

A stiff bourbon and a J later, I rallied enough energy to take off my clothes. Except for my shirt. The pain meter in my arm was moving towards excruciating. I knew it would take two hours for Nina and Jimmy to drive so I started for the bathroom.

Then I saw the leather bag.

I sat on the bed and opened it. It was packed with cash. The Vandal's four hundred thousand dollar bounty on me and Nina.

Large sums of money will make you paranoid. I took the bag with me into the bathroom while I attempted to shower.

It didn't work out very well.

First of all the towel bandage was stuck to my arm. It hurt like hell to remove and when I did my arm started bleeding again.

Examining the wound I saw the shotgun pellets had dug a trench in my forearm and part of my bicep. I would need to see a doctor right away or lose it.

I wasn't able to really stand in the shower and ended up crouching under the water. After a while my stiff, wrenched muscles began to loosen enabling me to get up and clean my ravaged arm.

Every drop of water was agony. Finally I drenched a towel in peroxide, took a deep breath, and dropped it on the wound.

Despite my gritted teeth I let out a loud yowl. The peroxide was a temporary measure. There was dirt and who knows what on a wound that had been exposed for hours.

I sat on the bed, took three aspirin, poured a large bourbon, and knocked it back.

The next thing I knew people were knocking on the door.

***

Nina and Jimmy took me back to San Francisco.

Jimmy called his colleague Doctor Henry Ku to sew up my wounds at the Pacific Heights house. He explained I had been shot helping rescue his daughter from Shark Boy.

Doctor Ku bought the story and neglected to report the gun wound. I was able to rest and recover for four days until Jimmy's friend came back from his vacation to claim his mansion.

After which, at Nina's insistence, I moved in with her and she nursed me 24/7 until I was semi healthy.

***

I left an anonymous tip with Detective Albert Lee concerning the dead bodies in Mai Sun's flat. I made sure he understood Dr. Wayne Sutter's DNA would connect his to the strangled escorts. He kept me on the phone for a while digging for more details. I gave him what I could secure in the knowledge that when he traced the call he'd find it came from Honolulu.

Whatever misgivings he may have had about me were brushed aside by the benefits of my info. He was credited with tracking down the man the media dubbed 'The Chinatown

Strangler'. However the matter of Dr. Sutter's business relationship with Ky Sin got somehow lost in the translation.

The day after Jimmy and Nina brought me back from Santa Cruz, I visited Bob Lowell in the hospital. He seemed glad to see me despite my being responsible for losing his car and nearly his leg.

"Max, you look terrible."

This from a guy with one heavily bandaged leg in traction and tubes flowing from his arm.

I grinned. "You look great yourself, how do you feel?"

He grinned back. "Ready to get out of here."

"How bad is it?"

Ever the embodiment of a shy cowboy Lowell turned away in embarrassment.

"The pier was blocked. When the bastard came at me I jumped behind the Mustang. Suddenly my car just exploded and a piece of the hood caught my leg. For that they're awarding me a goddamn citation for breaking up an international smuggling operation. Everything from guns, to drugs, to girls."

He shook his head. "I really didn't do anything. I didn't even fire a round. All I did was follow you and block the pier."

It hurt to not laugh.

"How many times have you gotten shit for doing the right thing?"

He looked at me and chuckled. "Plenty."

"And let's not forget, you didn't just follow me. You risked your life and your job. The whole thing could have blown up in your face and it did. You lost your Mustang and took a hard hit for the team. I for one am grateful and forever in your debt. Thanks."

"That's citation enough for me, Max."

We gripped hands, a bond forged in two battles.

"Anytime," I said, wincing a bit at what I was about to say. "You know the FBI will be talking to you very soon."

"Ah yes. They've already contacted me. In fact they're the boys awarding me this citation."

"You might leave me out of the report."

He lowered his voice. "Max, I understand, you're undercover. But how do I explain the dead bodies aboard that boat? They told me four."

I had to count. "Three. But I have a plausible cover story."

Lowell nodded, square-jawed and solemn. "Let's hear it."

"One of the dead Vandals is a bodybuilder type with big biceps. His gang name is 'Guns'. Let's say Guns was your informant out of Petaluma. You went to Half Moon Bay on his word. He was supposed to bring you evidence so you could call in the Coast Guard. You heard gunshots and blocked the pier. Things went wrong. Guns killed the guy on deck and an armed crewman then must have been assassinated by Duke."

He thought it over. "Keep going."

"That's your guess. After all you were blocking the damn pier when Duke blasted your car."

For a long minute he didn't answer. Then he smiled. "Good story. I'd buy it." Then he got serious again. "How's Jimmy? Doc told me his emergency treatment saved my leg."

"He's good. Still a little shaken up. Until a month or so ago his life was nice and quiet."

"Then what?"

"Developers. They used the Tongs to force out long- time residents in Chinatown. He was targeted."

"And you helped him."

"Seems like we all help each other."

"So what happened to Duke?"

I told him about tracing him to Pescadores though Nina's phone, the meth factory, Duke stealing my fucking car forcing me to chase him down and blow the Green Ghost off the road. As I told it my heartbeat soared past agitated.

"Let me get this straight," Lowell said. "You took out a smuggling boat, a human trafficking operation, and a meth lab? In the same night?"

I wanted to tell him it was actually The Preacher who wreaked such havoc but then Bob would know I'm batshit crazy and rethink our relationship.

So I just shrugged.

Chapter 32

"Life is a series of comebacks."
— Hershel Berry

Today marks *LazyBonz's* first year as a legitimate establishment. And our first anniversary as a legitimate couple.

Of course Nina's hinting at marriage now.

Women.

However we do make an excellent team.

Nina has family in Zlhuatanejo which enabled us to become major partners in a bar restaurant Nina named LazyBonz. Her uncle runs the kitchen, two cousins are waitresses, and Nina and I run the bar. One of the perks is I get to choose the music.

I took the four hundred thousand bounty I recovered from Duke and invested in a new life. Only fitting since the money was on *my* head. I offered to share with Lowell and Jimmy but they both refused. So I bought Bob a new Mustang and put fifty grand in a college fund for Jimmy's daughter.

The discovery of six bodies in a Chinatown cellar, including a biker and a respectable developer, made headlines for weeks. It ignited a war between the Vandals and the Tongs which is still raging. At any rate it keeps the heat off me.

Oddly there was no mention of Albert Chan aka Shark Boy or the case with the million dollars. Which means he might still be out there. My guess is it would take more than a bullet to stop that tank.

To make sure Shark Boy keeps his head down I hacked his personal financial accounts and sent them to the FBI. If he's smart he's back in Hong Kong.

Oh yes, before leaving town I posted the video of Taylor Kingston and Mayor Yen in flagrant heat. It instantly went viral and Taylor Kingston's yoga ass beamed on every TV scandal show and celebrity sex web site around the globe—eventually becoming YouTube's most watched.

It also started a recall action on Mayor Yen and stopped the developers cold. For the moment.

Money never sleeps.

Stability seems to agree with me. Not only have I recovered from my various injuries (which included three cracked ribs and a severely gouged forearm) my rehab routine propelled me into the best shape of my life. I suppose I work out with the same ferocity displayed by my pal The Preacher.

But he hasn't been around for a long time. Thank God.

I manage to handle any trouble in the bar with discretion—and the help of Nina's two hundred fifty pound uncle.

Only problem is… it's all about to go up in smoke.

This is how it began.

***

I had just taken a two mile run along the beach and was trotting back to our house when I spotted him, lounging under a straw umbrella, a Pina colada in his hand.

He was wearing a panama hat, a pink button down over khaki shorts, penny loafers without socks. Prep school conservative to the end.

Delaney.

At first I couldn't believe it. Delaney never took a vacation. And he ends up here? For a flustered moment I wondered if Grace my ex-wife, now his bride, was with him.

As my shock cleared so did my brain. It dawned on me that it wasn't a coincidence—and this was no vacation.

So when he walked into LazyBonz I was ready.

It was just six and my regulars were assembled around the bar enjoying happy hour. I saw him in the mirror and kept mixing my signature drink: one part tequila, one part Absinthe, add a dash of blue gin, shake with ice and pour neat. I call it Blue Limbo and the customers seem to like it. Delaney took a seat at the bar behind me.

I served the drink and lit a cigarette. Bad sign.

Always notice when you reach for a cigarette.

I had lost a step already but at least Delaney didn't know that. "Hello, Sam."

I kept my back to him and put the cigarette aside.

"Hello, Alvin. What'll you have?"

"Martini. Dry."

Slowly I turned and met his eyes. Like blue steel doors to a morgue. He was older, jowly but his bulldog expression remained firm.

I always thought he bore a passing resemblance to J. Edgar Hoover but with the new tan he looked more like Mitt Romney's ugly brother.

He gave me an admiring grin. "You look real healthy, Sam. Guess you cleaned up."

I started building his martini. "If you're here you know my name's not Sam."

"Of course, of course," he took out his phone and made a great show of studying the screen, "Max LeBlue isn't it?"

"Mexican olive okay?"

"Hold the olive, Sam."

I set his martini down and leaned on the bar so my face was six inches from his.

"The name is Max and you can hold the bullshit. What do you want?"

He didn't flinch. "You owe me, Sam."

I leaned an inch closer. "Sam owes you. Max doesn't."

Delany disengaged and made a show of tasting the martini. "This is damned good uh, Max."

That sounded like a concession. I leaned back and nodded. "How did you find me?"

"Cops in some town called Pescadores found a Sig Sauer near the site of a meth lab explosion along with two dead bikers. They ran the prints on the Sig and up comes Sam Devine DEA. Look, Max, whatever your name… the prints are yours."

"Which proves…?"

"That you're alive, Max." He took a long sip of his drink. "Oh by the way bullets from that same Sig were found in two bodies found aboard a smuggling boat in Half Moon Bay. Jesus—you've been a busy son of a bitch."

He half lifted his glass in a toast. "I'm impressed."

I turned away to tend to some customers. When I came back Delaney had finished his drink and there was a large envelope on the bar.

"What's this?"

"Twelve years back pay and the dismissal of all charges against you signed by the National Director himself. That's me. I've been promoted."

My stunned brain riffled through my option cards. I stared at the envelope, reluctant to pick it up. Delaney was a wily motherfucker and he had no reason to do me any favors.

I was beginning to hate it when people gave me large sums of money. It usually meant I had a life expectancy of thirty seconds.

Suddenly I wanted a drink—and another cigarette.

"What the fuck do you want?"

"I want you to come in out of the cold and go back to work."

"For you."

He nodded. "For me. But you get to keep your new identity."

"But not my life."

"Right now you're a fugitive. I pull the plug and we take you in."

"We're in Mexico, Alvin. Doesn't happen that way."

"But it happens." He pushed the glass my way. "How about a refill?"

I busied myself with the martini, my mind racing furiously. I set his glass down along with my rebuttal.

"How's Grace?" I said.

He seemed half surprised that I knew he'd married my ex-wife.

"She's doing fine, Max, why do you ask?"

"You knew I was alive when you officially declared me deceased. And you let my ex-wife collect all that insurance and pension money. Take me in and you're on the hook for it: fraud, embezzlement, the whole nine."

He sipped his martini.

"We've been divorced six years now. Yeah she still collects your pension but I don't profit in any way." He drained his glass. "Fact is I lost money on that deal. I'll be back tomorrow for you answer…Max."

So much for my hole card.

For a long time I didn't touch the envelope Delaney left behind.

I cleared Delaney's glass, half tempted to stash it in a plastic bag for prints and DNA.

Leaving my own prints on the Sig was unprofessional. However at that particular moment I had a damaged arm, three cracked ribs, swollen fingers, and a .45 in my good hand while chasing a dangerous kidnapper who just stole my car.

Give yourself a break, I thought angrily.

While I had damned good reasons for tossing the Sig, all through the rest of my shift I cursed my lapse in judgement.

It had been a slow night and as I stacked glasses the envelope caught my attention.

I approached it as I would an IED.

Wiping my hands on a towel, I studied it for a long minute before sliding it towards me. The envelope was sealed. I took a nearby paring knife and opened it.

As advertised inside was a check attached to a financial statement and a sheaf of papers purporting to clear me of all charges and reinstate me as a special operative of the DEA at full salary plus benefits.

After taxes my accrued pay came to three hundred and twenty three thousand.

The shifty bastard had something in mind.

I had no idea what it was. And unless I intended to pack up tonight and get in the wind there was no way I could refuse his offer.

Shark Boy would think it funny. But he was dead. As I stood there staring at the check I felt the same way.

When I left the bar I was tilting heavily toward the get in the wind option. The hard part was how to tell Nina. I decided to wait until after I met with Delaney the next day. By then I hoped to come up with a better plan.

Nina knew things had changed right away.

"You're hiding something from me, Max, I can tell."

I put my arms around her and caressed her perfect ass. "I'm hiding the fact that I'm skimming the profits, not to mention the owner herself."

"Be serious, Max."

She slipped out of my embrace and sat at our kitchen table. "If you won't tell me I'll have to hide my secrets too."

"Like what secrets?"

"Like I'm pregnant."

My smile dropped and so did I. On one knee beside her chair I pressed my face against her belly.

"I found out two days ago," Nina said softly, "didn't know how you'd take the news."

"It's wonderful, great..." I babbled, overcome with a surprising surge of emotion.

She took my face in her hands. "Now let's hear your secret."

"Actually it affects *your* secret in a big way."

As I told Nina about Delaney tracking me down her face registered fear, relief, anticipation, and uncertainty.

Her uncertainty about me.

"So you won't be a fugitive, charges dropped right?"

"Supposedly."

"Supposedly?"

"Delaney is a double-crossing son of a bitch. Could be a hoax to get me across the border without a long court battle."

"The big check he gave you seems valid. Once you put it in the bank it's official."

Good point.

I got up and pulled a chair next to hers. "I just got the best news in the world—and the worst news—at the same time. Our having a baby changes everything."

Her eyes got moist. "I hope you're happy."

"Beyond happy."

It was true. In one compressed moment a whole new universe had exploded into my consciousness. New emotions washed over me, healing the scars of my violent past. An hour ago I was prepared to run.

Now I had too much to give up—a meaningful existence.

Since childhood there had always been a void in my soul. Suddenly it was full of hope.

Except for Delaney.

His offer of amnesty was a form of slave labor. Working undercover for the DEA was tantamount to being a fugitive. Same bleak, loveless life. Not to mention the fact that the whole fucking drug war is ridiculous. Guys on prescription drugs chasing guys on street drugs.

But nobody wants it to end.

It's a billion dollar cash cow and everybody drinks the milk.

Look at me. I had just made three hundred grand for going AWOL.

Delaney wanted me real bad.

"You know if I sign up for this I won't be home much."

"Home is where we are, Max. The three of us."

I gently caressed her belly. "Life on the run is no way to raise a kid."

"Unless we run far enough."

"Like where?"

Nina shrugged and leaned closer. "Brazil maybe, Venezuela, Costa Rica…at least we could live like normal people."

The flaw in that scenario is there are no normal people. Humanity is a discordant note in the otherwise harmonious chaos of the universe.

Okay, granted I'm overthinking it a bit. But normal?

"I thought we had that right here," I said.

"Then we stay."

"Run or stay," I murmured, nuzzling her neck. "Which is it? I'll do whatever you say."

She pulled away slightly. "Oh no, Max. You've got the ball on this one." She took my face in her hands and met my eyes.

"Whatever *you* decide we'll do it together."

That night we made love as if for the first time.

Or the last…

The author would like to thank my loving mainstay Ellen Smith, Shane Mackenzie for his sharp editing skills, the amazing author/attorney Larry Townsend, Christine Roth and Rob Cohen for their continued faith and support and to Al Chan for his insights.